To My Friends,
Donna & Joey,
Study &
Enjoy —

Bill Hunt
July 31, 2009

A FULL-GROWN MAN

BILL HUNT

ILLUSTRATIONS BY
CAROLE FORET AND CLAIRE KAYSER

iUniverse, Inc.
New York   Bloomington

A Full-Grown Man

Copyright © 2009 Bill Hunt

All rights reserved. No part of this book may be used or reproduced by any means, graphic, electronic, or mechanical, including photocopying, recording, taping or by any information storage retrieval system without the written permission of the publisher except in the case of brief quotations embodied in critical articles and reviews.

This is a work of fiction. All of the characters, names, incidents, organizations, and dialogue in this novel are either the products of the author's imagination or are used fictitiously.

iUniverse books may be ordered through booksellers or by contacting:

iUniverse
1663 Liberty Drive
Bloomington, IN 47403
www.iuniverse.com
1-800-Authors (1-800-288-4677)

Because of the dynamic nature of the Internet, any Web addresses or links contained in this book may have changed since publication and may no longer be valid. The views expressed in this work are solely those of the author and do not necessarily reflect the views of the publisher, and the publisher hereby disclaims any responsibility for them.

ISBN: 978-1-4401-5010-4 (pbk)
ISBN: 978-1-4401-5008-1 (cloth)
ISBN: 978-1-4401-5009-8 (ebk)

Printed in the United States of America

iUniverse rev. date: 7/1/2009

DEDICATED TO
GRACE DUPUIS HUNT
and our children and their children.

TAKEN FROM AN INTERVIEW
WITH
Benjamin Bennefield and Anna Mancini
FROM
A FULL-GROWN MAN
January 2009

Interviewer: Ben, this is your story, isn't it, about your life?

Ben: Yes, mostly, I suppose, but it's about others, too: the people around me, those who affected my life from the time I was a teenager. Some were the demons who haunted me, made life miserable, but interesting. Yeah, it's mostly my story, and I tell it.

Interviewer: As you recalled the events, spoke the words, breathing life back into the people, the characters, how did you feel, what were your thoughts?

Ben: At times, I was saddened. At other times, recalling old memories upset me, even kept me awake a few nights. Later, when reading the manuscript, well, often I had to read the words several times before I could reconcile to what drove us, and how we managed the way we were back then, the way we lived. And my life, well, my spirit had been badly broken, and I was angry, tormented by what had been handed me at such an early age. In reality, I was a kid wandering around in an adult's world.

Interviewer: And you, Anna, tell me how you felt back then.

Anna: Well, without a doubt, I was upset and angry, too. I had plans for my future, and they were infringed upon, so I had good reason to be angry. But I was determined to move forward, so I adjusted my plans and my life as best I could. Some will say I was selfish, but I didn't see it that way.

Interviewer: Do you feel you accomplished all that you wanted in your career?

Anna: I really can't say for sure. But for years, I felt I needed someone or something to blame. And looking back, I played my best hand at every turn. Some worked out and others didn't. So, I would say I dealt with whatever confronted me, hoping my career might bloom. Luckily, there were a few bonuses handed to me, for which I became grateful.

Interviewer: Tell me about Mrs. Margaret. She was an important figure to both of you, from the very beginning. What about this remarkable woman?

Anna: Of course, to me she was most important, and to Ben, also, I'm sure. Looking at the early years, she was an anchor that held steadfast. Her husband Frank even knew that, although it never stopped him from being the awful fellow he was. And when I remember Frank, I end my thought with a prayer for him, "God rest his soul," as does everyone else who knew him.

Interviewer: And Ben, tell me about Ava. Who was she? Such a strong person. And how did she fit into this incredible journey?

Ben: Ava and I had a love for each other, and we understood each other, so there were no lingering questions or loose ends. Our marriage? Always good. And yes, absolutely, a strong and vibrant woman, a good person. I'm sorry she can't be here today and share in this interview.

Interviewer: What about your mother, Ben? Should I ask?

Ben: No, don't, please! She was far too complicated, and besides, the iniquity surrounding her. Well, I think the readers should decipher Hester. And the Gold Dust Bridge, also; what an applauded character it is.

Interviewer: Ben, why did you choose to tell your story, after so many years?

Ben: Because of the lessons I had to learn, I suppose. They're life lessons, and a reader can benefit by seeing and hearing them from the person who lived them.

Interviewer: In a couple of sentences, how would you sum up your life? How did it turn out?

Ben: It was difficult at times, but eventually, I became a full-grown man. That's only one sentence, isn't it?

Interviewer: Yes, but wow! That could be the title of the book: *A Full-Grown Man*. Thank you both. It's been a real pleasure.

One

"You've been foolish, Benjamin, and you're gonna pay the price for a hell of a long time." Her words cut through my brain. *Son-of-a-bitch*, I said to myself and closed my eyes.

Her knife turned inside me. My body shook. Her lips were pursed tightly. I opened my eyes.

Through the openings in the curtains, narrow rays of sun cut across me while I lay on her bed. My thoughts rambled, hazy and bitter. A slit of light pierced one eye. I turned my head from it.

I wondered what might have been, what my life would be like, had Anna's letters reached me three years before. *Maybe in New York*, I thought. "No," I said to myself, "not New York." The room was cold. But surely, with any heart at all, Hester would have been happy for her flesh and blood, for her son. "No," I said. *She didn't care about me*, my mind said. "She felt she was the victim, and she fought back," I said softly. *And everybody around here figured her to be a good person*, my mind spoke again. "Yeah, I did, too, for most of my life," I said under my breath.

I laid the letters neatly in front of me. Three letters, mine, taken and hidden. And the third letter, Anna's last, tore my heart apart. Looking at the envelope, my eyes dampened and my throat ached. But the messages in the letters were old now, and the circumstances that Anna had written of had changed. As surely as the sun brightened the room, I knew her words were locked in my mind. My head throbbed.

I crushed the letters in one hand. My life, as it had turned out, could not be by the grace of God, but by the meanness of a selfish and conniving woman, Hester McGinnis Bennefield, my mother.

I stood up quickly beside her bed, wrapped myself in the quilt, then headed toward the hall, but stopped abruptly at the door. There on the wall, framed exquisitely in a gold frame, was a quote my mother often spoke, though she seldom set foot in a church:

"Let he who is without sin, cast the first stone."
John 8:7

I read it a second time, mumbling the words out loud. The glass shattered when I slammed my fist against it.

Midway down the steps from the front porch, Lucy and Jake met me, with tails wagging from side to side. I called their names and knelt, wrapping my arms around their necks. As she usually did, Lucy licked my cheek with two big swipes. I glanced around the yard at the blanket of frost-burned green beneath the oaks, then walked with my dogs to the gazebo where Barbara and I played when we were kids and where we learned to swim in the slow-moving waters of Edward's Creek. I looked upstream through a thin white fog; the Gold Dust Bridge in the distance stood tall, like a monument to a great event or a memorial for a person of importance. The morning air was moist, and the fog moved slowly above the water. The sun hung in the southeast, low in a winter sky. I looked back toward the house at the light filtering through the spreading limbs of the oaks. Dim shadows crossed the yard. The slight breeze from the north carried a chill that seeped to my bones, making me pull the quilt tighter around me.

A Full-Grown Man

At the far side of the gazebo, deep water moved slowly, while Lucy and Jake played in the rocky shallows along the edge of the creek. I sat in an old rocker and read each letter out loud, hearing Anna's voice as I spoke her words. The first two letters I tore one at a time, dropping the pieces onto the water, but the third seemed nearly a living thing, like something I should hold and care for. I brought it to my face, took a deep breath, and held it. Through misty eyes, I looked to the other side of the creek at the leafless trees. Springtime was far away, but I knew it would come again; then there would be summer, and fall, and winter; time would go on. I looked at the letter, knowing I would repeat Anna's words over and over for the rest of my life.

Right then, I hated myself, for what I had done and who I was, and there was nothing I could do to change it. Cursing under my breath, I ripped the letter into small pieces, scattering them in the breeze, and watched as they fluttered to the water below. I sighed deeply and then closed my eyes, reciting the words Anna had written.

I pulled the quilt tighter around me, leaned against the back of the chair, and listened to the sounds of rippling water. Moaning howls of a hound echoed through the trees along the creek, and I closed my eyes.

The sun was warming. Sleep came easy.

* * * * *

Two

Four Years Earlier

For all of my seventeen and a half years, I crossed Edward's Creek by way of the Gold Dust Bridge, which we believed was held together by a thousand coats of dark red paint. But the old bridge was really a work of art in iron and wood. Many who grew up in the area crossed it for the last time when they finished high school, leaving home to find a job and a place in the outside world. A few stayed, only because their families owned the land and grew the cotton in the wide, flat fields around Gold Dust. Less than a half mile from the old bridge, I lived with my mother and father in a big house on a farm that had been in my mother's family for nearly a hundred years. Because the rich, sandy soil on windy days rose in clouds that moved across the fields, the air turned golden in the evening sun. That was the reason, I figured, why our quiet little village was called Gold Dust.

Gold Dust was home to several small stores where we bought our groceries, our clothes, and almost anything a person needed; there was a doctor's office, a post office, and a fine railroad depot warmed by a big iron stove, where, on winter days, old men sat around, chewing tobacco and telling stories about cotton crops, big ones and little ones, and incessantly telling lies about women. But the old bridge, referred to by everyone as the Gold Dust Bridge, seemed to be the heart of our town. When you crossed it coming in, you left time behind, and when you crossed it while leaving, time started over.

On bright sunny days, the bridge's geometric arrangement of iron cast shadows, which moved in odd configurations, keeping the minutes ticking along the wooden floor. When evening came, and the skies turned pink and amber, the old bridge stood tall and proud with its peak lit up by the last rays of the big orange sun dropping slowly behind the woods far off. The Gold Dust Bridge was a place of "first freedoms" for me and my friends. We gathered there in the evening, laughed, and picked on each other. We learned things mamas and daddies never told us about and learned a lot of forbidden words; we tried a cut from the newest brand of chewing tobacco and inhaled from our first cigarette. And we shared beers stolen from Dad's icebox, while swinging our legs from the tailgates of pick-up trucks. On any hot day during the long summer, it was a right of passage when young boys tested their daring and impressed the girls by jumping from the old bridge into the cool water below. When July Fourth came around, or any time a politician stumped the area, the Gold Dust Bridge was a place of celebration; a band played the marches of John Philip Sousa—always Sousa—and from side to side, the bridge was strung with long bright banners, Stars and Stripes waving from its highest peak. But then, on quiet Sundays after church, the beautiful water beneath the Gold Dust Bridge became holy when the Baptists or Methodists prayed and baptized their new believers.

Doc Foster brought me into the world in my mother's bedroom, on a cold December day a week before Christmas in 1934, and I was given the name Benjamin William Bennefield. Everyone around called me Ben, but by my eighteenth birthday, I was known also as the boy who had lost his heart to the Yankee girl who spent her summers in Gold Dust. Her name was Anna. Anna Mancini.

Her hair was auburn, her eyes were green, and I fell in love with her the first time I saw her. I was only twelve then. That was five years ago, and it was on a Tuesday evening on the east end of the Gold Dust Bridge. I remember it well because I thought it strange the last day of school that year was on Monday, and Anna arrived for her summer visit the day after school let out.

Anna stood apart from the kids who were born and reared around Gold Dust. She hailed from Philadelphia and came every summer to stay with her aunt, Miz Margaret, and Miz Margaret's mother, Miz Elnora. Together, they owned the best grocery store in Gold Dust. Anna was an artist, and she spent much of her time drawing and painting; at other times, she wrote poetry about people and things she discovered during her long summer visits.

Both Miz Margaret and Miz Elnora had come from Pennsylvania in the 1920s. According to local hearsay, the day after arriving in Gold Dust, Miz Margaret married one of the homegrown fellows, Mr. Frank Smitherman. Only in whispered conversations on the front porches on Sunday afternoons did anyone ever question the match-up between Miz Margaret and Mr. Frank. Mr. Frank seemed always disgruntled, obviously obnoxious, and at least three steps below the beautiful and elegant Miz Margaret. But he was a flag-waving veteran of the first big war, claiming he had been "gassed in the trenches," and this undocumented fact was viewed by most as an absolute plus for Frank Smitherman, who needed a lot more than "gas" as an excuse for his behavior.

Miz Margaret and Miz Elnora had very different ways from those of the local people, who raised the cotton around the Gold Dust Bridge. Naturally, they carried an air about them, revealing their big city and, most assuredly, Northern upbringing. Also, they were the only Catholics around. That alone seemed odd to the Baptists and Methodists, but like my mother, Hester, reminded me often, "Let he who is without sin, cast the first stone," and no one dared refute her quotation.

A Full-Grown Man

The first time I saw Anna Mancini I thought she was the prettiest girl I had ever laid eyes on, with a magic that seemed to draw everyone to her, especially me. Many times I had wanted to talk to Anna, or at least say "hi," but for the first two summers I was never able to say anything at all. She was far too fascinating and sophisticated for the likes of a country kid several years younger, and being somewhat shy, I figured I might never be able to talk to Anna, because to do so would have been far beyond the scale upon which I had placed myself. So I stood by and watched as she entered our lives every summer, and when summer was almost over, she would disappear, returning to her world far from us and, I figured, far from the way we lived in Gold Dust.

She didn't know it, but by the end of that first summer, when I was twelve, I excitedly counted Anna as my girlfriend, and that was a secret, my secret, which I confided to no one, not even my best friend, James Bartlett. I loved Anna Mancini as much as any boy could love a girl, and in my thoughts, I held her hand, looked deep into her big green eyes, and I kissed her lips with unabashed passion, as the feather pillow on my bed could attest. Anna knew none of it, but when school let out at the end of each spring, I waited anxiously for her arrival in Gold Dust.

Ben Bennefield

Three

"Well, good evening, Ben," Miz Margaret said, smiling.

"Hi, Miz Margaret," I said, with my hand held up. "Could I have an orange pop, please ma'am?" I smiled and held my dime between two fingers.

For a while now, I had come to recognize Miz Margaret as a very beautiful lady. Her hair was black as coal, cut short and curled tight. Always, she spoke softly, smiled quickly, and held her smile far longer than most people. Her skin appeared smooth and soft, the color of cream, and always, her lips were painted a shade of red. That day, she was prettier than usual. She wore a blouse that, to me, looked like pure silk and was the color of the sky outside, and her dark eyes sparkled. She looked happy and pleased. I wanted to ask her when Anna might arrive, but wishing not to appear overly eager, I dropped the dime into her opened hand, looked at her, and smiled.

"Sure, Ben," she said, as she shoved the pop across the counter. "Anything else today?"

"Thanks, Miz Margaret." Quickly I took a swallow from the bottle, cooling my throat and quenching a thirst that had started long before leaving the cotton field. Miz Margaret's smile lingered as usual, but today there was something really different. She hummed a little tune as she focused wide-eyed at me through her gold-rimmed glasses. When I moved a step in one direction, her eyes moved with me. *Maybe*, I thought, *there was something wrong*. I had said "ma'am" and "please," and had already said "thanks." Quickly, I turned, glancing down to make sure my fly was buttoned, and it was. Still, I couldn't figure her out. Feeling my face redden, I glanced back and forth between her and the floor. She kept on humming and watching me.

I cleared my throat, making ready to ask about Anna's arrival, but I stopped short, figuring I'd wait one more day.

"Ben," she asked, "is there anything else?" She smiled, taking in a deep breath.

"No, ma'am," I said, shaking my head. "I don't guess there's anything else today." I turned and started walking toward the screen door onto the store's front porch. "See you later, Miz Margaret," I called back, raising my hand. "Thanks."

Just before kicking the screen door open, I heard her voice: "Well, hi, Ben. Don't run off before I can say hello." It was Anna's voice, the sweet sound I'd waited for days to hear. Turning quickly, I bumped into a braid of garlic hanging from a wire strung across the aisle, and stuttered, "Fine, fine, Anna. I'm fine." I smelled the garlic. Immediately I felt stupid, realizing she hadn't asked how I was doing, but Anna Mancini had arrived in Gold Dust, and she had spoken to me. My thoughts bounced wildly, and my breaths shortened.

As Anna walked slowly toward me, my eyes scanned from her feet to her hair, settling quickly on her face. *Beautiful Anna*, I thought, smiling to myself; so pretty with those big green eyes and dark red hair, but she appeared a little older than I expected, when I remembered how she looked at the end of last summer. Standing as tall as I could, stretching and raising my chin, I hoped I looked older, too, at least eighteen; nineteen or twenty would have been better, I figured.

"So how is Gold Dust, Ben?" she asked, as she came closer to me. "It looks the same to me." I flinched when she placed her hand on my arm, then quickly she reached to my chest and snapped the strap of my dusty overalls. Smiling, she removed my cap. I ran my fingers through my sweaty hair, already made blonde from the hot sun. She smiled, and again, she looked at me from my head down to my boots, over my entire length, and again, I felt my face turning red, getting hot. My knees felt weak, and my breaths were short. My heart thumped.

"Gold Dust?" I stammered. "Oh…oh, it's good," I said, shrugging. "Same ole place, like always. When did you get here, Anna?" I smiled nervously, almost laughing out loud.

"A couple of hours ago, but I haven't seen anyone yet. You're the first, Ben, and you've changed so much," she exclaimed as she smiled, bringing her voice into a higher pitch. My breathing quickened more, while she glanced up and down again as though to verify how much I had actually changed. "I'm going to take a nap and walk down to the bridge later," she said. Her smile broadened, with her eyes now on my face. "I'd love for you to meet me there, Ben," she said softly, as she reached toward my orange pop. I handed it to her and watched her lips as they rounded around the bottle's opening. My lips rounded, too. She took a sip then handed the bottle back to me. I raised it quickly to my lips and held it there, feeling the round opening with the tip of my tongue. Quick, short breaths and my imagination ran wild. My lips were touching where Anna's had just been. I took in a swallow of the orange pop then held the bottle in front of me, hoping she would reach for it again.

"Anna, I'm sure glad you're here," I said nervously. "We'll be at the bridge after a while, and I'll be glad to meet you there."

"Wonderful, Ben," she said. "It'll be nice to see everyone."

"Great!" I said, nodding my head. "Really glad you're here, Anna." Then I leaned toward her slightly, hoping she'd hug me, or at least reach for my hand. I wanted to touch her, feel her skin, let her scent seep up to me, but she ignored my gesture.

Smiling, she handed my cap to me. "See you later, Ben," she said, as her eyes rolled upward, meeting mine. Anna turned and walked slowly down the aisle leading into the kitchen at the back of the store. Frozen in place, I sighed deeply and listened to the old wood floor squeak under her heels. I hated the sound of her walking away. The door into the kitchen closed. I licked my lips slowly, then held my fingers to them, while looking at the bottle in my other hand. I cut my eyes toward Miz Margaret, who was still in the spot where she had been when Anna and I met, never moving while she watched the entire event. Miz Margaret kept on smiling, appearing as though something else was going to happen. Glancing again at my nearly empty pop bottle, I pressed it against my lips, leaned my head back, and emptied it, then stepped to the counter directly in front of her and slammed the bottle onto the counter top. "See ya later, Miz Margaret, thanks," I said, grinning, and walked quickly toward the front door.

When the screen door closed behind me, I heard her call. I stepped back inside. "Tell your mother to come by the store tomorrow when she comes to the post office. Would you please, darling?"

"Yes, ma'am, I'll tell her," I said, raising my hand with my cap in it. "I'll tell her!"

Anna Mancini

Four

That evening I was the first to arrive at the bridge. On the east end, I leaned against the railing, where I could watch for Anna when she stepped from the store's front porch. Several friends came by, and we talked while I continued to glance toward the store about a hundred yards away. I said nothing about Anna. I wanted to be the only one to know; I wanted it to be my secret until she appeared at the bridge, and then I would *present* her to my friends. Bobby and Jenny walked up holding hands. After gabbing for a couple of minutes, they went on to the middle of the bridge where several other friends had gathered. I felt pretty sure Bobby and Jenny would marry as soon as they finished high school next year, and then leave Gold Dust to find a job somewhere. The bunch in the middle of the bridge was laughing and joking around, passing a couple of beers from one to the other. Someone called to me and held up a bottle. I motioned back that I didn't want any.

Disappointed that Anna had not yet come, I began to worry she might be too tired from the long train ride from Philadelphia. Or maybe she didn't want me to wait for her or to be there at all; maybe she had changed her mind about coming. I picked up some rocks and threw them one at a time into the water, watching the ripples grow into wide

A Full-Grown Man

circles. The circles grew bigger then disappeared, and I thought Anna might be a ripple, too, in my mind, a ripple that had grown bigger with every summer, and eventually, it'd disappear. "Hell, no," I mumbled to myself, glancing back and forth from the water to the store, "that's not gonna happen; I'm not gonna let it happen." Then I said to myself, "I love Anna, and one day she's gonna love me, too."

At once, I threw all the rocks in my hand into the water, far out, then turned away to see my friends waiting for me in the middle of the bridge. I cursed under my breath, sighed deeply, and leaned against the railing. "Dammit," I said to myself, then spit as far out as I could and watched it fall until it hit the water. I glanced to look for Anna. Instinctively, every muscle flexed and tightened, and I stretched tall and straight, my fingers spread wide, and I smiled. Anna was on her way to meet me.

The Gold Dust Bridge

Five

Our meeting at the Gold Dust Bridge each evening had become something I waited anxiously for every day. Thoughts about Anna were always at the front of my mind, and for a week now, each day in the cotton field seemed longer than the day before.

At daylight on Friday morning, Dad called from the bottom of the stairs. I said nothing, waiting until he called a second time. "Okay, Dad," I yelled, throwing the sheet back. It was damp from the moist night air pulled across my bed by the attic fan. I sat on the edge of the bed, stretching as I glanced around the room, then rubbed my eyes, and I wished I could sleep some more. I stood, stretched long and hard, then began putting on my work clothes. Deliberately, I dropped one of my boots on the floor, then again, signaling to Mom I was out of bed; otherwise, in no time she'd be yelling from the bottom of the stairs. When I reached the kitchen, she was at her usual place, cooking my breakfast at the stove, and like every other day, she had on her blue jeans and blue work shirt. Her short-cropped hair, coarse and thick, was streaked with gray and free to fly with the breeze. Unlike Miz Margaret, Mom never used anything on her face, like powder, or rouge on her cheeks, except on a very special occasion when she might wear a little bit of pink on her lips. Mother was a strong, robust woman; she loved the outdoors, her animals, and farming cotton. A cup of hot coffee was waiting on the kitchen table. I sat at my place, stretched again, and yawned big, but said nothing. My stomach growled while I leaned over the cup, taking in the aroma.

"Oh, poor boy," she said. I rolled my eyes, having picked up on the sarcasm in her voice. "You stayed out too late last night, didn't you?" When I glanced at her face, her lips were pursed tightly, and she was shaking her head in agreement, her hair bouncing. "I heard you sneaking up the stairs." Before I could think of a counter, she commanded, "You've got a lot to do today, Benjamin, so you had best perk up and get your butt moving."

"Like what, Mom? What's Dad got on his mind?" I asked, yawning again. Before she could answer, I added, "By the way, Miz Margaret said for you to come by the store after you pick up the mail today, Mom, and remember, I told you!"

She looked at me curiously for a second, as though there might be something else in the message from Miz Margaret, but she didn't ask. After a bit, she began her regular morning instructions about the day's work. "You've got ten acres of hay to bale and get in today. Your dad thinks it's gonna rain later, and you need to get it to the barn. You'll have plenty of help." She set my breakfast in front of me, touched my shoulder, and moved her hand quickly to tousle my hair, her routine of saying, "Good morning, how are you?" or whatever she wanted it to say. It made me mad when she did it, but I figured it was Mother's thing, and she would do it whether I liked it or not.

Baling and hauling hay was the worst job I knew on the farm, and right then I didn't care if the hay ruined. As for rain, I hoped a shower would come and we would knock off so I could go to the bridge early. And if Anna wasn't there, then I would go to Miz Margaret's store, and we would walk together.

"Son, I want to tell you something," Mom said, and I knew by the rush in her words and calling me "son," she was forcing herself to be nice, and she was about to say something I wouldn't like.

"What, Mom? What's up?" I asked, cutting my eyes toward her and holding my breath. I took a swallow of coffee.

"Well, Margaret has mentioned you've been meeting her niece at the bridge every evening; her niece, Anna. Is that her name?"

Mom knew Anna's name very well. "Yeah, we meet there. I saw her yesterday," I admitted and raised my cup to my lips again.

She poured a cup of coffee, then sat at the table. While running her fingers through her hair with a couple of swift jerks, she started, "Ben, she's a beautiful young woman. I've seen her many times, and of course, Margaret talks about her often. But I want to tell you this," she said, glaring straight at my face. "Anna is several years older than you and has a lot of ideas that are different from the way we live in Gold Dust." Her forehead creased. "Besides," she said, "she's too old for you, and experienced, Benjamin."

"Aw, Mom," I interrupted, in an attempt to stop the flow. "Don't worry. She's a pretty girl," then I lied, "and there are plenty of girls around here who are just as pretty as she is."

"Ben, listen to me," she said, bringing her voice almost to a whisper as she leaned toward me, and looked doggedly at me. "She's already been married, and they had it annulled. That alone should tell you something, boy!" She paused, pursing her lips again, then said, "You're too young for that woman, and you're heading in a bad direction, big boy. You're gonna get yourself in a heap of trouble and be hurt to boot, if you're not careful."

"Hurt?" I couldn't help but feel anger beginning to bubble inside. "Mom, now listen to me for a second. I'm almost eighteen, and I do the work of a man around here, without question or complaint, and I consider myself as much a grownup as anyone else in this house." Her hair seemed to stand straighter, her forehead creasing again, while her eyes squinted, holding straight to my face. "So, how do you figure a girl a few years older than me is going to hurt me, or get me 'in a heap of trouble,' as you put it?"

Her voice got louder and her words came faster. "Well, Anna is not a girl, and that's the problem. She's not a girl like you've ever known, and there are plenty of ways when a young, headstrong boy takes a liking to an older woman, especially one who has been around, as she has." She pounded her fist on the table, shouting, "And Benjamin, don't be so damned hard-headed; you've got a lot to learn, and all I'm trying to tell you is, don't do anything foolish." Her eyes were in slits, and her lips shut tight.

I heard my teeth grind as I looked her in the face. Her usual frown looked deeper, confirming how troubled she felt, but how determined she was to have her way with my life. Again she rushed her words. "I've heard some of the things girls around here think, and even say, about you. Their mothers are more than happy to tell me. And I'm telling you, Benjamin, just keep your damned pants buttoned."

I shook my head, feeling the blood rush to my face, making it hot, but I knew any attempt to reason with Hester Bennefield was a futile endeavor, a misadventure, and it was best to let it go. All day, a dark shadow with arms and legs hovered over me, yelling, and screaming. It was angry and mean.

But Dad was right, and I was glad. As we hoisted the last bales of hay into the barn loft, the clouds rolling in from the west grew heavy and dark. I drove the tractor with the trailer to the shed near the house, where I waited with three farm workers until the lightning passed and the rain slacked. At the first chance I got, I ran with my dogs to the house, figuring I would get cleaned up and walk to the bridge as soon as the storm was over.

Six

After a quick shower, I pushed my feet through jeans ironed stiff with starch, wondering if Mom had them done that way deliberately, making them miserable to wear. I pulled a T-shirt over me and slipped on my loafers, then stepped quietly down the stairs, hoping not to alert my mother, who was closed off in her bedroom. Along the gravel driveway, puddles of standing water glistened, reflecting the parted clouds, while the knee-high cotton stood up straight, its leaves having lost the sun during the rainstorm. After a few minutes, I came to the bridge, where everything was wet, still, and quiet. Standing alone in the middle of the span, I looked anxiously toward Miz Margaret's store. After a second, Anna came onto the store's porch and waved to me. I waved back and began walking fast to meet her as she headed toward the bridge. Moving closer with each step, I whispered, "Please, please," a wish that Anna would hug me when we met. I wanted desperately to put my arms around her, hold her close against me for a second, just one exciting second, and catch the aroma of her hair and body.

"Where is everyone?" she called out.

"Don't know … too wet, I guess."

Only a few feet from me, she stopped, her eyes moving up and down. "Boy," she exclaimed, smiling, "don't you look snazzy, Benjamin Bennefield."

I turned my wish into a prayer, saying to myself, *Please, God,* but she made no offer to hug me.

"Ben, look what I've brought," she said, and held up two bottles of beer.

"Great," I said, "from Mr. Frank's icebox, I bet?"

"Yes," Anna chuckled, "but don't tell him." We laughed, knowing Frank Smitherman would say a few choice words and demand payment if he knew. She handed me a bottle, then took my hand in hers and glanced at my face, letting her eyes stare into mine. I felt my heart beating in the tips of the fingers she held.

"I'm sorry no one's here this evening, Anna," I lied, and then winced at the sting of that first taste of beer.

"That's okay, Ben. You and I are here," she said, with the sound of happiness in her voice. She raised the bottle to her lips. I watched her. I took in a deep breath and let the air out slowly and quietly, wanting desperately to press her lips to mine. *Maybe,* I thought, *I should just grab her and kiss her fast, letting whatever happens happen.*

I was glad no one had come to the bridge. We were alone, and I knew Anna would give all of her attention to me, only me, and the idea of just the two of us, alone, excited me further. I took another swallow of beer then turned to lean against the bridge's railing with my elbows on top. Just when my breathing had begun to turn normal, Anna slid her arm through mine, making me flinch. I closed my eyes for a second, and then looked at her. We stood side by side, our bodies touching, with our interlocked arms atop the railing. The east bank of Edward's Creek was lit up by the rays of the sun shining through the breaks in the clouds; the water held blue and green reflections from the sky and the trees along the bank. I felt big, wound tight like a top ready to spin, and I wanted to yell and shout as loudly as I could, telling the whole world that Anna and I were touching with our naked arms laced together. My muscles quivered. Her skin was warm and soft. I closed my eyes for a second then took a deep breath, holding her scent inside me.

"Anna, I'm glad you're here in Gold Dust, really glad," I said softly, looking at her face. "Since you left last summer, all I've done is wait and count the months and days before you came back." I watched her eyes and her lips. "You're beautiful, Anna," I said, shaking my head, "the most beautiful girl I've ever seen."

She never looked at me, only stared at the water. "Thanks, Ben, and I'm glad, too, to be here again this summer," she said. "I've loved spending my summers here for a long time now." She turned toward me, placing her hand on my arm, and teasingly said, "You're grown up now, Ben, a man, big and tall, strong and handsome, and I can only believe every girl around here is after you!" She laughed softly as she patted my arm a couple of times. Then slowly, she moved her hand back and forth along my arm.

"No," I said quickly, denying her statement. "No, Anna, that's not so," I said, not wanting her to think in any way I might have a girlfriend around Gold Dust.

She socked me on the arm with her fist, laughed quietly, and looked at me straight in the face. "Well," she said insistently, "this summer they're going to have to leave you alone because you're going to be mine, Benjamin Bennefield. I've made up my mind." She held her eyes directly on mine, and I smiled back as her words sank in. I came closer this time to grabbing her and pressing her body against mine, kissing her quickly. And I wondered what would happen if I did just that, grab her and kiss her, and hold her close to me. But Anna chuckled, "But all good things must come to an end, as they say." She sighed, raising the bottle for another swallow.

What? I thought, then asked quickly, "What do you mean, Anna? What's coming to an end? The summer's just starting."

"Well, Ben, I think this will probably be my last summer in old Gold Dust," she said, lowering her eyes to the water.

"What are you saying, Anna?" I asked anxiously. "Why not next summer?"

"Ben, next summer I'll be studying in Italy. In fact, I'll be there for an entire year, hopefully longer. And as you might guess, I have family in Florence," she said, adding to my puzzlement. "I plan to get to know them while I'm living there." My mind raced, and my body stiffened.

Anna leaned her head against my shoulder, sipping the last of the beer. After a second, she tossed the bottle to the middle of Edward's Creek, making a big splash, then I threw mine as far upstream as I could. Looking into my face, she said straightforward, "My life is well planned, Ben, well planned, and as much as I love this place, I've never put Gold Dust in my plans." She smiled. "It's just a quiet place for me to come to every summer to keep out of trouble." She laughed quietly for a second and added, "Or at least that's what Isabella thinks."

I stared at her, and I didn't want to think about next summer, just this summer, right now. I couldn't make sense of anything at that moment, and suddenly a new name was thrown into the conversation. "Why, what—" I stammered. "Who's Isabella?" I asked. "Who's that, Anna?" I was desperate for the subject to change.

"Isabella Mancini, at home in Philadelphia," her words flew out fast, giving me reason to believe she didn't care to say more about Isabella. She slid her arm from mine, taking my hand. "Oh, come on, Ben," she said hurriedly. "Let's go for a walk before it rains again." Already, a drop of rain had hit my cheek.

It was impossible to find the right words. Here I was with Anna; touching her and looking into her eyes, sharing her thoughts and hearing her plans, and suddenly the idea of her never coming back to Gold Dust had stolen my words and muddled my mind. We left the bridge.

A Full-Grown Man

Walking slowly, we passed the Bartletts' house, barely visible in the late evening light, and hiding behind a row of trees. We turned toward Doc Foster's place about a half block away. I was still pouting.

"Anna," I said hesitantly. "Anna, I don't know what to say other than to confess outright." I shook my head while looking at her, forcing a smile, and waiting for a reaction. "I really want to tell you something, to confess."

"Confess? You sound so serious, Ben," she said, looking in front of us as we walked slowly along the gravel street.

"Oh, I need to tell you something you'll probably not believe, maybe think I'm a foolish kid, but I want to say it," I said. "I want to say it so you'll know how I feel, Anna, and you'll know what's on my mind."

"Well," she laughed, "I'm no priest, young man."

"Anna, it's not that kind of confession," I said softly. "I just want to tell you something, that's all, and I'm serious about what I'm gonna say."

"Well, you certainly sound serious," she said, smiling. We stopped walking. She turned and faced me, taking my hand and placing hers in mine. "Okay, confess, Benjamin."

"Anna," I said, while holding her hand tightly and, closing my eyes, facing her. "Anna, I've loved you since I was twelve years old, over five years now. I know you didn't know it, but it's true, and I just can't help it. Every day, all day, you never leave my mind. I think about kissing you, about holding you in my arms, touching you, listening to your voice, and looking in your eyes—"

"No, Ben," she said, jerking her hand from my grasp. I opened my eyes. "That's not possible," she said, while holding her hand to her chest, with her eyes wide open.

"Yes, it is possible, Anna, and I mean it, every word," I said, shrugging, "and that's how I feel. I love you, Anna."

"Ben," she said, catching her breath, "you're what, eighteen?" her voice suddenly shaky. She looked in my eyes. "Ben, I'm almost twenty-five," she said. She stopped, then added, in a whisper, "You're so young." She raised her finger and smiled slightly, still looking straight into my face. "But you know," she explained, "I remember those big brown eyes of yours back several summers ago, and now I understand why you were always around, right in the middle of everything. You never spoke, Ben, ever, and you know what? I thought you were in the way, a little kid, Ben, and you were in the way," her tone moved upward. She smiled slightly. "I see now what was happening." After a second, she continued, "Until a week ago when I met you in Aunt Margaret's store, I knew you only as a dreamy-eyed little boy." She looked at me as I waited, staring at her face while her smile grew bigger. "I'll bet now you do have all kinds of girlfriends around Gold Dust, Benjamin, with a line like that!"

"No, I don't, and I don't want any girlfriends," I said softly, quickly and firmly. "I want you, Anna, just you, nobody else, and I want you to believe it."

"Ben, you're bound to have dated, or are you saying you've never even dated? No girlfriends?" Her voice rose. "I don't believe it," she said, smiling.

"Sure, I've dated, dated plenty, but I've never had a real 'girlfriend,'" I said, emphasizing the word. "I've waited for you every summer, and I've waited for this summer, for this day, for this minute, Anna, right this minute, when we would talk about it … talk like this."

She interrupted, "Ben, no! We're not in grade school … we can't do this, sweetheart." Her words were rushing.

"Well, that's the way I feel, Anna. And we're not in grade school, but here we are; you're a woman and I'm a man, and I'm laying my heart out to you, telling you how I feel." I reached, took her hand, and kissed it. "Forget about all the summers before. This is our time, when we start, Anna, right now. We're starting at this moment." I smiled, looking into her eyes. I raised her hand, kissed it, and held it to my lips. "And we know who we are, Anna," I whispered, "and it's a lot more than a kid's thing, believe me."

"Ben," she said, looking very seriously, "you mustn't love me." Her eyes held to mine and began to tear. "We're too far apart in too many ways. Age, first: seven or eight years, Ben," she said, shrugging her shoulders. "Isn't that difficult enough?" I stared at her, slowly shaking my head, slightly smiling. "We're far apart in other ways: who we are, and where we came from. Certainly, you must realize that, Ben?"

I said nothing in reply, just held my eyes on her face, hoping she would make no further attempt to deny the moment, the first time I dared to talk openly.

We started walking slowly. I took her hand, placing her arm through mine. The aroma around her was sweet. Anna was quiet, keeping her eyes looking forward, but it was plain to see thoughts moving quickly through her mind. When we reached Doc Foster's house, big drops of rain pelted us, and thunder suddenly blasted the silence. "Hurry!" I said, grasping her hand tighter, running toward Miz Foster's garden house, only a few yards from the street, and mostly hidden by overgrown bushes and small trees. Doc Foster's old hound started barking, and I could see him standing, watching us from the porch. The door into the garden house opened easily and closed quickly behind us.

Anna began wiping the wetness from her arms and face with the hem of her skirt, then looked at me in the shadowy darkness. "We shouldn't be in here, Ben," she said, glancing around.

"Nobody will know," I said. "Poor Miz Mazie died a couple of years ago, and Doc Foster birthed everybody around here for forty years. He doesn't care." The rain was loud on the tin roof, and streams of water ran steadily down a lone window in the far side of the familiar little house. Lightning lit the window with a flash. The tall window overlooked the garden, which once was filled with flowers, where many times in the fall I raked leaves and helped Miz Mazie when I was a kid.

Carefully, I stepped through a maze of dusty pots and garden tools, left where they had been last used. I stood in front of the window. With my wrist, I wiped the dust from one of the panes so I could see the rain and watch the lightning light up the garden.

"This is a wonderful little house; it's so charming," Anna said while I peered through the glass. She came behind me and placed her arms around my waist. "Hold me, Ben, I'm cold," she whispered.

On a dusty windowpane, I wrote with my finger, "Ben loves Anna."

I turned and looked into her face, while wrapping my arms around her. Tears glistened in her eyes as she looked at me. "Ben; sweet, sweet Ben. You know we shouldn't." She placed her finger over my lips when I leaned to kiss her. "Ben, we don't have to do this."

"Yes, we do, Anna, we do."

Her body relaxed against mine.

"Because Ben loves Anna," I whispered in her ear.

Her hands caressed my face as she kissed me. I closed my eyes when again she pressed her lips to mine. Our breathing became short and quick. The thousands of thoughts I had had about Anna began to mesh in my mind and my body, and the dreams, which often ran wild and free in the middle of my nights, became real.

Thunder sounded again and again, and lightning lit the garden house with quick flashes.

And the rain came down.

The Garden House

Seven

During that summer, Anna and I were happy, always anxious and excited to be in the presence of each other. Uppermost during the day, we looked forward to meeting at the Gold Dust Bridge, where every evening seemed new, stirring our desires, which were rousing and invigorating. On days when the fields were too wet or there was little to do on the farm, we rode my horses through the broad expanses of cotton fields and explored deep into the woods in the east, where Dad and I had often hunted. Edward's Creek became our favorite place; we tied the horses and swam in the cool water, sometimes lingering in the quiet and seclusion for hours. We were as happy in those few weeks as we would ever be. But Anna never let go of what she considered to be her "plan," the plan she had already said did not include Gold Dust. Most evenings, we lingered at the bridge alone, sitting on the bank below it, talking about what the future might be with each other or away from each other, and listening to the cicadas sing their songs. When darkness set in, we would wander down the path leading to our secret place, the quaint little garden house left unattended for years. It wasn't long till we came to believe it was ours, left there, hidden from the world, just for us, for Anna and Ben.

But never did Anna commit herself to a future, or any part of one, that included me, a young man on a family farm deep in the Southern woods. At times, for reasons I didn't understand, sadness overwhelmed her, turning into sullen anger toward herself or her family. At times, she seemed annoyed by our closeness, our wanting, and it was those times that brought out the very best of her great talent in the drawings, paintings, and poetry she shared with me, of her deepest thoughts. Those times of sadness and anger weighed over her until something great came out, sometimes taking days, after which she would appear exhausted. Patiently I would wait, and always she returned to the Anna of my heart and my dreams, relishing our evenings beginning at the Gold Dust Bridge.

"Ben?" There was a question in her voice. Looking at her as we sat on the grass, I was overwhelmed by her beauty: the high cheeks and skin as smooth as silk, sculptured eyebrows over deep-set eyes, and hair the color of burned copper. And this beautiful woman was so close to me that I could touch her face, her hair, and take in the sweet aroma that always surrounded her. "Ben," she said again, as she leaned on one elbow, and nibbling on a straw of grass. I waited for her to say what was on her mind. "Ben," she said my name a third time, then leaned toward me, placing her hand on my cheek. "My time in Gold Dust is coming to an end, sweetheart," she said, and the spell I was under was suddenly broken. There was sadness in her voice. "What's going to happen to you, to us, when I leave?"

I held her hand against my cheek. "I'll be right here, Anna, waiting till you come back."

A slight frown appeared on her face. "No, Ben," she said, shaking her head. "You can't do that. That's not the way it should be." She glanced toward the water, then quickly back to me. Her words came out fast. "Just remember this summer; that's all you should do; that's all, Ben." She looked straight into my eyes, recognizing I was startled by what seemed to me was a sudden good-bye. "You'll have to let go and move on with your life. Move on, Ben; both of us have to move on."

We had had this conversation, I recalled, or parts of it, frequently in recent days, and I didn't want to hear it again. I tried to bring it to an end. "I'll be waiting, Anna. I've told you a thousand times. I'll be here, right here in Gold Dust. I'm not going anywhere."

She stood quickly and leaned over me, scolding, "No, no, *no*, Ben, you're not hearing me. I'm never coming back, so your being 'here' is not an answer." Her eyes filled with tears. "Do you hear me, Ben? I'm not coming back," she said calmly. "Do you not understand?"

I had already jumped to my feet and was reaching for her, but she pushed me away. "Just go to hell, Benjamin, and leave me alone!" she cried, holding both hands over her face.

Before she could move, I grabbed her and pulled her to me. She beat on my back with her fists, and her sobs began to come in heartbreaking gasps. "Stop, Anna. Stop crying, please," I said. She laid her head on my chest. "It'll be less than a year and we'll be together. That's the best we can do right now. Just a little time, that's all we need, and we'll work things out. It'll be okay."

"No, Ben," she said, "it's not going to be okay, and we don't have time." In her voice, there was urgency and fear, complicating my thoughts. Quickly she added, "And it's entirely your fault, Ben, entirely your fault."

"I know," I said jokingly, in an attempt to lessen the anxiety. "We should never have fallen in love, right?"

"No! No!" she said, glaring at me, with our faces only inches apart. "Benjamin, think back a little, just ten weeks ago, I didn't even know you, and look what you've done, what's happened to us."

"I've only loved you, Anna, just loved you with everything I have. You own all of me, every bit of me, and I'm not sorry about loving you," I said. I'd become impatient with arguing about something for which there was no immediate solution.

She spoke softly, "I know, and that's why it's your fault, Benjamin. I didn't love you then, ten weeks ago. I didn't know you, but you made me love you, you *made* me love you, and here we are, locked in something we created, but not prepared for. And there's nothing we can do about it." She wiped her eyes. "This is your world, Benjamin, Gold Dust, and I have no place in it." She shook her head, surprising me with her conclusiveness and the angry tone in her voice. "Let me go, Ben, would you please? I have to go," she said.

I opened my arms, and she pushed me away, glancing at me for only a second. Without saying anything, she picked up her drawing pad and pencils, and walked up the slope to the bridge, stopping at the top of the bank. From there, she looked down at me. "Go home, Ben. Go home, and forget about me; leave me alone." She turned and ran.

The sound of a car moving slowly across the old bridge caused me to look up and then down into the water, where a thousand little rocks were falling through the cracks of the old bridge's floor, making hundreds of ripples. The bridge moaned.

The last rays of the big, round sun, setting over the line of trees in the west, lit the highest peak of the Gold Dust Bridge, and like the sun, its peak glowed bright and orange, but it was silent. My head pounded, and all I could hear was the constant roar of the cicadas screaming from the trees along the bank. Their sound was tormenting, and mocking, too; so loud and as scornful as Anna's last words: "Go home, Ben, and forget about me, leave me alone."

I sat on the grass, hoping with all my heart Anna would return. I watched the deep waters of Edward's Creek flow slowly in front of me, going somewhere, away from me, from Gold Dust. To where? I didn't know. I had never thought about it.

A surge of darkness covered me, and my head and my heart ached.

I waited in the blackness of a night with no moon. The cicadas sang louder.

Miz Margaret's Store

Eight

According to my mother, the people around Gold Dust enjoyed and thrived on the gossip about Anna and me. Some wrote it off as a summer thing between two kids, but others whispered with cunning and maliciousness. That tended to be the impetus for the grimaces and the rolling of eyes. I didn't care, and I'm sure Anna gave the gossip no thought at all, but it weighed heavily on my mother's mind. At breakfast the morning after Anna left me at the bridge, Mom told me Miz Margaret had mentioned that several customers had said Anna was causing problems in our family. Mom told me she had denied any such thing to Miz Margaret, but I felt sure Mom was stretching the truth, being angered that Anna and I had no doubt become far more than just friends, and she was enraged by the gossip. I realized, too, Miz Margaret was keeping my mother well informed about Anna and me.

"Don't worry, Mom," I said. "Anna and I have to work a few things out, but I'm pretty sure everything's going to be okay." She was incensed by my words.

As she cooked my breakfast, she kept pounding her words on me: "Ben, you've got a lot in front of you for the next few years; your last year of high school and four years of college if we can get the money to send you. By then, that girl will be almost thirty years old and doing no telling what." I refused to look at her, despising the referral to Anna as "that girl." I gritted my teeth as she went on, "She's a big city girl, Ben, a big city girl, and Margaret will tell you exactly what I'm saying. There's a tremendous difference when you compare her to the sweet and innocent girls you know around here." I could tell by the tone of her voice and the expression on her face that I could say nothing to stop the cruel and unjustified remarks about Anna. She turned from the stove and raised her finger, pointing it straight at my face. "She'll never fit into the way we live here, and you're wasting your time if you think she would ever try." She stopped for a second and looked squarely at me, shaking her head in anger. "You're just like every man I've ever known, thinking about only one thing, and I don't have to tell you what that is, do I?" She hesitated. "You've been foolish, Benjamin, and now you'll have to pay the price for a long time to come, a hell of a long time."

My mother's predictions cut through my brain like a sharp knife, while her voice rumbled like thunder, rolling and tumbling. When I glanced up at her face, I cringed. Lightning was about to strike. Her fist was balled and ready.

While she yelled, I said nothing for fear of worsening the situation or prolonging her outburst. I realized she had come to the point of hitting me, and it dawned on me that, perhaps, her anger stemmed from something more than Anna and me. I waited for her to calm down, and when she finally stopped ranting, I stood and looked at her. "Mom," I said, calmly. "Be patient, would you, please? And right now, I'm going to see Anna. This is my life you're raging about."

She turned from the stove, slammed my breakfast plate onto the table, and stood waiting for my next sentence. "Mom," I said softly, "when Dad comes in for breakfast, tell him I'll meet him later in the morning, please."

A Full-Grown Man

My mother, breathing fast and shallow, her face tense, and her hair standing on end, appeared like a raging bull, hurting and desperate, and ready to charge.

I left the kitchen.

Nine

Holding the screen door until it closed, I waited while Miz Margaret finished speaking with an older lady at the counter. When the lady turned toward me, she glanced the other way, raised her chin slightly, and hurried, passing just inches from me, not speaking. Her heels tapped the floor with each little step. "Good morning, Miz Hazel," I called after her just as the screen door slammed. "And I hope you're doing well this morning!" I called out louder. Then, looking across the counter, I glared at Miz Margaret, and the sadness on her face told me something had happened. "What? What's wrong, Miz Margaret? What's the matter?"

Behind her glasses, I could see the redness in her eyes and the tears. "Oh, Ben, I'm so sorry," she said, speaking the words slowly while shaking her head.

"Sorry, Miz Margaret? Sorry about what? About what?" I asked hurriedly, leaning over the counter toward her. "What's wrong? Why are you crying?"

"Ben, darling, Anna left this morning, very upset and angry." Miz Margaret wiped her eyes. "I just don't know what's going to happen to my sweet Anna." Her chin quivered.

My mouth opened but nothing came out. "Left?" I said, finally. "Where'd she go so early? I need to talk to her." Louder, I demanded, "I have to talk to her, now!"

"Oh, no, Ben, she caught the first train to New Orleans. She's on her way home, to Philadelphia. She hadn't told you, darling?" Miz Margaret removed her glasses, wiping her eyes again. "Bless her heart," she said, "I know what she's going through," and while fitting her glasses on her face, she added, "I know what she must be thinking."

I felt as though someone had knocked the wind completely out of me. I could think of nothing, only Anna. "Why?" I asked softly. "Why would Anna leave this way?"

"Ben, you're so young, darling; just a boy. You'll understand one day, in time," Miz Margaret said, tears in her eyes again.

I glared at her. *A boy, I'm just a boy, and I'd understand one day,* I thought, *What would I understand? That Anna had plans, but not for me. That she didn't want me? No,* I thought, *I understand it now, right now.* I turned, slowly making my way to the front door, feeling sick to my stomach. Before I could kick open the screen door, she called after me. "Here, Ben," she said, stepping in my direction, holding a small white envelope toward me. "This is for you, darling. Anna asked me to make sure you got it."

I walked across the porch, stepped onto the gravel, and stopped. Through the tears, I could see the Gold Dust Bridge standing in the bright sun, a hundred yards in front of me. It cast shadows, confusing shadows from its iron beams, and it stood waiting for me to come. Twenty feet away, I stopped until an oncoming car crossed its rotting wood and rusting iron. As the car passed in front of me, the old bridge groaned quietly, assuring me it knew everything about Anna and me. And high in its beams, it held the passion of young lovers, our secrets, and our wishes. It groaned again, and I knew that every time I crossed the Gold Dust Bridge I would replay in my mind every moment of the events of that summer. And forever the old bridge would stand in mockery of what Anna and I had, but now it was gone. Anna had vanished from my life, and suddenly, the only thing left was a small white envelope I did not dare to open.

Lonely and cold, but sweating in the dampness of the warm morning air, I stood in the middle of the bridge, looking upward, searching through its rusting iron for something, anything to help me understand what had happened. The sun was there, already bright and hot, and in anger, I cursed it: the bridge, and this place, Gold Dust. And I cursed myself.

Time stopped for me when Anna left, and I knew I was no longer the kid I had been when she arrived that summer. My childhood had long ago passed; I misplaced my youth, and rushed into the certainty of manhood. And Anna left me, and with her, she took it all, even my heart.

Ten

THE STAIRS SEEMED STEEPER than usual, and my legs felt heavy. Sitting on the bed, I turned the envelope in my hand, glancing at the beautiful writing on the front. Only two words, two words: "Ben Bennefield," written in delicate strokes by an artist. Still, I didn't want to see what Anna had written inside, the words of someone I loved who had angrily told me to leave her alone and go away. The words tore at my heart.

I jumped when Mom's excited screams suddenly came charging up the stairs. "Benjamin, come quick! It's your dad! Hurry!"

I dropped the envelope on the bed. From the panic in my mother's voice, I knew something had happened, something bad, and I charged through the hall and down the stairs as she called again.

My mother was kneeling on the kitchen floor, fanning Dad with a dish towel, as he lay still and white beside the table, so white I knew it was too late. Life was leaving my father as I dropped to the floor beside him. He raised his hand, whispering his last words, "Take care of this farm, Ben, and be careful."

"No ... no!" I could hear myself yelling, and as the tears flooded my eyes, I looked at Mom kneeling beside me. "Why, Mother? What happened?" I yelled at her. "He's too young to die."

She stared at me but said nothing, shaking her head, with her eyes locked on my face. She stood. I heard her sigh, deep, letting the air out fast. I looked up at her. Her lips were tightly pursed, and her eyes, dry and piercing, glared down at me.

"Get up, Benjamin," she said. "Get up, boy," she demanded. Her lips turned down.

Will Bennefield was a strapping man, and tough, but a kind and gentle man whose time had been too short. My father was my hero, and though I had never told him in so many words, for all of my life I believed he knew it. *Take care of this farm, Ben*, his words slammed inside my head. I closed my eyes as I knelt on the floor beside him, and like lightning in a stormy night, his words, *Be careful*, lit up my thoughts, like a warning, a warning for my future. For the second time that day, my heart had been torn out of me and crushed.

Over the next few days, I thought of his last words a thousand times. They were a whisper at times, and at other times a demand in my father's usually strong voice. Each time they crossed my mind, memories, too, struck hard in my heart, memories of my favorite times with him; when we stood for hours, back to back, fly-fishing the shallows along the bank of Edward's Creek, almost without words; and the hours we sat against the trunk of a big tree deep in the canopied woods, when he gave me my first gun, explaining the patience of a hunter. I was ten years old, my birthday, a cold, damp day near the start of winter.

The day we buried our father, my older sister Barbara arrived from New Orleans with her husband and three children, their first visit to Gold Dust in several years. Ours was obviously a strained relationship; we greeted each other and hugged, but Barbara and I had little to say to one another, as the commonality of our childhoods had long been laid aside. It appeared to me, and I despised the thought, that our father's death was a great imposition to Barbara, her husband, and her children. Seldom through the years had they made the trip to Gold Dust, where our mundane life was far removed from their lives in New Orleans. In their thinking, every place outside of the city was "the country," and everything anyone could possibly want or need was in "the city." Five minutes after the minister said "Amen," they bid a quick good-bye to Mom, and I walked with them to their car. While I held the car door open for Barbara, she turned to me with tears in her eyes, a surprise to me, hugged me, and whispered, "I love you, Ben. Be careful, and take care of yourself." They drove away.

The direct route from White's Cemetery to our home was a short distance, but after the funeral, I chose to drive the long way back to avoid crossing the Gold Dust Bridge. Mom said nothing about the change. She looked through the open window at the long flat fields, at the cotton that gave us our livelihood from one year to the next. The breeze through the truck's windows was hot and dry, and the white fields were beautiful like new-fallen snow, but what I saw when I looked across them was the hard work ahead and the upcoming task of getting the crop out of the fields before winter.

Mom's hand moved from her lap to her dark blue hat, then she turned to look at me. "I'm sorry, Ben, so sorry," she said.

"Me, too, Mom. He was a good man, and I loved him, and I'm gonna miss him. Look at all the people who came to the funeral, everybody from miles around." I was sad and lonely, in a bad dream, unable to fathom the death of my father. Already I missed him, but not yet realizing how much and for how long.

"I know, Ben, and I'm sorry your dad's gone, but my heart—" she stopped in mid-sentence, and I glanced to see her face. "My heart cries for you, my boy, for you, and there's nothing I can do to change it."

She took her hat off and set it on her lap, looking again across the fields. Her hair blew free and wild.

Frowning, I looked toward her, questioning why she would be so distraught about me. I was young, and I had my whole life in front of me. "Why, Mom, what about me?" I said. "We just buried Dad and … and, what's the matter?"

"Oh, Benjamin, you're so young," she said. Her hesitation and the look on her face made me anxious. "I'm sure you realize you're gonna have to take over the farm, take your Dad's place, don't you?" Again, she stopped, but before I could say anything, she went on. "It's yours to work now. You're the only man in the family, and we have a lot going on."

We looked straight into each other's face, my mouth open.

"Mom! School's starting in a couple of weeks, and I—" but before I could get the words out, she continued laying out a plan, which sounded conceived long ago. A puzzling, slight smile crossed her face, and while I drove, I glanced back and forth between her face and the road, waiting for her next words.

"I suppose you'll have to stay out of school at least till the cotton's in, then maybe you can start in November or December, if you think you need to." Again, she looked out the window, while shading her eyes with one hand placed on her forehead.

My mother's words, with the reality of the consequences of my father's sudden death, shook me, stirring anger as her words sank in. I stopped the truck on the side of the road and leaned forward, letting my head rest against the steering wheel, and trying hard not to say anything that would make the conversation explode. After a second, I felt her hand on my shoulder, then slowly, she moved it up and down my back, mocking me. "Oh, poor Ben," she said, "you're suddenly a full-grown man, whether you like it or not, and we'll just have to weigh all of the responsibilities of the farm and our lives against what might have been otherwise." Her voice was grating and humiliating.

I jerked away and pounded the steering wheel with both hands. She knew I was stunned by what she had said. "Oh, don't be angry, Benjamin. Plans change people, and people change plans all the time." The tone in her voice rose. "And our lives are changing," she said, "and you're the only one I have now, the only one left." My breaths were short as I searched in her face. "But I'm going to take care of you, Ben; don't worry, son."

I looked at my mother in disbelief that she intended for me to forgo my last year of high school, knowing my father would not have allowed it to happen. But I believed completely she expected I should, without question, follow through with her plans, plans I was sure were punishment for my summer with Anna, and *sentencing* for being the son of Will Bennefield. Feeling the blood rush to my head, I hit the steering wheel with both hands, and shouted, "And where is my letter, damn it? What did you do with Anna's letter, Mother?"

She glared at my face, her eyes in narrow slits, and her lips moving into a slight smile. "Letter?" she said calmly, never blinking. "Ben, what are you talking about, son?"

"You know damn well what I'm talking about, from Anna, it was in my room. I had it when you yelled about Dad," I said. "And I want it, damn it!" My breaths were short and fast. My head throbbed. Mother sighed, raised her chin, and turned to look across the wide, silent fields of white, shading her eyes with one hand, while biding for time. Whatever came out of her mouth next, I was certain, would be a lie.

"No, Benjamin," she said, holding her stare to the distance. "I don't have your letter, and unless you put it away somewhere, it probably was thrown in the trash and burned when your room was cleaned." I wiped my hand across my parched lips. And I knew, as far as my mother was concerned, her plans were laid out, the rules were set, and the talking was done.

I pounded the steering wheel again, and let out on the clutch. The truck jerked, and the engine roared while the wheels spun in the dirt and gravel. Hester never flinched.

Anna. I thought about Anna.

The Depot

Eleven

BEFORE THE MIDDLE OF November, we sent the last of our cotton to the gins. The railroad depot was laden with bales waiting for boxcars to take it to the mills up north, to Alabama, Georgia, and the Carolinas. Without a doubt, the crop that year was the largest in Gold Dust's memory, making the harvest that year, long and tiring. Dad would have been proud had he been around, and by the time Christmas came, he would have begun planning for spring, the time for planting.

There was no talk about my senior year of high school, and it wasn't long before it was lost in the everyday work of running a large farm. I had erased the idea of going to college from the list of my plans, Ben Bennefield's future. Before the harvest season ended that year, I had become a farmer, a seventeen-year-old cotton farmer who moved cautiously from one day to the next, hoping time and weather would not overtake his lack of experience. Mom continued to give most of her attention to taking care of the livestock she counted as her own, but she insisted the horses both Dad and I had loved be sold in the spring, another punishment, in my mind, for the summer just past. She continued the role she always seemed to relish, keeping control of her house and handling the usual amount of business associated with the farm.

I came to realize my mother's strength, an innate power that made her who she was. But it appeared, and I believed, my father's death had changed her, not as a grieving widow, but quickly, in other ways I was yet to understand. Never was I able to predict her thoughts and ideas about the farm, or about our relationship. Early on, she seemed emboldened and excited, but after a few short months, she became more demanding and controlling. At other times, finding her alone in the silence of the dark living room, she seemed burdened and almost apologetic for being, for existing. She left home far less frequently, and retrieving the mail by daily visits to the post office in Gold Dust was the highlight of her day. She appeared angered, however, when only a few pieces or no mail came, ranting that the postmistress was "hiding her mail," or giving it to somebody else. Bitterness began to seep into her mind, manifesting as paranoia, making her sullen and suspicious of everyone's intent.

By the time the cotton was gathered the following year, her physical health had begun to fail badly, which brought on more bitterness, and frequent bouts of mental anguish. She often complained about a fence, a fence she felt surrounded her. It had no gates and was too high to climb, and the enclosure was getting smaller, almost by the day. Unbelievably to me, visits to Miz Margaret's store had nearly ceased. Soon, she seemed always angry, lamenting she had long expected "everyone she chose to love" would abandon her. Often, her emotions triggered days of fury toward whoever was nearest to her, most often me, and frequently my sister Barbara, who never made any attempt to soothe Mother's heart and mind. Mother's memories of times in her youth, as she would off-handedly comment, were frequently re-created in her mind, setting off vengeful ideas about Dad and me and jealousy regarding the marvelous and loving relationship my sister and I had had with our father.

In the spring of the next year, on a beautiful afternoon, I left the fields early with the two farm hands I had hired full time, Henry Brown and Bo Johnson. I felt good, with a sense of accomplishment, rejoicing after having planted the last eighty acres on land we had purchased from a retiring neighbor. We knew in about ten days the sprouts of new plants would suddenly mark the long rows with bright green lines, a particularly gratifying moment in the springtime for a cotton farmer.

The brakes on the truck squealed as I brought it to a halt at the end of the brick sidewalk leading to the back porch. Lucy and Jake jumped from the rear bed and waited happily, with tails wagging and ears laid back, for me to open the truck door, greeting me as though they hadn't seen me for several days. Just as I knelt to hug my dogs, a blast from the house rocked me, causing both dogs to suddenly bark and whine. The screen door onto the porch slammed back when I flung it open in my rush to the kitchen door. I stopped abruptly at the threshold. Lying on the floor beside the table, I recognized my mother by the work clothes she always wore. Her body was jerking as life left her. In her hand, she clutched a piece of paper.

My legs weakened as I looked at the scene on the floor. Breathless, I picked up the gun—both barrels had emptied—and leaned it against the wall. Why, I wondered, had I not arrived only a minute sooner? Happenstance, I figured. If only I hadn't played with Lucy and Jake, but I always did. And my mother was gone in an instant! In my mind, and for a reason I couldn't explain to myself, I felt as though I had been placed here deliberately; I was the center of this terrible happening. But still, I wondered where I had failed so badly, why I had not seen it coming, and what I could have done to stop my mother from killing herself.

Slumping into a chair at the table, I took a deep breath, covering my nose to shield the stench of open flesh and blood. I looked up to the speck-marked ceiling and then covered my eyes with my other hand, wondering if anything else so horrible and tragic could possibly happen in my life. I sat up straight in the chair, my hands shaking, as I opened the note I had taken from my mother's fist. Surprisingly, I said her name out loud, slowly, "Hester McGinnis Bennefield," and I couldn't help feeling my throat tighten, while tears came into my eyes. I wished, again, I had seen it coming, and wondered why I hadn't. "What," I said out loud, "did I do to cause this?"

The smell of spent gunpowder and blood overwhelmed the room. I lay the piece of paper on the table, smoothing its wrinkles with my hand, and read the words in silence.

Dearest Hester,

Money is not the problem, and I believe you. But you have your son and I have others who need me. Leaving is far too drastic a change this late in my life. I'm very sorry.

"M"

At the time, the few words written on the paper meant nothing; no clue why my mother had taken her life. People would say it was a choice she had made and condemn her to hell, but I knew her reasons were far reaching, very deep, private, and hidden.

Crushing the note in my fingers, then wadding it into a tiny ball with both palms, I let it drop to the floor. Slowly, it rolled, stopping against my mother's hand, a fist on the linoleum of black and white squares. I cursed myself, again.

Cotton

Twelve

Two days later, I stood in White's Cemetery at my mother's burial, looking into the freshly turned dirt. I questioned myself, wondering about the oddity of the course my life had taken; almost a stranger now, from the summer when Anna was with me, through the deaths of my father and my mother and the estrangement of a sister who left long ago. I had no one to touch or to touch me; no one to listen when I spoke my heart, or to hold me when I cried; no one to love, and no one who loved me. And everything that happened pressed on my mind, my emotions heavy. I felt myself stretching as I stood; holding up my chin, looking at no one; trying, I suppose, to pull myself above the anger, bitterness, and overwhelming self-pity. Like my friend Anna, I had made plans, too, but events and circumstances over which I had no say or control had changed the direction of my life. Who I was that day, and where I was in time, just happened, and happened by chance, by a stroke of fate. My eyes wandered across the hundreds of tombstones set in memory of lives long ago lived and now silent and cold, and I thought to myself: Maybe Benjamin Bennefield could justify and validate his own life by saying simply, "Here I am by the grace of God," and let it be. I shook my head, wondering.

A Full-Grown Man

In times of trial or torment, my thoughts most often turned to Anna and our summer together. Sometimes foggy, at other times clear, the memories were always good, bringing excitement, joy, and sometimes laughter; and then, the kid, the small pieces of my youth still lingering quietly inside me, would stir and cry for what might have been. And when I had wanted and needed someone to listen, to touch me, and to hold me, it was Anna who came to mind, exciting me, and bringing up my spirits.

Deep in thought as I was, and with a clouded mind, the minister's words reached me like sounds coming from far away. I winced when I felt a hand grasp mine and not let go. At the same time, I was stunned when the preacher read, "Let he who is without sin, cast the first stone," my mother's favorite quote, and one she had used at will. At that very moment, it seemed exceedingly meaningful. "Amen," he said, as I glanced at Miz Margaret, holding my hand.

She looked up at my face, and I could tell she had been crying. "Oh, Benjamin, I'm so sad about your mother," she said in a whisper. "She was dear to me, and I always enjoyed her coming to the store. And I'm—" she stopped and looked to the casket in front of us. "I'm going to miss her dreadfully. It's just awful. I feel so bad about it." She looked at my face with a faint smile. "Ben, you were closest to her, but don't feel guilt or anger about what she did. Just try to think the very best about her. In time, it'll all seem better." Sadness and sincerity showed plainly on her face, but her words, which should have been comforting, seemed needless and empty.

"Thanks, Miz Margaret, you're kind to say so, and I thank you."

She didn't smile as she dropped a folded paper into my coat pocket. "Read this, Ben, the first chance you get, darling," she said. "My aunt in Philadelphia sent it to me last week. You'll be proud." Forcing a faint smile again, she continued, "Come see me, Ben. Don't wait so long. Bye now." She raised her hand and set her glasses over teary eyes, then reached to place a single red rose atop my mother's casket. Watching as she walked toward the front gate of White's Cemetery, I felt bad that I hadn't set foot in her store since the morning Anna suddenly departed Gold Dust and my life.

At White's Cemetery

Thirteen

THE RIDE HOME WAS quick, and I spent most of it pondering Barbara's troubling absence at our mother's funeral. I opened the door into a freshly cleaned kitchen, reached into the pocket of my coat, and pulled out the folded paper Miz Margaret had placed there. I put it on the kitchen table with my keys, then fumbled through the refrigerator for a beer. After a few seconds, I unfolded the paper and saw it was a clipping from a newspaper, but before I could settle into a chair and read it, a car came to a stop at the end of the sidewalk. Standing at the screen door, I waited while my sister walked toward the porch. She stopped at the bottom of the steps and looked up at me.

"You're too late," I scolded. "I've already buried her."

Barbara was alone. Her purse dangled down to her knees. I could see the sadness and weariness on her face. After a couple of seconds she said, "Ben, for your sake, I'm sorry I missed the funeral, but I didn't decide to come till late in the morning, and the traffic was terrible."

"Why? You haven't been a part of the family for years, Barbara. To be perfectly honest about it, I figured you wouldn't show up." I made no offer for her to come up the steps.

"Ben, I must tell you. I didn't come here to go to the funeral, or cause a fight. I came to see *you*." Then she asked, "Are you going to let me come in?"

I held the screen door open. Slowly, she ascended the steps, neither of us saying anything. She crossed the porch, moving slowly to the kitchen door, and stopped at the threshold. She looked into the kitchen for a second, then stepped inside, and stopped again. Her eyes scanned the room, up and down and across. "Don't worry," I said, "there's nothing left of her in here. We've cleaned up the mess."

Barbara said nothing as she walked to the table, laid her purse to one side, and dropped into one of the chairs. Nervously, she smiled, glancing at me as I continued to stand. She broke the silence, teary eyed, "I'm so sorry, Benjamin, that we're no longer friends, brother and sister friends." She sniffed, then reached for her purse. "And the blame for that misfortune, I know, is mine." She cut her eyes up to me.

I had waited for this moment, when I could put into words what had been on my mind. "Sister, let me tell you this," I started, with my finger pointed toward her face. "I hardly know you at all. You've been gone for a hell of a long time, a hell of a long time," I repeated, slowly. "I was only ten when you left for college, and I missed you. I missed you a lot." Hesitating for a second as my voice began to break, I continued, "Now tell me how a friendship builds when a little kid hasn't heard from or seen his sister but two or three times in ten years? Barbara, that's nearly half of my life."

In the softness of her eyes and the sadness on her face, I could see she was sincere and hurting. "Ben, please sit down," she begged, "and let me tell you all of it, everything; things I'm sure you've never known." I pulled a chair up to the opposite side of the table, sat, and waited, with my eyes locked on her face. She placed her fingers over her lips then removed them. "By the time I left Gold Dust, I was becoming a sour and mean young woman, much like our mother." I shook my head at her words. "Ben," she said, questioning the frown on my face, "she had been trained by her mother to shield herself from everybody, to be distrustful of love, and to care for no one … to give no love nor take it." Barbara shook her head; the tone in her voice rose, "She never had fun, and resented anyone who did," she said. "I never heard my mother laugh. She couldn't. And I was being trained to be the same way."

"Trained?" I shot back, angrily. "What are you talking about, Barbara? You were spoiled by Mom. Even at my age, I could tell."

"Yes, spoiled, too, or whatever you want to call it," she said, "but believe me, there was a purpose to all of the attention she paid me, a purpose, which eventually I came to recognize." She stopped for a second, frowning. "Ben," she said, "Mother never loved Dad; in fact, she came close to hating him, and she often criticized and ridiculed him, cursing him for no reason at all. Even tidbits of gossip about any man around here sent her into a rage she would turn on Dad and use on me, about how evil all men are, and how they take advantage of unsuspecting women." I rolled my eyes skeptically. She continued. "Benjamin, Mom hated men, all men. It didn't matter who they were, and that's the way she wanted me to be, too." Barbara's eyes filled with tears. "Her mother was the same way, Ben. Mom talked about it often." She stopped and sighed heavily, smiling a little. "She liked you, Ben, because she birthed you; you belonged to her … and you were just a little ole boy, not a full-grown man."

"You came all the way from New Orleans to tell me this garbage," I said. "What are you doing here, Barbara? Mom is gone and never coming back, so what … what does it matter anymore?" I said, shrugging.

"It matters, Benjamin," Barbara replied, "it matters to me because I was old enough to see how badly Dad was hurt when she accused him of things he never did, to me, his daughter. Over and over she lied to me, and over and over she tried to convince me how evil he was, how evil all men are, at least in her thinking." She wiped her eyes. "It isn't easy to say these things about her, but she was different, Ben. Even small things, like when Dad would hug me. Right in front of me, she would forbid him from touching me, and later she would try to convince me he was abusing me." Again, she touched her eyes with the tissue. "Can you imagine her doing that?" she asked. "And I knew he wasn't abusing me. The whole idea was ridiculous."

By now I was concerned. Barbara continued, "Ben, Mom's mother's older cousin had abused her when she was around seven or eight years old, and for years Grandmother blamed Mom. Later, Grandmother tried to cover it over, explaining to Mom that men did those things, and anyway, it was a family matter, and no one's business around here." Barbara began to cry. "And when Dad died so suddenly, and he was no longer around to bear the brunt of her anger and bitterness, I figured you were old enough, and she would soon turn her hate and resentment on you."

What I had just heard from Barbara was far more than I wanted to hear, especially about my mother, whom I had buried that morning. My mind was running fast, picking up on conversations with my mother and angry arguments I had had with her, confirming some of what my sister was saying. I shook my head, grimacing.

Speaking slowly and calmly, I told her, "It doesn't matter now, Barbara. Dad's gone and Mom's gone, and all of the misery and hate you may have seen is behind us. It's you and me here now, and I'm sorry if I appear unconcerned." I wanted to reach out to her, but at that moment I wasn't ready, and couldn't do it. "Sister, I have so much in front of me right now, so many things," I said, leaning my head into both hands with my elbows on the table. "And I don't much give a damn, not any more."

Without saying anything, Barbara reached over and took my hand, holding it. We looked at each other, and she said softly, "I'm your sister, Ben, your sister who loved you when you were a little boy, and I loved our father as much as any daughter could ever love her dad, but I was being made into the likes of a deceitful and self-centered woman. I really hope you were never a part of the problems with our mother, and now that she's gone, I want a chance for us to start again, from where we were before I left Gold Dust."

In silence, we looked across the table at each other. Suddenly, a loud knock echoed through the house and then another. I stood, looking at my hurting sister. "Another well-wisher with a plate of food, I'm pretty sure. I'll see who's there," I said, while walking out of the kitchen.

Before I could reach the front door, another knock rang out. "Coming," I yelled, quickly turning the latch. I opened the door to find a basket of fruit, beautifully wrapped, held up to hide the face of the bearer, but instantly, I recognized her. "Ava, come in, come in," I said.

The basket lowered slowly, revealing Ava Koller, smiling. She set the basket on the floor at her side, then standing on tiptoes, she wrapped her arms around my neck and pressed her lips tightly against mine. When she released her kiss, I felt her sweet breath on my neck as she whispered in my ear, "Oh, Ben, you were so busy at the funeral, darlin', and I was so sad for you, so I decided I'd come by here and cheer you up." She wiped the lipstick from my lips with the tip of her finger. "How are you, sweetheart?"

"Oh, I'm fine; everything's okay," I said softly. But before either of us could say another word, Ava dropped her arms from around me and stepped back as Barbara approached behind me.

"Hello, I'm Barbara, Ben's sister," she said, extending her hand to Ava.

Still obviously taken aback, Ava glanced at me, smiled, and reached toward Barbara with one hand while fidgeting with her blouse with the other. "I'm so sorry," she said. "I didn't mean to interrupt a family meeting."

"No family meeting, Ava. We're just visiting," Barbara said, shaking Ava's hand as she examined her, from her hat down to her shoes.

Ava, still flustered by Barbara's sudden appearance, held her chin up, smiling and holding her eyes on me. "Oh, I had almost forgotten you had a sister, Ben," she said. Then she looked back at Barbara, "But it's certainly good to meet you, Barbara, and I'm so sorry about what happened to your mother."

Barbara smiled nicely. "Thank you, Ava. It was a shock to us and everyone around, but everything's going to be okay. That's the way we feel."

"Well," Ava said, fumbling with the latch on her purse. "I must be on my way. It's nice to see you, Barbara. And Ben, darlin', I'll see you later."

Ava turned quickly and crossed the porch. As she moved down the steps, I called after her, "Thanks for the basket, Ava! Talk to you later! Oh," I quickly reminded her, "I have a phone now! 5-1-0. Call me, it's five-ten! Remember!" I glanced at Barbara, who, with a discerning smile, was watching Ava as she walked down the sidewalk toward her car.

"Well, she's a fine one, Ben, and lively, too," she whispered. "Look at that strut; she knows we're watching." Barbara looked at me, smiling, and then she chuckled. "She'll call, 'darlin', before the sun goes down."

I picked up the basket of fruit, saying nothing as we returned to our places in the kitchen. From across the table, and with her lips partly opened and smiling, Barbara waited, looking at me.

"What?" I asked. "What do you want to know? Go ahead, ask me."

I waited, looking at her face and smiling also.

She tilted her head a little to the side. "So, who's Ava, Ben … tell me about her, and are there other Avas poking around you, little brother?"

"She's Ava Koller," I said. "You remember. Her dad owns the old Star Plantation up the road a few miles. She's a nice girl, spoiled a little, but she's great." I shrugged.

"Great! Great where?" she asked, chuckling, and added quickly, "Oh, Ben, I'm kidding," and she brushed her hand toward me. "But I'll bet there are others standing in line out there, waiting, and hoping for their turn to pounce on my little brother. Am I right, Benjamin?"

"Why am I telling you this?" I questioned, sighing. "It's none of your damn business, but yes, there are a lot of girls out there in the bushes." Shaking my head, I said, "But believe me, they're all just alike, every one of 'em's the same; well, except Ava," I added quickly. "She's different, in fact, a hell of a lot different." How strange it felt to be talking to my sister about myself, about what was happening in my life. Never before had I had anyone to talk to this way, not even my close friend, James Bartlett. It felt good, and I repeated, "Yeah, they're all alike."

"What do you mean, Ben? Alike, how?"

"Well," I sighed, "they're three-kissers. That's what I call them." I smiled.

"Three-kissers, Ben?" she asked, frowning. "What are three-kissers?"

"Well," I gestured, holding up three fingers. "After the first kiss, she wants you to meet her parents; as soon as the second kiss is over, she wants to talk about getting married." Barbara began to laugh. "And as soon as you open your eyes, but before you catch your breath after the third kiss, she starts telling you how many kids she wants."

She laughed out loud. "Oh, Ben, you've got to be kidding," she said. "It sounds more like girlish infatuation with a little desperation thrown in. But listen, boy, you're a good catch."

I interrupted. "I'm not kidding, and believe me, that's the way it is around here," I said. "And no, I'm not a 'catch,' Barbara, not now, anyway."

Barbara shook her head a little. "Ben, you're a fantastically handsome young man, and what, twenty now, and a big-time farmer with lots of land? Wow!" Her voice went into a higher octave. "And you're a darn good fellow, so yes; you're a great 'catch,' Brother." She nodded, then warned, "Just be careful, Ben, or one day you'll find yourself in a snare, trapped by one of those 'three-kissers.'" She laughed out loud.

"You know," I said very seriously, "everyone leaves. Everyone leaves from around here, except me. You first, then Dad, and now Mom, and most of the friends I grew up with. They're all gone. Oh, I have a few friends scattered around, and we get together for a beer or maybe a barbeque at someone's house. I guess I'd call it my 'social life,' but I've never left, and I'm pretty sure I'm tied here, probably forever, plowing the dirt, year after year, growing cotton."

Sadness covered her face, as though she might cry, and I continued, smiling, "Ava Koller's been good for me, a beautiful girl with a great personality, so I'm not really complaining," I said. "But it's different around here, you know. It's not New Orleans, not much to do, so," then I raised my hands in the air, "here I am, and here, I'll be."

In the silence that followed, I glanced to the floor then back at Barbara's face. "Barbara," I said, "I'm really glad you came. Thank you." She reached across the table and patted my hand, then took my fingers in hers. "Sometime, somewhere, I'll think about all you've told me, and yes, I see where you're coming from. But honestly, I was too young to be aware of all the bad things around me and the way you saw our lives back then. And yes, Mother had problems, a lot," I said. "But for quite a while now, I've had my share of events that 'happened,' crazy things I never knew how or why they came about. And I've had to deal with them the best way I could." I looked at my sister again. "There's a lot yet for me to understand, and I'm trying. And believe me, there are disappointments. But I'm pretty sure somewhere down the road, I'm going to figure out what my life should be. Until then, I'll just take what's in front of me and do the best I can."

Barbara stood, then walked around to my side of the table. "Hug me, Ben. Put your arms around your sister like you used to do," she said. We hugged, holding close to each other, and I remembered the warmth and secure feeling I had felt many years earlier from a kind and loving older sister who kissed my finger when it hurt, who picked me up when I fell. And again, the smattering of the kid lingering inside me wanted to cling to the moment and hold it, at least for a little while.

After a second or two, Barbara gently pushed away, her eyes set on mine. "Benjamin Bennefield, whether you realize it or have even thought about it, you're an unbelievable man to be so young," she said. "Find yourself a good woman to love and let her love you back. And enjoy life, Ben, look for joy and excitement. It's there, believe me."

She picked up her purse, stepped to the door, then crossed the porch, and walked down the steps. While I stood where we had first met that day, she looked up at me, and in a voice I remembered from a long time ago, she said, "See you later, Ben; I love you."

I watched till her car reached the main road. My mind and heart were drained, feeling tired and empty, but I smiled to myself, repeating out loud Barbara's advice, "Find yourself a woman to love, and let her love you back."

Immediately, my thoughts found Anna, Anna Mancini.

I sat at the table and took a sip of the beer I had taken from the refrigerator a few seconds before Barbara arrived, and nearly choked when I looked closely at the newspaper clipping Miz Margaret had placed in my pocket. Right before me was a picture of Anna. Beautiful Anna with the same dark hair and smile. My heart quickened as I recited the words just spoken by my sister. "A woman to love. A woman to love, and let her love you back."

I looked down at the clipping, reading it closely.

New York, NY April 10, 1954

**THE MUSEUM OF AMERICAN ART
IS PROUD TO ANNOUNCE AN EXCLUSIVE EXHIBIT
OF THE ART OF
ANNA MONTAGNE
DECEMBER 21, 1954
BY INVITATION ONLY
(WATCH FOR FALL ANNOUNCEMENTS)**

As I read the words and looked at Anna's picture, memories nearly three summers old, and heart wrenching, flooded my mind, flashing and quick, like my breathing.

Anna, a famous artist, and guessing from the name on the announcement, Anna must have married. "Anna Montagne, December 21," the announcement said. Eight months from now, after the cotton is in. Anna Montagne. *No, I don't think so. But I've never been to New York. That's Christmas anyway.*

Right then, I knew Anna's face would be at the forefront of my mind for weeks to come, and the memories would replay themselves over, and over, and over.

Fourteen

Remembering I was to help Henry with the chores that evening, I hurried up to my room to take off my black suit, my "funeral suit" now, since that was the only occasion for which I had worn it: two years ago when my father died, and the second time, to my mother's burial.

At the bottom of the stairs, I stopped with my hand on the railing, waited for several seconds, staring at the closed door to my mother's bedroom. This was a door never left open, and it was a room you dared not enter unless invited, a room that you eventually forgot was there. Slowly, as though waiting for someone to reprimand me, or perhaps a sudden bolt of lightning to hit me, I turned the knob and lightly pushed the door. Its hinges cried softly as it opened. Standing in the doorway, I glanced through the big room, expecting to hear Mother's yell, "What the hell do you think you're doing?" There was eerie silence.

Glancing from wall to wall and floor to ceiling, I was awed by the room's beauty and completeness. Slowly, I stepped to the middle, to a diamond in the center of a thick Persian carpet at the foot of the bed. According to my mother, the carpet was a gift sent by a cousin in Ireland and placed there by my Grandmother McGinnis many years before. Against the front wall, between two windows, was my mother's bed: a tall headboard, elaborately carved, with a crown at the peak in the center. Sitting beneath the windows on both sides of the bed, were large, ornate chests with four drawers, painted green with touches of gold. A tall lamp, a sculptured bronze lady, stood on each chest. On the wall opposite the bed was a fireplace surrounded by dark green marble, with a mantle of the same supported by marble columns. Above the mantle hung a mirror framed in a massive wood carving, meticulously gilded.

Mother's writing table and chair were placed in front of two windows very exactly so she could see easily across the flower garden, all the way to the gazebo on the bank of Edward's Creek. Two large, comfortable chairs—one had been my father's and the other one, my mother's—with a table and reading lamp sat facing the fireplace. Bookcases, with glass doors and holding hundreds of books, stood on each side of the marble mantle. Pictures of Mother's father and mother hung on the wall near the door. The room felt private, for a private individual, I understood; a place whose sanctity I could feel and, at that moment, was being violated by my presence. Slowly, I backed out of the room, pulling the door closed until I heard the latch click. Again, I stared at the closed door, realizing my hands were shaking, and knew that someday, perhaps when enough time had passed, I must go there again.

Fall came early that year, surprising the farmers. The rooftops around Gold Dust were whitened by the first frost on Halloween morning, and it lingered for several hours. Much of the cotton was still on the stalks. We knew that only a couple of weeks after the frost, the rains would start regularly, every two or three days, and there would not be enough time for the cotton to dry. My neighbor and friend Charles White sent his new mechanical cotton picker to run through the back acres on Saturday and Sunday two weeks after the frost, so we managed to get the first picking out before the cold rain set in. But the first week in December, the wetness turned into sleet and ice, lasting for two days, an unusual event in south Louisiana. The rain followed and continued for several more days, thus making the second picking of little value. Though our crop that year didn't match the abundance of the year before, it was considered another good year for cotton farmers. Nevertheless, at the end of every season, good or bad, a couple of older landowners usually decided to give it up and retire, offering outlying acreages of their farms to their adjoining neighbors. That year, I managed to add nearly two hundred acres to my farm, now a spread of over eight hundred acres of some of the finest cotton land for miles around the Gold Dust Bridge. I also built two four-room houses on the south bank of Edward's Creek, one for Henry Brown and his family, and the other one for Bo Johnson and his family. Like my father would have done, I rejoiced in the effort and celebrated the accomplishment. He would have been proud, and I knew it.

Fifteen

FOR NEARLY EIGHT MONTHS, my thoughts often centered on Anna, tempting me and exciting me about going to New York. I was puzzled by her new name, Montagne, but it was extraneous to my memories of our summer together and the strong desire to see her. When December finally came, I still had not decided, but in the middle of any night, I would awaken, unable to sleep, and attempt to make a decision. Anna, I knew, had long ago become an obsession, which at times became an excursion back to our summer together, and then at other times, it proved mood altering and interfered with relationships I wanted with others for whom I cared. But the long hours of solitude in the fields often seemed shortened and were made bearable by my passion for Anna.

Her show was only two weeks away, now. Both Henry and Bo encouraged me to make the trip to New York, assuring me everything would be fine while I was gone, and their encouragement was the impetus that clinched my decision. A visit with Miz Margaret secured the invitation I needed.

The weather was unusually warm for the twentieth day of December in 1954. From Gold Dust, I drove my old truck to New

Orleans, where I caught a plane to Washington and then to New York. Around midnight, a taxi delivered me to a hotel several blocks from the Museum of American Art, and when I stepped from the cab, a light snow was falling, accumulating along the sidewalks. The streets were shiny with wetness. *New York City*, I thought, *New York City*. I stood under the long, green canopy, wondering about the tall buildings, the shiny streets, and the smells surrounding me.

When daylight peeked around the edges of the heavy, dark draperies the next morning, I had already been awake for nearly an hour, lying in bed and wondering how to begin the day. And I was thinking about what I would say and how Anna might react when she saw me.

Near ten o'clock, I slipped on my usual attire, a cap, blue jeans, a sweater pulled over a T-shirt, and boots, and knowing I needed to find appropriate clothes for New York in December. I stepped through the hotel's front doors onto the sidewalk under the long canopy and looked around, deciding a direction I should take. A slow-falling snow like I had never seen—flakes the size of my thumb—excited me as I glanced up and down the busy street. Less than a block away, I found a shop that would have a suitable coat and whatever else I needed, including cuff links, which I had failed to pack with my shirt and funeral suit.

The man at the shop fitted me into a dark brown, wool coat. A long scarf as white as the snow outside was displayed on a rack nearby, and I bought it also, and a pair of soft leather gloves the color of the coat. And a set of gold cuff links. The gentleman chuckled each time I spoke and commented that my accent revealed my origins. He seemed to ask questions merely to hear me speak, eventually asking why I had come to New York. I told him about Anna Montagne's show at the Museum of American Art. He was well aware of the publicity surrounding the up-and-coming young woman whose talents, as the man quoted from a recent news article, "had fascinated, and captured the hearts and imaginations of many New Yorkers." When he asked how I knew her, I shrugged and said, "Just a friend from a time back." The expression on his face and the rolling of his eyes made clear he doubted I really knew the artist, but his questions ended. Very nicely, he thanked me for my purchases, and I left the fancy little shop, wearing my dark brown coat, the gloves, and the long white scarf, and holding a black umbrella to shield me from the snow.

The sidewalks were crowded, and the constant sound of horns and thousands of cars running the streets kept my senses at a peak. The buildings were tall and big, and lights, millions of Christmas lights glimmering through the falling snow, created a scene I could never have imagined. I smiled to myself with excitement and walked briskly to nowhere, my breaths coming out in white clouds. Every now and then I stopped, and taking in a deep breath, I relished the smells of the city. Strangers whose eyes never looked my way, their voices in a thousand tones and accents, flew by me, arousing my curiosity about a world I had never seen. *This is New York*, I thought, *and here I am, Benjamin Bennefield, right in the middle of it.* Fascinated and wound up, I walked for several miles before I realized time had overtaken me and I had to hurry back to the hotel.

In New York

Sixteen

Around seven that evening, dressed in my suit with my new coat, scarf, and gloves, I got in a cab hailed by the doorman to take me to the Museum of American Art. Seeing the line waiting to enter, I asked the driver to let me off a couple of blocks past the museum so I could take a walk back. A light snow had continued to fall, accumulating along the curbs and sidewalks, while the windows of the shops and restaurants were fogged from the warmth inside. By the time I got back to the museum, the line outside was gone; everyone had made their way in. I walked up the steps and pulled on the heavy glass door. The lobby was crowded, my heart beat faster, and I began questioning the wisdom of coming to Anna's opening. I let go of the door and slowly backed away, watching the crowd through the glass. I tried to convince myself to return to the hotel, but the thought of seeing Anna and talking to her kept pushing me forward. When I glanced to the bottom of the long set of steps, I stopped abruptly. A black limousine settled into a reserved parking space at the curb. A man in the front seat stepped out, quickly opened a large umbrella, adjusted his coat and hat, then opened the rear door. A woman in a black fur coat down to her ankles stepped from the car onto the sidewalk and waited under the umbrella as another man in a black coat got out of the car. She took his arm, and the three of them began the slow climb up the steps to where I was standing. It was Anna, I was sure, but her hair and part of her face were hidden by a wrap, and she was sheltered by the umbrella.

My first thought was to move away before she saw me, but there was no place to go. Neither my mind nor my heart was yet prepared to suddenly come face to face with Anna, not at the door with a man on each side. Quickly, I wrapped my scarf around my face and waited. While one of the men held the door open, Anna moved forward, passing so close to me the sleeve of her coat brushed against my chest, and I smelled her perfume: sweet, rich, and powerful. Then, as she stepped through the door, she quickly looked up at my eyes, only an inch or so above the hem of the scarf, and stopped for a second with an expression of sudden surprise. She glanced downward and then looked quickly again at my partially hidden face. "Good evening," she said, smiling. Holding on tightly to the arm of the man in the long black coat, she walked confidently into the lobby of the Museum of American Art.

Applause erupted, and tears, big tears, moved slowly down my cheeks. All of me, it seemed—my mind, my heart, and my soul—were stripped from me and I stood naked, breathless, and shivering. While hiding behind a long white scarf, I realized this place, New York, the tall buildings, the snow, the shiny streets, and the millions of lights, was far, far from home. It was intimidating and foreboding.

Seventeen

As soon as I had time to consider Anna Montagne's royal entrance and the fact I was standing where I was, I ran, almost in a panic, down the steps to the sidewalk below. When I reached the bottom, I stopped, turned, and looked upward through the glass to the massive chandeliers with a thousand lights sparkling from the ceiling of the museum. Without a doubt in my mind, I knew Anna Mancini, too, was in that place. I knew she was there because in a split second I had seen her eyes and her smile. My heart pounded and my mind ran in circles while I argued with myself. Surely, I had come too far, much too far, to let the unknown stop me.

I ran up the steps, flung open the door, and stepped into the lobby.

"Yes, ladies and gentlemen, Miss Montagne has captured the essence of time and place in her extraordinary work, from Fisherman's Wharf in San Francisco, up and down the streets of our own New York, all the way to the profound beauty and far into the soul of the Deep South." A tall, thin man in a black tuxedo held the attention of the crowd as I fumbled with my scarf and unbuttoned my coat. "Few artists, at any time in their lives, have ever been able to achieve such great depth of heart and spirit, and to paint onto a canvas, in vivid color, the fundamental nature of man, how we have lived and evolved through time, where we have been, and even where we might be going." I sighed and thought about what this fellow had said. He continued. "At this point, ladies and gentlemen, please feel free to visit through Carrigan Hall, then turn into Weston Hall, and we will gather in the Tower Room, where Miss Montagne will speak to us and will officially open this extraordinary exhibit. Thank you." A few people applauded as the man bowed prissily two or three times.

Slowly, with the crowd, I moved through Carrigan Hall, looking at Anna's art. I watched people as they pointed to this or that, whispering, some holding a glass of wine or a drink, some speaking much louder than I felt they should have. Everyone was dressed as though they were going to a party, a fancy party, a ball, maybe.

Rounding the first corner, I came to a complete halt in front of four drawings, twenty feet away, framed in black and perfectly hung on a white painted wall. I moved closer. The first drawing was of Miz Margaret's store; the next was of the depot, laden with bales of cotton. Then there was a drawing of me, up close, a boy I remembered well; I could see the sweaty hair and, on the face, smudges of dust from the cotton field. And the fourth drawing was of a little house with a tall pointed roof. It knocked the wind out of me; instinctively, I wanted to touch it. *No, Anna*, I thought, *this is our place, a secret place only you and I should know, and it has a window looking across a garden, and on one of the panes it says, "Ben loves Anna."* Suddenly, my stomach turned, and my heart beat faster. I glanced away.

On the wall below the group of drawings was a small plaque with gold letters reading "Artist's collection." Without thinking, I reached, trying to touch the plaque, but it was too far away, protected by a railing polished as bright as gold. A fog surrounded me; voices became muted and garbled. I was overwhelmed by thoughts and memories, and I didn't want them to burst out, not then, not in that place. Slowly I backed away, bumping into a woman who looked at me with indignation. I apologized. "Sorry … I'm sorry, ma'am," I stammered, then turned and walked toward Weston Hall, only glancing at drawings and paintings along the way. After a few seconds, I walked through the door into the Tower Room, where a crowd had gathered, all facing the far wall. The chattering was a constant hum, like bees swarming.

On the far wall hung a red velvet curtain, drawn shut over a very large painting, which I presumed was the showpiece of the exhibit. The same lanky man who had spoken to the crowd in the lobby was pacing nervously from one side of the curtain to the other, wringing his hands. Every now and then he talked to people standing nearby, motioning toward the curtain and looking back and forth toward a door to his right. Standing at the back of the crowd, I leaned against the wall next to a tall clock, its ticking made me anxious. I took a deep breath. The air was thick with perfume.

After a couple of minutes, a man in a black suit emerged from the crowd, stopping directly in front of me. "Your invitation, please?" he said. While I fumbled through my jacket, two other men in blue uniforms approached and stood on either side of the man. I finally found the invitation tucked in an inside pocket of my suit and handed it to him. Squinting, he glanced at my face, then at the invitation. "Thank you," he said, and all three turned quickly and marched in perfect step out of the Tower Room.

Suddenly, a voice rose from the direction of the velvet curtains, and I stretched to look. The man raised both hands, adjusting his black tie. Then smiling, he quieted the crowd with a couple of loud throat clearings, a wide grin crossing his narrow face. "Ladies and gentlemen," he said, "thank you very much for accepting our invitation to this exclusive exhibit. Miss Montagne will be here shortly, but before she comes in to say hello, I want to make an important announcement, which will make plain to you what we at the Museum of American Art believe, and that is this: Tonight we are sharing with you a landmark in what will someday be one of the greatest and brightest careers in contemporary American art. Miss Montagne's work will, one day, grace the halls of many galleries, museums, and private collections around the world. If you harbor any doubts, they will vanish when these drapes are opened. The painting is not for sale," he said, smiling and clasping his fingers together. "In fact, because of our confidence in the talent and artistry of this young woman, Miss Montagne, the Museum of American Art has secured an option to buy this painting and make it a permanent piece in our collection." The crowd hummed with awe and excitement. "In the meantime," and my stomach turned as the tall, prissy man continued, "Miss Montagne has agreed to let it adorn this wall in the Tower Room, right here, for two years." With that, the man bowed a couple of times, and then stretched out his right arm, his finger pointing toward the glow of the spotlight on the red curtain. Slowly, the curtain opened and applause broke out as people craned their necks to look at the painting. Then came another deeper wave of applause, and I stood as tall as I could to see over the heads in front of me as Anna emerged from the door to the right of the painting.

Beautiful Anna, trim in a flowing, long black dress. Her hair was blonde and pulled back from her face. Her smile was brighter and more beautiful than I had remembered. I knew I had to make the best of what was playing out in front of me; I sighed deeply, applauding with the crowd. Tears came to my eyes as she crossed gracefully to the other side of the painting and stood by the man. Again, with a smile on his face, he gestured toward Anna, calling out, "Well, here is Miss Anna Montagne," his voice trailing upward to a much higher pitch, holding the note. Again applause burst out, and the man's smile grew bigger. Anna stood motionless, but her eyes searched across the room, back and forth, quickly, several times. Her hair and face were meticulously styled. I hated the feeling inside me; my heart was racing, and my stomach was turning.

Anna glanced to her painting and brought her fingers to her lips, then quickly looked again across the crowd. "Thank you so much for your kindness and for being here tonight; I expect one or two of you may have come from a far distance," she said. She hesitated for a second. "I have little to say. You, my friends, will be the judge of everything you see here tonight, and that is the way it should be. This painting here," and she motioned toward the picture with one hand, turning back to the crowd with a slight smile, "this is a painting of a place and a time unrecorded except in the memories of a few people. It is a part of my own life." She paused, then spoke slowly. "Unfortunately, I doubt I will ever be able to settle, or resolve, those times for many years to come, so … it's a painting of my heart, a heart reminding me of a place and a time that will forever be part of me." Several people applauded. Anna bowed her head slightly, then raised her eyes toward the row of bright lights above her. She looked at the audience. "I named it … this painting, I've named it," she said, her voice softened. "Well, to me, the name speaks for many people about the past; for others, about the present; and for some, about the future." Her smile disappeared, then reappeared quickly. "It's the center of joy and excitement, which I left one day, and now, I wonder if it will ever come again." She stopped, looking across the crowd for a second. "The name," she said, "the name is *The Gold Dust Bridge*. Thank you."

Applause broke out. She raised her hands, then lowered them, clasping them together at her waist. *Beautiful Anna*, I thought with pride, while shaking my head.

Applause died away as people moved closer to the large painting and surrounded the artist. Yet I could feel the penetrating force of Anna's eyes; they had found me, and they were focused on me, where I stood, far in the back of the room, alone in the dim light and the shadows. I looked at the floor, then back, just as the tall clock struck the half hour. Anna never wavered from the demands of her task. She shook hands, spoke to her admirers, and gave autographs, willingly and graciously and beautifully.

For the first time, I recognized the distance between Anna and me; a distance not measured in miles, but the distance in a life in Gold Dust and a life in New York. And in this large assembly of people, I was alone, but there in front of me was Anna, the woman I knew and loved. And in the depths of the loneliness I was feeling, I heard her voice and felt the warmth of her touch, while we held each other, in a dark little house with a tall pointed roof, very far away from the Museum of American Art.

Like time, my breathing had stopped, too. I gasped for air and took a deep breath, letting it out slowly, and left the Tower Room.

Eighteen

"Wait, Ben, stop!" I heard Anna call after me as I walked slowly through Weston Hall. I moved to the nearest wall on which I could lean, and in a second, she was in front of me.

She looked at me, smiling, and asked, "You were going to leave without saying 'hi' to me?"

"I'm sorry, Anna, I realize now," and I shook my head slightly, "this is a long way from Gold Dust."

She pressed her fingers to my lips. "Oh, hush, Benjamin Bennefield. I'm glad you're here, and besides, I recognized you at the front door when I came in. Did you think I wouldn't know those eyes, Ben, peeking over that scarf?" And she reached up and removed the scarf from around my shoulders. "This is for me, isn't it? Ben brought me a long white scarf!" She smiled, laughing silently, and suddenly I began to feel, truly, that Anna Mancini was standing only inches from me. She tied the scarf around her neck, and beautifully, it became part of her. "And besides, Mr. Bennefield," she said, "I know how you got the invitation." She raised her eyebrows, tilting her head. "I know more than you think, big boy." My heart raced.

"Anna, I'm very proud of you. A big-time *artiste*, right in the heart of New York City, Miss Mancini," I said, then quickly corrected myself, "Oh, sorry, Miss Montagne."

"Oh, whatever name you like. At an event like this, they always make you look important and great, and Montagne is the name I—"

"Where's your beautiful hair, Anna?" I asked, interrupting her. I touched her blonde strands lightly and, again, smiled as best I could.

"Oh, Ben, you have to do a lot of things for public perception," she said, smiling, "and that's just one of them right now. Believe me; the people who come to these events make you who you end up being. I just want them to like my work and fork up the money. I have to make a living, you know, sweetheart." She glanced around, laughing, then patted my cheek, whispering, "It's so good to see you, Ben. You look wonderful, and as handsome as ever!"

Two ladies walked by us, watching Anna. Even though I smiled, I was sure disappointment showed on my face. Quickly I commented, "The old bridge at Gold Dust … a great painting, Anna. I was surprised to see Gold Dust right here in New York, and you brought it here. I'm proud of it."

"You should be, Ben, because you and our summer together are laid out in full color on that canvas, in every brush stroke, right along with the old bridge, whether you see it or not." Before I could say anything, she said, "Ben, I understand you're a big-time farmer now. How wonderful!"

"Well, that's what they say, but like you said, 'public perception.'"

Suddenly, her expression changed, like a cloud had moved over her. "Oh, Ben, I'm so sorry about your dad and, so soon, your mother, too. And you're alone now, aren't you … poor Ben?"

"Thanks, Anna. Time changes things, and you, of all people, should know," I said. "Yeah, it's just me, now. I'm alone."

She tilted her head slightly, looking at me. "Some things time can't change, Ben." She waited a second, choosing her words carefully.

"Maybe it bends us a little here and there, and … we have to make a few adjustments, but … there are no absolutes." She smiled again, laying her hand on my chest, and looked into my face. "Well, Ben, they're waiting for me, all of those wonderful people in the Tower Room." She sighed, smiling slightly. "I have to proceed with my duties here tonight and mingle with these rich folks. Maybe they'll fork up a little of that green stuff before the night's over." She laughed quietly, kissing my cheek. She reached and placed her hand where she had kissed, looking in my eyes as a quivering smile appeared. I clasped my hand around hers and held it. "Bye, Ben, my sweet, sweet Ben," she whispered, shaking her head. But then, quickly, she pulled her hand from mine, and added, "But I'm very angry with you. You should know that, Mr. Bennefield! Ignoring my letters!" She tapped me on the chest again and turned quickly, raising her gown above her ankles, and began moving at a fast pace down Weston Hall.

Ignoring my letters. Ignoring my letters. Her words, so quick and unexpected, slammed into my head, startling me, making me wonder what she meant.

"What? Anna, what are you talking about?" I called after her. She raised one hand in a fluttering wave, but continued without looking back, in a slow run. I hurried after her, but when I turned the corner, the doors to the Tower Room were closing.

I waited in the lobby till eleven o'clock. The snow was still falling when I left the Museum of American Art to walk to my hotel. Again, Anna's plans had not included me.

The night was cold.

The Museum

Nineteen

A STRONG NORTH WIND was blowing when I arrived in Gold Dust the next night, near ten o'clock. Droplets of frozen rain sparkled on the bare limbs of the bushes and the grass along the side of the road. And Christmas Eve was only two days away. I slowed the old truck almost to a complete stop as I turned from the main road into the long driveway leading directly to the front of the house. The headlights shone brightly, and I could see the house beyond the big trees. It was tall and ghostlike, lonely, and appeared to be sleeping. Stopping at the end of the sidewalk, I turned off the ignition, leaving the headlights on, and glanced about the yard, recalling the events in New York. Looking down through the truck's window, and barely visible, Lucy and Jake waited anxiously for me to step from the truck. I turned off the lights and got out, and in the pitch dark and cold, I bent low and hugged both of them while they licked my cheeks. Lucy barked a couple of times while looking at me with her ears back, welcoming me home. And with Lucy on one side and Jake on the other, I walked through the quiet blackness to the old house.

The big living room was cold, so I lit a fire and settled into a big chair with a beer, hoping to unwind. It had been a long and tiring trip from New York, having been routed through Chicago instead of Washington because of bad weather, and after a couple of stops, to Memphis, and finally to New Orleans. The flames grew while my mind continued to ponder the events of the night before.

"Ignoring my letters," Anna had said. I remembered the letter Miz Margaret had given me the day Anna left Gold Dust so unexpectedly … a letter I had not read when Mom called to me about Dad. And according to my mother, the letter was thrown into the trash and burned. *According to my mother*, I questioned. Suddenly, I sat up in the chair and looked into the red flames roaring in the fireplace, remembering her saying, uneasily, "thrown into the trash and burned." At the time, I felt she was lying, and didn't believe her. I leaned back in the chair and watched the shadows of the flames dance around the walls and the ceiling of the room.

Bolting from the chair, I rushed to my room upstairs, realizing my bureau was a logical place she might have hidden the letter, for me to find later. The first small drawer at the top was empty except for a piece of pencil and several paper clips, and the other small drawer lined with green cloth held my tie tacks, cuff links, and several award-day pins I had accumulated through school. Quickly I dug through every drawer in the chest, but nothing, nothing. There was no envelope, no letter.

I was tired and cold. Maybe tomorrow, my mind would be cleared and rested, and I would search again for my letter, maybe in my mother's bedroom.

I stripped down to my skivvies, fell into bed, and pulled the covers up to my chin.

I closed my eyes. My mind was running, jumping from one thing to another. New York, Gold Dust. And Anna's face.

Sleep came slowly. The night was long and restless. And troubling.

Twenty

Far off someplace, a bell was ringing, and I opened my eyes, looking at a blue wall. At first, I thought I was still flying, but the bell sounded again, two short rings, and then I realized it was my phone telling me and the other three parties on the line we shared that the call was for me. I threw back the covers and ran down the stairs to the main hall while the phone kept ringing. I found the receiver, and in a hoarse voice I said, "Hello."

"Oh, Ben, I bet I woke you!" The voice sounded familiar.

"No … yeah … but, but it's okay," I mumbled. "I needed to get up anyway."

"Well, guess what, Ben? If it's okay, we're coming to spend a few days with you."

"You are? Well … well, who is this?"

"Benjamin, it's your sister, your sister, boy. You need to wake up; it's almost ten o'clock."

"Barbara, oh, Barbara, sure, I'm … I'm a little crazy right now and … and you're coming to Gold Dust?"

"Yes, if it's okay with you."

"Yeah, sure … that'll be fine, I guess. When?" And my body began to shake in the cold of the unheated hall.

"We'll arrive around three on Sunday, Ben, the day after Christmas. Are you sure it's okay?"

By this time in the conversation, I was awake, and I wondered what in the hell I was going to do with Barbara, her husband, and three kids in the house. Then my lips began to quiver.

Hurriedly, I said, "Sure … sure, y'all come on."

"Well, it'll just be Mary Ann and me. James and Leigh are going to stay home with their dad. He's on call for the next three days, but they'll do fine."

"Sure," I said. "I'll be looking forward to it, Barbara. That's great."

"Okay, then, we'll see you on Sunday. Bye, Ben." The phone went dead.

Standing nearly naked in the front hall, I wrapped my arms around my body, figuring I needed to get my mind and thoughts in order. Shivering, I glanced to the far end of the long hall, where the window was bright with sunshine. I hurried up the stairs to my room, jumped into bed, and pulled the covers over me.

A letter, my letter, I thought. *What happened to my letter?* And at that moment, I figured I would never know what Anna had written to me on the day my dad died.

They were angry, I could tell from the sounds of their barks. Lucy and Jake had found something to fuss about.

Twenty-One

I NEEDED GROCERIES BEFORE Miz Margaret closed her store on Christmas Eve. Still a little restless from my trip, I approached the bridge, stopping in the middle of the span. I stepped out of the truck and looked up into the iron girders, wondering how much longer the old bridge would stand. It had always been a fascinating structure; I had studied it from the time I was a kid. It had been a part of many lives, of everyone who had been born in or lived around Gold Dust. I glanced upstream toward the north; the usually slow-moving water was a murky, brownish color, swirling, churning, and moving rapidly because of the recent, heavy rains. It was a different sight from the tranquil setting in the painting I had seen in New York three nights earlier. I pulled my jacket collar tighter around me just as a horn beeped from down the road. I jumped in the truck and left the bridge, parking at the steps in front of Miz Margaret's store.

The wooden door opened easily, and I was met by the warmth from the big iron stove in the middle of the store. Warming my hands, I stood beside the stove and waited, wondering why Miz Margaret wasn't behind the counter. She was always there. For as long as I could remember, Miz Margaret was the one who waited on us, handed us our pops, and asked us how we were doing; but today, the day before Christmas, her husband, Mr. Frank, with his overgrown, black eyebrows and thin, white hair that made him look at least twenty years older than Miz Margaret, stood looking across the counter at Miz Lewis. Mom had often said she would never tell Frank Smitherman anything she didn't want everybody in Gold Dust to know, and she often reminded me he couldn't be trusted. When I watched him drop some coins in Miz Lewis's hand, I figured she should probably count her change. Mom said he was lazy, too, that he hadn't worked a day in his life; she said he had been "paid off" years ago, and lived off the kindness of Miz Margaret and her mother. I never knew what she meant by him having been "paid off," and when I asked, she always evaded the question with the degrading little statement, "You wouldn't understand," and always ended with "One day I'll tell you, when you're old enough." I figured, however, it was just another mean way of showing her contempt for her distant cousin Frank Smitherman.

I glanced toward Mr. Frank just as his eyes caught mine, and he grumbled, "Watcha need, Bennefield?"

"Mornin', Mr. Frank. How are you?" He said nothing, so I continued, "Just pickin' up a few groceries I might need during Christmas."

"Well, git whatchu' want and bring it on up here," he said, never moving from his stool behind the counter. As his glassy eyes followed me, he reached and picked up his cigarette from a dirty ashtray then took in a deep, long drag, making the end of the cigarette light up a bright red. I watched through the corner of my eye to see how much smoke would come out of him, but he immediately took another drag and deliberately mashed the cigarette in the ashtray, and then, from his mouth and nose, he let out a billowing, bluish cloud, enveloping him.

I wandered through the store, picking up several items: four or five cans, a loaf of bread, and three candy bars. I placed them on the counter, then asked him to cut a nice roast from the hindquarter in the meat box. He looked up at me and stood up, grunted, then slowly waddled toward the back of the store, shaking his head as he went. I picked out a half dozen Irish potatoes from the open bin and set them next to the cans. On the merchandise counter was a scarf laid out with several items of winter clothing, a scarf very similar to the one Anna had taken from around my shoulders a few days ago. "How much is this scarf, Mr. Frank?" I called to him.

"For you, Bennefield, it's real special. In fact, M had it made just for you, boy," he called out. "She has it marked somewhere; look for a tag."

On a small tag pinned to one end was the price, $2. I had just paid $15 for a similar one two days earlier. I folded the scarf and placed it neatly next to my groceries, thinking it would be a nice Christmas present for my sister. Then I chose a small, metal airplane with a propeller that turned and wheels that rolled, and placed it on top of the scarf. I liked airplanes … maybe Mary Ann would too.

"That about it, Bennefield?" Mr. Frank asked in his gruff, raspy voice as he shuffled to the counter from the back of the store.

"Yes, sir, that's about it. Where's Miz Margaret today, Mr. Frank?"

His bushy, black eyebrows rose as he sat back on the stool, and he glared at me as though I had poked in his personal affairs. He answered, angrily, "Look, fella, I've been running this damn place for four days now, and I've got a belly full of it. Damn it!" He coughed a couple of times. "M's old mama's bad off, probably won't make it much past Christmas." He coughed again.

"Oh, I'm sure sorry to hear that. I haven't seen Miz Elnora for a long time." Mr. Frank started writing my purchases down in my charge book, and I pushed a couple of items toward him, thinking I should watch him closely.

He stopped writing, looked up at me, and said, "Well, that old gal, over eighty, I guess, been dying for almost as long as I've known her, 'round twenty-five years now, and Lord, she's mean." He resumed writing as he talked. "She's been mad for a long time, was mad about her havin' to come down here and live, when her old sister kicked 'em out of Philadelphia, her and Margaret both." He giggled. "Yeah, 'exiled to a foreign country,' that's the way she put it." He shook his head, and looked at me while I attempted to make sense of what he said, trying to fit together the people he was talking about. "Ain't anybody left in Miz Elnora's family now, except her old sister, Isabella, another mean one," he went on. "That woman took Anna when she was born, just plain took her from her mama, and adopted her, then sent M and Elnora down here." He grinned from ear to ear, leaned across the counter closer to me, and in a teasing voice asked, "You know Anna, don't chu, Bennefield? Yeah, I don't need to tell you nothin' 'bout her, the one you took a likin' to a time back." He chuckled, causing his big stomach to bounce. He raised his heavy, black eyebrows as he smiled, showing his smoky brown teeth. I said nothing, but wondered where he might be taking this very unusual and revealing conversation. Finally, I answered, mostly for Anna and me, "Yes, sir, I liked Anna very much. She's a great person."

Immediately he said, "Yeah, Miss Anna; I always called her 'Miss' to pick at her. Kinda' high-falootin' girl, a big city girl like Elnora's sister." He strung out her name, "Miz Isabella Mancini," raising his nose, mocking the lady. "Yeah, Anna's a pretty girl, 'bout as pretty as Margaret when I married her. But you sure knew Anna, didn't you, Bennefield?" And his eyebrows rose again while he chuckled. He leaned toward me from his stool, looked straight at me, and asked, "And why in the hell didn't you marry her, boy? They got more money than you'll ever see in your whole lifetime, just rollin' in it. I know it fer a fact, and Anna's gonna git it all one day."

I was jolted. *Marry her?* I thought. Anna ran away from me, left me, and it was none of Frank Smitherman's damn business. Surely, it wasn't something I would ever talk about with him, the old bastard. I felt anger beginning to rise and my patience thinning. He shoved the bags of groceries across the counter to me. I grabbed them quickly. "Tell Miz Margaret I'll check back in a day or two to see how Miz Elnora's faring out."

"You do that, Bennefield," he said. "I know M would sure want you to know as soon as Miz Montagne passes. She's got a likin' for you, kinda' like a son, I guess." He chuckled again, plopped down on his stool, and reached for the pack of cigarettes, as he mumbled, "Especially after your mama shot her head off." His smile was wide; his stomach bounced as he chuckled. I gritted my teeth.

In less than thirty minutes in his presence, Frank Smitherman had confirmed all of the bad things I had ever heard about him, even the words my mother used most often: "He's a real son-of-a-bitch."

But the second Mr. Smitherman said it, *Montagne,* I caught it. *That's Anna's name now,* I thought excitedly. *She's not married. She just took a family name.* Instantly, my thoughts ran wild, and I could feel the blood rush through me. But when I heard Mr. Frank call Miz Margaret 'M,' I thought back to the note Mother was holding in her hand when she died.

Just when I stepped away from the counter, the front door flew open, slamming against a shock of brooms standing in a can; the can and the brooms fell over, making a terrific racket. "Merry Christmas, Frank!" a man shouted, and several people walked through the door, talking loudly and laughing. He shouted again, "How 'bout a beer, buddy? You got any left?"

Hearing a grunt, I glanced back at Mr. Frank just as he was taking a sip from a bottle stashed in a brown paper bag. He looked me straight in the eyes again, swallowed quickly, and mumbled, "Take that damn bunch with you, Bennefield. Christmas Eve, and Lord have mercy, I need to git outta' this damn place."

Twenty-Two

I SET THE BAGS of groceries on the kitchen table, took the roast, and placed it on the front of the main shelf in the icebox, then searched for the jar of my favorite food. On two slices of the fresh bread I had just bought, I spread a layer of peanut butter and finished it with grape jelly spread on top. After pouring a glass of milk, I placed my supper on a tray and cautiously moved through the dark dining room into the main hall, where a single lamp near the front door lit the way to the long stairs. In my bedroom, I lit a fire in the fireplace, probably for the first time in more than a year. At the foot of the bed, my suitcase from the trip to New York stood waiting to be unpacked and was covered over by the hanging bag holding my suit and new coat. I sat in the big chair facing the fireplace, balancing the tray across my knees. The fire popped and crackled while I watched the flames grow tall and red. *A glass of milk and a peanut butter and jelly sandwich*, I thought, *two of my favorite foods*. Through the windows, the night was black and deep. And it was Christmas Eve.

Christmas Eve, my thoughts rambled, *and as soon as I finish this fine meal, tucked neatly into this warm room with a blazing fire casting dancing shadows across the walls, I'll unpack that suitcase holding day-*

old underwear and dirty clothes worn while I walked excitedly along the snowy streets of a great city. I smiled, rejoicing in my thoughts, and I felt Anna's hand on my cheek.

After hanging my suit and new coat behind the door, I placed the suitcase on the side of my bed and opened it. On top of the clothes sat a small box holding the cuff links I had bought. I snapped the lid back and admired them for their uniqueness and beauty, a remembrance of my trip. Rattling them like dice in my hand, I figured they should go in the drawer in the chest with the other cuff links, tie tacks, and trinkets. I walked to the chest and pulled the small drawer completely open, glancing at its contents. Catching my eye, barely visible beneath the jewelry and the trinkets on top, was a white piece of paper, folded to fit tightly in the bottom of the drawer. I jerked the drawer completely out, dumping its contents on the bed. Carefully, I worked the paper out of the bottom of the drawer. It was an envelope. *My letter*, I thought, holding it in one hand and the drawer in the other. I took a deep breath. Turning the envelope several times, I looked again at my name, Ben Bennefield, written in the delicate strokes of an artist. The envelope had been opened, torn badly, and was smudged with soot. I took the note out and pressed it to my face, searching for the unmistakable scent belonging to only one beautiful woman: Anna Mancini.

August 6, 1952

Dear Ben,

I'm sorry to leave without saying good-bye. Last night at the bridge wasn't as sweet as I had wished, and I'm sorry for that, too. Please forgive me, Ben.

I must return home as there are situations to which I must attend.

Come to Philadelphia before school starts. If not, as soon as you can. I'll await your reply. Write me at home: 122 North Marion St., Philadelphia, Pennsylvania.

We have much to catch up on, Mr. Bennefield. I love you, Ben.

Love and kisses,

Anna

With the letter in hand, and puzzled by her words, I lay across the bed on my back, looking at a white ceiling, and feeling my heart beating fast. *Maybe she loved me after all*, I thought. I sighed deeply, then read Anna's letter again. *Come to Philadelphia. I love you. Much to catch up on.* I brought the letter to my face and, as sweet as I remembered, Anna's scent filled my mind, rushing my thoughts.

"Anna," I said out loud, then closed my eyes. I wanted her right then to lie next to me, hear her laugh. I wanted to wrap my arms around her, touch her lips with my fingers, and feel her breath on my cheek, her lips on mine. And I wanted her hair to fall across my face while our bodies pressed to each other. Flashing memories made me ache, unleashing a long pent-up desire. Like a smothering blanket, overwhelming anger settled over me. I yelled at the top of my voice and beat the bed with my fist.

"Anna Mancini," I said softly, with a question lingering in my mind. "Son-of-a-bitch," I screamed.

The fire died, and my room turned cold.

Twenty-Three

My lifelong friend James Bartlett was home from college for the holidays, and he had invited me to join his family for the grand dinner his mother would serve on Christmas Day. After reading Anna's letter at least twenty times, I put it in my hip pocket and took it with me, figuring if the time and place seemed right, I would read it again, and again.

Just when the last glasses of wine were emptied, an unexpected knock at the kitchen door stopped the chatter and laughter around the Christmas table. Miz Bartlett quickly stepped through the kitchen and opened the door. The familiar, coarse voice of Frank Smitherman carried all the way to the dining room, and I could picture his black eyebrows moving up and down as he spoke. "I hate to bother y'all, Miz Bartlett, but I'm goin' 'round to tell everybody Margaret's mama died 'bout ten this mornin'. M's gonna bury her on Monday mornin' at White's Cemetery. 'Bout ten, I believe."

"Oh, I'm so sorry to hear that, Frank. Thank you for coming by to let us know."

"You're welcome, ma'am. If you see anybody out, tell 'em 'bout Miz Elnora, please ma'am."

"I certainly will, and you tell Margaret I'll pray for her and her mother tonight, Frank; thank you for coming by."

When the kitchen door closed, right away I knew I must go see Miz Margaret, to express my sorrow; she would know if Anna would be coming to Gold Dust for the funeral. Miz Bartlett returned to her place at the dining room table, and right before she sat, I stood and thanked her for having me to Christmas dinner. James walked to the door with me, and we said good-bye.

I parked my truck across the street from the Smitherman house, next door to Miz Margaret's store. Several people had already been by, but before I could knock on the door, it opened. "Oh, Ben," Miz Margaret said, reaching up to hug me, "thank you for coming so soon. Frank said you had been by the store yesterday."

"Yes, ma'am, and I'm sure sorry about Miz Elnora."

Miz Margaret was obviously tired from having spent her days and nights taking care of her mother. She spoke slowly, only glancing at my face every now and then. "Oh, thank you, Ben," she sighed, "but she was getting up in age and had been in poor health for a long time." Her words flowed like they had been memorized. "But anyway," she sighed deeply again, "I'll get to see Aunt Isabella; she's a couple of years older than Mother, and they'll be here by late tomorrow evening sometime." She stopped and looked at my face, then placed her hand on my arm. "Aunt Isabella adopted Anna when she was born," she said. Her eyes were teary. "I'm sure your mother must have told you, Ben. Aunt Isabella raised her … and yes, Ben, Anna is coming tomorrow, in case you wanted to know." She touched her cheek where a tear had run. "I'm so grateful Anna will be here with me." She wiped the tears from her eyes as she looked at me. "You're a good man, Ben, but I knew very well your mother never liked the idea of you and Anna together. To Hester, Anna was a threat, taking you away from her and the farm … poor soul." She shrugged and shook her head, appearing to be in a stupor as she slowly backed into the room.

"Thanks for telling me about Anna coming, Miz Mar—" but the door closed before I finished getting her name out.

While crossing the street to my truck, I smiled at the thought of Anna coming the next day. Then I remembered my sister would arrive, also, around three. That would be complicated, and for a moment I wished Barbara wasn't coming. But I knew it had been a long time. So, what the hell; I'd work it out.

By the time I reached the Gold Dust Bridge, I had already taken Anna's letter from my pocket, to read it one more time. I stopped in the middle of the bridge, looking upstream then downstream. Edward's Creek wound its way past the houses of many friends who lived on the creek's banks, making their living from the sandy fertile lands, and called Gold Dust their home. I knew everyone for miles around, and everyone knew me. While looking down to the water in Edward's Creek, my breath came short for a second, realizing that now, like everyone else, the land, the cotton, and the people had seeped into my blood, into my life. This was my home. The old bridge moaned softly; I smiled, then looked up into its massive iron. But I couldn't help but laugh out loud, gripping the steering wheel with all my might, thinking, *Yes! Anna! She'll be in Gold Dust in just one day.*

When I let out the clutch, the gears of the old truck rattled and then hummed, making the tires squeal as they spun on the wooden runners of the old bridge.

I went home.

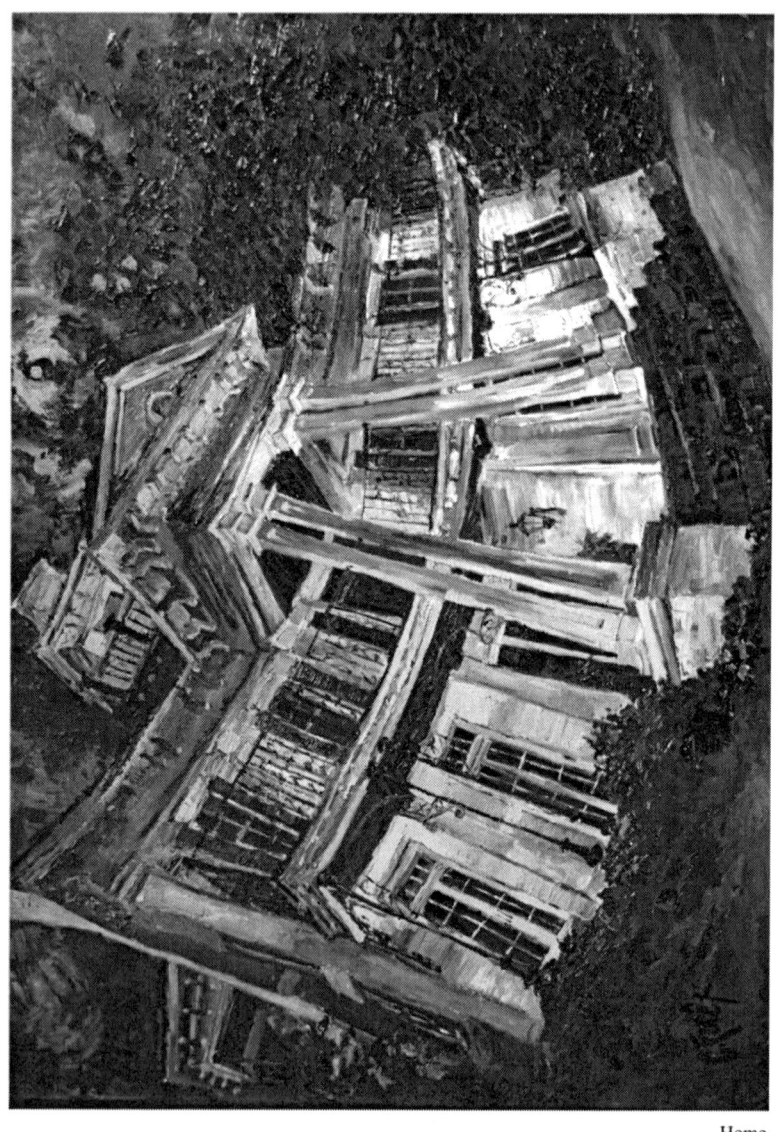

Home

Twenty-Four

Two long beeps from a car horn sounded, and I knew Barbara and Mary Ann had arrived. Anxiously, I hurried through the dining room into the hall and opened the door.

"Well, here we are, Ben, just like I said!" Barbara swung open the screen door and hugged me. After so many years, and so much anger, I was happy to have my sister in my arms. "And this is Mary Ann, whom you've met once before, a little bit bigger than the last time, but still Mary Ann." Barbara smiled.

In the two years since Dad had died, my niece had grown into a beautiful young girl; she was tall for her age, which I guessed to be around six, and had all the features of the Bennefield blood. She was very much as pretty as her mother, and like her mother, she smiled easily. Only later would I see that Mary Ann had inherited the saintliness of a quiet demeanor, like her father, the doctor. Extending my hand toward her, I said, "Hi, Mary Ann."

"Oh cut it out, you two," Barbara quickly interjected. "Get down there and hug each other like uncles and nieces are supposed to do." I bent down and hugged my young niece, who smiled and hugged me back, neither of us saying a word.

"Come in, come in," I said after a second, happily leading them to the living room, where a dwindling fire kept the room comfortable. In the middle of the couch, I had laid out the white scarf and the airplane. "These are for you two. Merry Christmas!" I said, pointing to the sofa, waiting anxiously to hear their reactions.

Barbara smiled as she looked at the scarf and the airplane. "Oh Ben," she exclaimed, "how thoughtful! But Christmas is already over. So sweet, Ben, thank you. I love my airplane."

"Oh, the plane's for Mary Ann, the scarf is yours," I said.

She laughed and placed her hand on my arm. "Just pulling your leg, little brother," she said. "But it's very sweet of you to do that." She smiled as she draped the scarf around her shoulders, primping in front of the mirror over the fireplace.

We laughed and sat down for a chat that lasted for several hours. I told them about Miz Margaret's mother dying and decided she and Mary Ann would go to the funeral with me. They understood when I told them I needed to visit at Miz Margaret's later in the evening to express my condolences, and I suggested Barbara prepare supper while I was in Gold Dust. That would be a treat for me.

Twenty-Five

Just as I crossed the bridge, a black car stopped in front of Miz Margaret's house, and I recognized immediately it was Anna arriving. I pulled to the side of the street and turned off the truck's engine. After a couple of seconds, the front doors of the car opened, almost at the same time. Anna stepped out of the passenger side and stood there, surprising me when a small child appeared in the car's door. She reached and picked up the child. A tall man, who had gotten out of the driver's side of the car, walked around and took the youngster in his arms. Then a rear door of the car opened, and a woman I figured was Anna's mother appeared to struggle to get out. After a few seconds, the four people proceeded up the sidewalk to Miz Margaret's porch. I watched from my truck window until the hellos and hugs were done and everyone moved inside. Again, I took Anna's letter from my pocket and looked at the handwriting on the envelope, but folded it and put it away. By then, I had memorized every word in the letter. *I love you, Ben.* But again, my thoughts were confusing. *Anna, a man, and a small child.* I sat quietly in the truck, wondering, figuring everything I had hoped for had been blown away. *Anna, a man, and a small child,* I said to myself, and waited in my truck until darkness set in.

Barbara had figured out a way to turn my groceries into a dinner the likes of which had not been seen in my house since Mom died. While she cleaned up the kitchen, Mary Ann helped me bring in a few sticks of fresh wood, and I stoked the living room fire. We talked a bit before she began playing with her airplane. A few minutes later, Barbara came in with a pot of tea and several tea cakes she had brought from New Orleans. "Now, Ben, these wonderful tea cakes are your present from Mary Ann and me," she said. "We're going to share your present with each other. Isn't that thoughtful?" She smiled while she poured the tea.

Before I finished the tea cake, Barbara asked, "Well, Ben, have you done anything with all of Mama's stuff?" I shrugged my shoulders and continued nibbling on the cookie. I didn't want to think about Mama's stuff. I thought about Anna, a man, and a small child, and like a song stuck in my brain, I kept repeating it over and over, in rhythm: *Anna, a man, and a small child. Anna, a man, and a small child,* and hoped my emotions weren't apparent to my sister.

"Ben!" Barbara said loudly, making me flinch. "Have you done anything with Mama's belongings?"

"No, no ... no, nothing yet," I said quickly, shaking my head and watching the fire.

"Benjamin, what's wrong with you?" she asked. "Your mind's wandering somewhere."

"Oh, nothing, nothing, just thinking, I guess." I looked at Barbara and commented, "Well, I've been in her room once since she died, for a few minutes, and closed the door. I really don't want to fool with her belongings." I looked at the fire, my thoughts returning to Anna, a man, and a small child.

"Well, maybe we should start right now, and at least look around. I can help you," Barbara said. "I plan to leave after the funeral."

"Well, that's okay with me," I said, "if you've got the guts to do it. I'm not sure, but I'm thinking Mom still hangs out in there."

"Oh, Ben, don't say that," Barbara whispered, rolling her eyes toward Mary Ann, who was flying her plane in front of the fireplace.

"Don't 'Oh, Ben' me," I whispered back to her. "You're the one who's been haunted by her for years."

"Oh, stop it," Barbara laughed, "I haven't been haunted by my own mother. It's just … well, the way I saw her, God rest her soul." Barbara smiled and continued, as she looked at me, "But haunting me? No, not for a long time, Benjamin. Not anymore."

Twenty-Six

For reasons I didn't want to express in words, I hated the idea of picking through my mother's belongings. With Mary Ann holding close to Barbara, we left the living room, crossed the hall, and opened the bedroom door slowly as though we might disturb our mother. I reached through and flipped the switch, and the big chandelier lit the room. Cold came through the door. Looking around, we moved slowly to the center and stopped in the middle of the rug at the foot of the bed.

Barbara attempted to smile, but tears already began to show in her eyes. Mary Ann appeared to wonder about her mother's tears.

"What a beautiful place, this room," Barbara said, brushing the wetness from her cheeks, and in a soft voice she spoke directly to her daughter. "Darling, I remember this room was always beautiful; Mother kept it this way, but always off-limits to everybody."

"Yeah, no doubt about it. That's why I haven't been in here but once since she died," I said. "This is crazy, but there's something about all this." I motioned around the big room. "Knowing this was hers and it's all right where she left it … like it's ready, just waiting for her to come back." I shook my head, frowning. "I don't like the feeling I get when

A Full-Grown Man

I'm in here, but Mom ... God, she loved it, that's for sure." I looked at Barbara, who was taking in everything around her. "It can stay like this, just like it is, forever, as far as I'm concerned."

"Yeah, I suppose so," Barbara said, examining each piece of furniture, the walls, and corners. Her eyes moved quickly. "Maybe it's her atonement to us, Ben. She always hid so much from us, her life and the truth, most of the time. So hard to understand her! This was her sanctuary, where she hid out." She stopped for a second. "Poor Dad. I really don't know how he managed to put up with her all the years he did!"

"Dad," I said. "Yeah, I miss the fellow. I haven't set foot in the woods since he died, or fished either, for that matter." I watched Mary Ann as she stood still, holding her small hands with her fingers locked together, surveying the room as her mother was doing. "Yeah, this place is like something you would see in an old magazine," I said jokingly.

I moved toward one of the chests at the side of the bed, then pulled on a drawer's handle. "Looks like we're gonna have to search for a key." I tried the other three drawers, and they, too, were locked.

Barbara moved to the chest on the other side of the bed, and she too pulled a drawer's handle. "We have to find two keys. These are locked, also," she said. "Ben, my curiosity is about to kill this cat here. Two big chests and all the drawers are locked tight. Something's strange; where in the world would she hide the keys?" She shook her head, again in exasperation, and asked, "And wouldn't you have expected she would make it hard for us?"

"I don't know! Don't even think about it!" I said. "Everything I've felt about her lately has been strange. So, I'm not surprised she locked her things away and hid the keys." I sat on the edge of the bed while glancing around in search of a place Mother might hide a key, possibly a crevice around a door frame, or a secret cut-out in the marble on the fireplace.

"Uncle Ben?" Mary Ann asked, in a sweet, girlish voice. "This is a pretty little box, Uncle Ben." She picked it up from the desk, turned toward me, and the lid slid off. Startling her, she dropped the box. Two large keys bounced out of it. Mary Ann glanced at me, then ran and wrapped her arms around her mother.

"Well, I'll be darned," I said. "Those are the keys, I bet. Wow, Barbara! Look. Mary Ann found the keys. Good job, Mary Ann!" I grabbed both keys in one hand while picking up the box with the other. Stuck inside was a note. I glanced at it, then shoved it into my shirt pocket. I held one of the keys toward Barbara, as she held Mary Ann in her arms, soothing her. "Here, sweetheart," I said to Mary Ann. "I want you to have this little box for finding the keys for us, okay?" and I handed it to her. "You really did a fine job." Before she reached for the box, she sniffed, smiled slightly, and wiped her tears with the heel of her hand.

Barbara moved to one chest, and I moved to the other. We inserted the keys, but the drawers wouldn't unlock, so we exchanged keys from across the bed and tried again. The locks clicked, and the top drawer of each chest slid open easily. In the drawer that Barbara opened, she found my father's pipe, his last driver's license, his wallet, and a money clip holding a few dollars. Barbara moaned and sat on the bed as she examined each item carefully. In the drawer I opened were several old bills, invoices, and papers tied with a string around them and, to one side, two small stacks of twenty-dollar bills, also tied with string. After gathering the papers together, I placed them on the edge of the bed, figuring I should check to make sure the old bills had been paid.

Barbara opened the second drawer. "Oh, my God!" she gasped. Neatly arranged were rows and stacks of twenty-dollar bills, filling the drawer to the top. Most stacks were tied with string; others were wrapped in the paper ties banks use. I hurried to Barbara's side of the bed and helped her unlock the other two drawers. Both were filled with twenty-dollar bills, all tied neatly with string, much of which had yellowed with age. We sat on the edge of the bed, looking back and forth at the money and at each other. Barbara began to laugh, but neither of us said anything.

"Mother, are we rich?" Mary Ann asked, gently tapping on her mother's arm.

"Oh, no honey," Barbara answered nervously, still laughing quietly. "This is such a surprise to find all of this in Grandmother's room, that's all." Barbara leaned toward me, whispering, "Maybe all of the talk and gossip around Gold Dust was true. We just didn't believe it." She smiled, shaking her head. "Can you imagine her hoarding money this way?" I shrugged in silence, then walked around the bed to the other chest and unlocked its other three drawers, opening them only halfway. As I had expected, they, too, contained thousands of twenty-dollar bills, stacked neatly and tied with string. We sat back on the bed and looked at the chests and back and forth at each other, laughing quietly, amazed at the discovery.

"It's a guess," I said, "but I think a great deal of this was hidden here by somebody else. Grandmother, I suppose, a long time ago." I frowned. "You know we never made any money that I can remember, not like this," I said, glancing to Barbara's face. "Mom just did the same as her mother."

"Yeah," she said, "just like her mother, for sure ... afraid of the banks ... everybody back then had the Great Depression syndrome." Barbara sat up very straight. "Poor Dad, he had to know about all of this money; why did he let her control everything the way she did?"

"Maybe he thought he had no choice," I said. "The farm was mother's inheritance, but he was never concerned about money anyway, not Dad. He loved the land and the cotton, and the people around him. That was what he lived for. Mom handled everything else, the house, and apparently the money."

As she looked at me, Barbara commented, "You can't imagine what all I had to do to get through four years of college on my own after I left this place, and to never have been given a penny to help me along." She pointed to the chests, then looked at me. "Here it is, Ben, my college, your college, and—" She shook her head. "What in the world motivated that woman?" she asked, grimacing, then gritted her teeth. "Ben, I'm so sorry for you. It's all right here, and thousands and thousands more." Barbara stood and placed her arm over her daughter's shoulders. She wiped the tears from her cheeks. "And according to Mama, we never had any money, just dirt poor." Barbara appeared exhausted and almost breathless as she glanced around the room. She bent slightly to embrace Mary Ann. "My darling, just look at this room," she said. "It's like something you might find in a grand manor in the English countryside, elegant, lavish, and beautiful, a monument built by your great-grandmother and protected by my mother." Her face was red, her eyes glassy. "But it's as cold and hard as Hester Bennefield herself. What a woman she was, honey, a selfish, devious, and mean person."

"No, no, Barbara, stop," I said, getting up and shaking my head. "Just think! Think, Sister, and listen to me, please. All of the bad things about the way we lived, everything you saw and hated, you're passing them right along to another generation, right this minute." I looked at Mary Ann, then at Barbara, as she brought her hand over her mouth. "Mom's gone now, and there's no need to say those things to anyone. Who's to gain by it? No one, absolutely no one, Barbara." She began to cry. "Mom was who she was, and that will never change. But we should think about the good things we knew. And Barbara," I said, "I can't stand in judgment. I don't want to judge her, not now or ever." Placing my arms around her, I said, "And above all, we have to understand, regardless of everything, we're part of her; I want the good part to stay alive in us, all of us." For a moment, we stood in silence, looking at the open drawers holding thousands of dollars. "And we've gotta do something with all of this," I said, pointing toward the two chests. "Maybe we should just lock it up and start over when the bank's open."

Barbara said nothing as she moved back to the bed, sitting again on its edge. "Ben, you're right," she said. "I've been so foolish, not seeing what I was doing. I'm so, so sorry." In an instant, she started gathering the pile of papers I had placed on the bed, quickly glancing through them while she cleared her eyes with her fingertips.

"They're old bills," I scoffed, wanting to hurry and get out of the room. "I need to go through them to make sure they've been paid." While I waited impatiently for her to drop the papers back in the drawer, I took the note from my shirt pocket, and saw Margaret Smitherman's name imprinted on top. And signed, "With much love, M."

Saying nothing, I returned the note to my pocket just as Barbara looked up at me with a frown on her face.

"Ben?" she said. "Look, Ben, these letters are addressed to you, all of them. There are one … three here, from somebody named Anna Mancini, in Philadelphia."

"What?" I said, then stammered, "You're … you're kidding!" and she handed the letters to me. Each was addressed to Benjamin Bennefield. They were mine.

"Anna, Anna, Anna," was all I could say as I shook my head. "Her letters," I mumbled, and I dropped onto the bed. As I looked at the envelopes, my breathing became shallow, and heat, extreme heat, shot through me, making me sweat.

Barbara looked at my face, and I stared into hers.

"Mary Ann," she said, taking her daughter's hand, "let's go, darling. We'll wait for Uncle Ben in the living room."

The door closed quickly and softly.

Twenty-Seven

Alone in my mother's secret place, I felt as though I had been pushed into a deep pool of murky water, holding my breath while attempting to rise to the surface; then suddenly, I took in the cool water, and a quiet calm came over me. Closing my eyes and holding the envelopes to my chest felt good. *Or maybe*, I thought, *maybe I've drowned.*

I stared at the three envelopes from Anna. They were old now, and I hesitated in trepidation for what I might find inside, thinking, at this point, it may be best not to read them at all, and return them to their hiding place. Then, in the midst of it all, plaguing me, was a letter I had unexpectedly found in a small wooden box, a letter I knew was surely a key to my mother, her life and her death. A letter from "M," my friend Miz Margaret, to her friend, my mother; the very thought caused my stomach to turn.

Without thinking, I crumpled the letters in my hand, desperately suppressing the thoughts running through my mind, and feelings of sadness, sorrow, and anguish, growing into bitter hate.

For a long time, I lay across my mother's bed. I pulled the quilt over me, then glanced through the windows over her desk into the blackness of night. It was deep and impenetrable.

A Full-Grown Man

Again, I looked at the envelopes with my name on them, then turned to lie on my back. The big chandelier hanging high above me sparkled, its prisms casting sharp spots of color on the ceiling and the walls. I stopped counting when I reached a hundred red spots, then opened the first letter.

* * * * *

Twenty-Eight

THE CHILL IN THE breeze blowing through the gazebo was beginning to penetrate the quilt I had wrapped tightly around me before I fell asleep. I felt a nudge on my arm, followed by the warm touch of Lucy's tongue gliding across my cheek. I sat up in the rickety chair and leaned forward to hug my yellow dog. She wondered, I suppose, why I had lingered there for so long. Jake sat next to her, whining, with his ears laid back. I glanced at the blue-green water below the gazebo, believing, after a long and untimely journey, my letters from Anna had reached, yet again, an unintended place, but this time, a final one.

Still in my hand, I held the fourth letter, Margaret Smitherman's letter to my mother. I pondered giving it to Barbara, but concluded no good would come of it. It was very personal and private, a letter I felt guilty for having read, and revealing it would do nothing but cause others more heartache, distress, and anguish. Without further hesitation, I tore the letter into small pieces, throwing them high. With Lucy and Jake sitting beside me, I watched as the pieces fluttered, falling slowly onto the water, and then floated away on Edward's Creek. Lucy barked twice, looking at me.

"Ben, come on. It's time to get ready," Barbara called from the porch.

"I'm coming," I called back to her, realizing I had become restless and anxious at the thought of going to White's Cemetery for Miz Elnora's funeral and seeing Anna. There was little order to the thoughts tumbling through my head, as I attempted to come to grip with the facts, some of which were evil and dishonest, causing my life to be captive to the will of others. I had hoped, at times unbendingly, at times tenuously, some way my life would return to a summer at the end of my youth and to the woman I loved.

Standing from the chair, I looked upstream to the Gold Dust Bridge in the distance. Stretching hard and long, and with my eyes holding true to the old bridge, I reviewed the events that had brought me here, to this place in time, this moment in my life. I thought of the words in Anna's letters, which now were hidden in the rocks and the sand at the bottom of Edward's Creek. With them, I hoped, lay an obsession begun when a twelve-year-old boy fell in love, an obsession that lasted nearly half his life. I realized now it was time to come face to face with the person I had become, but I wondered still if I would ever be, as Hester Bennefield once said, "a full-grown man."

I smiled when I looked at Lucy and Jake waiting at "ready," and surprisingly, I felt the excitement of a twelve-year-old kid playing with his dogs. Slowly, I rolled the quilt into a ball and placed it under one arm. I took a deep breath and yelled, "Go!"

I ran as fast as I could, racing them to the house, but Lucy and Jake were waiting, excited and barking, when I reached the porch.

Twenty-Nine

BARBARA, MARY ANN, AND I sat with a small group of friends of the Smithermans. A few yards away stood the tallest monument in White's Cemetery, an obelisk cut from gray granite, twenty feet tall, bearing my family's name. Newly engraved below it was my mother's family name: McGinnis. My mother had demanded the addition when we buried my father. The smell of the flowers in front of us made my nose tingle, and I blamed the flowers when tears gathered in my eyes.

In the family section on the other side of the grave was Frank Smitherman, moldy, old, and bulging above his belt; Miz Margaret leaned away from him, and rested lightly against Anna, both women dressed in shades of black and brown. Seeing them side by side made clear the true relationship between the two women, their similar features identifying a mother and daughter, both obviously beautiful, each at her own time. Miz Margaret and Anna were only two pieces of a large and complex puzzle entwining a rich, old family from Philadelphia down to a tiny village in the Southern woods; *exiled to a foreign country,* as Frank Smitherman had quoted Miz Elnora saying. Next to Anna was Miz Isabella Mancini, sister to Miz Elnora Montagne. She was dressed far more elegantly than anyone in the group, all in black, from her small round hat to her shoes, striking a distinguished, commanding figure. A thin black veil, covering her white hair and her face, draped over her shoulders onto her back, folding on the grass around her chair. She was jeweled like royalty and, obviously, had long ago been heralded as the family matriarch. In her lap, her right hand moved slightly while holding a silver rosary. Her gloved left hand sat atop her scepter, a gold walking cane, which stood purposefully, separating her from a man dressed in a dark brown suit, who I assumed was Anna's husband. Immediately, I recognized him as the man who had directed the crowds through the halls of the Museum of American Art. On his lap, he held a beautiful child with eyes as green as his mother's, a young boy who squirmed and wiggled until the man finally put him down in front of him. Anna reached and took the child's hand, guiding him to stand directly in front of her, to lean against his mother's legs. She whispered a few words to him, then he laid his head on her lap. The breeze blew her hair across her face.

My heart beat mercilessly.

I looked to the ground, reached, and found my sister's hand. I closed my eyes, and silently began reciting Anna's last letter:

April 3, 1953

Dear, dear Ben,

Benny came on February twenty-first: bright green eyes and it appears he'll have your hair, but maybe darker. His smile is big, and already, his legs are long and muscular, a miniature of Benjamin Bennefield. Maybe he'll one day dive, too, from the railing of the Gold Dust Bridge.

Ben, my thoughts often bring back our summer, which gave me you for too short a time, but gave me Benny, too. And with him now, you and Gold Dust will forever be part of my mind and heart. One day Benny will ask about you, and I will tell him.

In June, I will marry Jacob Steinman, who is a buyer for a gallery in New York. He's a nice man, and marriage will be a fantastic arrangement for both of us, outstanding for me. He'll be a good friend to Benny.

Love always,

Anna

Moving my eyes back and forth from Frank and Margaret Smitherman to Anna and the young boy, to Mrs. Mancini and Jacob Steinman, I thought about my mother and me, about our place in this lineup of people. Our lives had touched one another, intertwining, making complex and unexplainable attachments, attachments that were questionable as to why and how they came about. I could find no evidence, in my thinking, where any one of us had contemplated the consequences of our relationships.

I started over:

Dear, dear Ben,
Benny came on February …

At that moment, the priest said, "Amen," and the small group stood quickly to hug and shake hands. Barbara and Mary Ann walked toward Miz Margaret, who was greeting friends. I walked slowly toward the front gate of White's Cemetery.

"Ben, wait up." I turned, finding Anna and the boy only a few feet behind me. She immediately kissed my cheek. "Well, Benjamin, always leaving before I have a chance to say hello. Naughty, Ben." Smiling, she pressed her gloved hand where she had kissed.

"I'm sorry, forgive me," I said, unable to utter her name. "Things on my mind; you know how that is." I looked in her eyes. The words I wanted to say were difficult to hold, but were useless and meaningless after so much time, and now, those words, and the reasons why her letters were never answered, belonged only to me, to hold, to handle, and the reasons were heavy and burdensome. "Anna," I said, simply, "I'm sorry I never answered your letters. Please forgive me."

"Forgive you, Ben?" she asked, barely smiling, her eyes squinting. Anna sighed, shaking her head, and spoke slowly, looking straight into my eyes. "I'm sorry, too, Ben, but forgive you?" Her smile faded completely. "I'm sorry, Ben," she said. She glanced to the child holding her hand, then back at me. "I want you to meet our son. This is Benny." I closed my eyes for a second, before looking at the boy's face, a face hauntingly familiar. My hands were shaking, my heart pounding as he smiled up to me. I bent toward him. Confidently, he held out his hand for me to take.

"Benny, huh?" I said, examining his hand in mine. "That's a mighty good name, young fellow, almost like mine. My name is Ben." Determinedly, he shook my hand, and smiled. I was taken aback when suddenly he reached up for me to take him. I picked him up. Immediately he wrapped his arms around my neck, then kissed my cheek. When he let go, I glanced at Anna, placing my hand where he had kissed. "He's friendly, and he's beautiful, so very beautiful."

Her eyes glistened as she motioned toward the man approaching us. "Ben, I want you to meet my husband." The man from New York extended his hand, and a smile was fixed perfectly across his face. I reached for his hand. "Ben, this is Jacob Steinman. Jacob, this is Benjamin Bennefield." She had barely said my name when the child repeated slowly, "Bennefield, that's my name, too." Again, he wrapped his arms around my neck, holding me.

I felt my legs might buckle. There, very close to me, was Anna, Mrs. Steinman, while I stood holding our child. My heart cried for Anna

Mancini and cried for my son; I wanted to take him in, to look at his lips, feel his hair, see his naked body, his legs, and let him run with me, holding my hand. I wanted to press him against my bare chest, holding him there, until I felt his heart beat. We looked at each other for a second, then I put him down to stand at his mother's side. He wrapped his arms around her legs and looked up at me, holding his eyes on my face. Haplessly, I looked across the expanse of White's Cemetery.

Flashing through my mind was the lineup of people I had seen, and I wondered about us, and who we were. Each of us seemed to fit neatly into our own box, to have our own place, each in our moment. And I was saddened for Anna and felt sorrow for Jacob Steinman, a match for convenience only; and I felt a deep sorrow for my friend Miz Margaret, for the loss she suffered of two people she loved. And when I thought of my mother, I felt a singularly piercing sorrow for her, a tormented soul whose childhood innocence was stolen; she had lost her way and was unable to find happiness and contentment with who she was. And Benny, young Benny. I glanced at him and knew, with certainty, that one day I would see him dive from the railing of the Gold Dust Bridge into the deepest waters of Edward's Creek.

"Good-bye, Benny," I said, brushing my fingers across his cheek. He stared intently at me, half hidden behind his mother. "Good-bye, Mr. Steinman, Mrs. Steinman." I turned and began my walk to the gate where Barbara and Mary Ann were waiting, but I stopped and turned around to look, one last time, to see if maybe, just maybe, Anna Mancini might be there. Thinking about the letters, the years lost, I cursed silently and watched Jacob Steinman walk briskly toward their car, with Anna following, holding our son in her arms, and looking down at the ground.

A breeze from the south blew across White's Cemetery, whistling softly through the tall cedars. Glancing up to the cloudless, blue sky, I frowned when a ray of sun shot through my eyes. Barbara smiled as I approached, placing her arm through mine. As we walked toward the car, she mumbled something.

"Ben?" she questioned. "Ben?"

"What?" I asked, frowning. "What'd you say?"

"I asked about the child, that beautiful boy, and his mother. Didn't you know her at one time, darlin'?"

The wind cut through my coat. I cursed under my breath.

"No," I said. "No … no, I never knew her … not Miz Steinman."

Thirty

Barbara and Mary Ann left on Monday to return to New Orleans, as she had planned.

I was restless and anxious all day, remembering the events at White's Cemetery. I awakened around four the next morning, with my mind set on the cache in my mother's bedroom. After three cups of coffee, I sat at the kitchen table, reading and nervously watching for the sun's rays to come shooting through the trees along Edward's Creek. At the first glimmer, I moved to the front hall and confronted the door to my mother's room. I turned the knob and pushed lightly, listening to the hinges whine until the door stopped against the wall. Before crossing the threshold, I scanned the room; the crystal prisms were dark and absent of color; the two big chairs faced the blackness of the cold fireplace. I stepped inside the shadowy space with a burlap sack in one hand and moved to the chest on my mother's side of the bed, taking the key from my pocket. I glanced around the room again, then turned the key, unlocking the first drawer. My hands were shaking. I was cold.

The first two drawers in the green and gold chest held exactly $80,000 in twenty-dollar bills, I counted. Most small stacks of fifty bills were still tied neatly with string, but others were loose because the string had dried and broken. The bottom drawer was somewhat deeper, and when I removed it from the chest to set it on the bed, one end slipped from my hand, and the money scattered across the floor. I hated the feeling when I dropped to my knees to retrieve the money, glancing around as I counted and placed the money in the sack. The drawer held $70,000.

"Good God a'mighty," my thoughts burst out, shattering the quietness; a perfectly rounded number, easy to remember. I figured my mother had not unlocked the drawers for a long time, but no doubt, she knew exactly how much was there. A total of $150,000, and I looked at the other chest yet to be counted. "That'll wait for another day," I said softly to myself. A flash of heat shot through me, and I could feel the dampness on my forehead as I brushed my hand across it. My heart beat fast.

I wrapped the long end of the sack neatly around the money, slid the bundle under the bed, and stood upright. On instinct, my eyes searched around the room. There was a presence there, of something, someone. I could feel it. My first impulse was to leave fast and get out. *A thief*, I thought … I felt like a thief, digging in a grave, robbing the dead. The feeling ate at me, and I covered my face with both hands. I sighed deeply and, in anguish, let out a loud yell, a yell of absolute frustration. Hurrying, I walked through the door, turned quickly, and slammed it closed; I held the knob, making sure it wouldn't open.

I could hear Lucy and Jake barking from the front porch.

A few minutes before nine, I placed the burlap sack on the seat of my truck, close enough to ride touching my hip during the ten-mile drive to Bunkie. The gravel on the road seemed deeper in places, and my old truck swerved more than it usually did. I slowed my speed. Over and over, I thought about what Barbara said on the day we found the money, about atonement. And now, I decided Mother figured money, so much money, was atonement for all the bad things she had done.

"But, no," I said, "you took too much; more than what dollars can buy, Mother," and I glanced to the other end of the seat, "our lives … all our lives." The truck swerved badly, and slowly, I stopped the old truck in the middle of the road, sighed deeply, and pushed the sack of money to the end of the seat, away from me.

There wasn't a vacant parking space in front of the bank, so I parked about sixty feet up Main Street and waited until a green car pulled out from in front of the bank's door. Slowly, I moved the truck and parked in the vacant spot; I stepped out and proceeded to place a nickel in the parking meter. Before I could slip a second nickel in, I heard my name called from across the street.

When I looked up, Ava was crossing the street in my direction. Under normal circumstances, running into Ava was an exciting event, but as she walked toward me, I froze in my tracks. Smiling, and sashaying briskly around the truck, she asked, "What in the world are you doing in Bunkie so early, darlin'?"

With one hand on top of the meter, I replied rather sheepishly, "Oh, just a little banking business, that's all. How are you, Ava?"

She stood on her tiptoes and lightly kissed my cheek. There was no way I could rush Ava's visit.

"I'm fine, sweetheart, but you haven't called me for several days. What's going on?" she asked, tilting her head and smiling. "I've missed you," she whined.

Ava was stunning, with a bright red smile and blonde hair, loosely curled, framing her sculptured face. Her snug-fitting coat covered her completely and was tied tightly around her small waist. She stood only inches from me while I took in her perfume, deep, and held the aroma for several seconds. Through the glass in the truck's door, I could plainly see the burlap sack sitting on the seat. Ava's spiked heels scraped the sidewalk.

"A lot going on. You know Miz Montagne died on Christmas Day, and my sister Barbara came for a day or two," I said. My mind was locked on the sack of money.

"Yeah, I heard about it, but I didn't know the lady. Otherwise, everything's okay in Gold Dust?" Ava smiled, asking another question before I could answer the first. "I suppose that woman from Philadelphia came, Anna … Mrs. Montagne's granddaughter …" She shrugged her shoulders, exclaiming, "I'm confused about who she really is."

"Yeah, she came with her husband and Miz Mancini. They all came," I said, but not mentioning Benny. I moved to stand with my back to the truck door, figuring I owed no explanation about the relationships in the Montagne, Smitherman, and Mancini families, nor about Anna Steinman and Benny, whose face crossed my mind. "They're nice people," I said, hoping to dismiss the subject.

"I never knew any of those people, Ben, but everybody in high school knew about you and Anna," Ava said, smiling, "during the summer before your senior year." She patted my arm above my elbow, winking. "But I forgive you, Mister Bennefield, for giving that Yankee girl all your attention instead of me." She laughed quietly, then asked, "You're still coming Friday night, aren't you?" Only then did I remember the Koller's *cochon-de-lait* on New Year's Eve.

"Sure; what time should I be there?"

"Oh, around six, and dress casually. We'll be on the terrace out back, if it's not too cool." By then, Ava was backing away. "Mama's waiting at the drug store for me. About six, Ben." Her hand fluttered sweetly, and not moving from where I stood at the truck's door, I watched till she was at least thirty yards away.

Thirty-One

I PULLED THE SACK from the seat and walked through the bank's door, setting the bundle at the end of a table in a room to the right. Several chairs sat neatly around the long wooden table. Before I could turn around, a voice asked nicely, "May I help you, Mister Bennefield?"

"Oh! Yes, ma'am. Hi, Miz Nona," I said. "I have some money here that we need to count and I want to deposit it." I removed my cap. Miz Nona was enthralled by the sack on the table. She looked at me.

"Yes, sir, I'll help you," she mumbled slowly, pointing to the sack. "There's money in that sack, the whole thing?"

"Yes, ma'am, the whole thing."

"Well," she said, her eyes fluttering, "I think Mister Cal needs to see this, Mister Bennefield. Excuse me for a minute, please." She backed out of the room, pulling the door closed. Holding my cap in my hand, I glanced around the cold room, paneled with dark-stained wood. *Probably oak*, I thought, *expensive stuff, like a bank would have.* I studied five pictures hanging on the side wall, figuring they were the past presidents of the bank. A couple I remembered, or at least remembered Mom talking about them ... bastards, they all were, according to Mom.

A Full-Grown Man

Only a few seconds passed before the door flew open, slamming against the wall. Mr. Cal stepped into the room and stopped just inside, tugging his pants above his belly. Rotund and quite short in stature, Cal Evans was wearing his usual dark blue suit, white shirt with collar tips curled upward, and a striped tie whose knot was shiny with oil from the roll of skin hanging over it. Holding a cigar between two fingers, he glared at the sack of money. "All that's money?" he asked, dragging out his words while pointing to the sack, and frowning. "Where in the world did you get it, boy?"

Boy? I thought, *He knows me; I owe him money from last year's cotton crop.* Nonetheless, I introduced myself. "I'm Ben Bennefield, Mister Cal, Will and Hester's son. I'm sure you remember my parents."

"Oh, sure, sure," he muttered quickly. "What'd you say … Ben, that right?" he said. "Oh, sure, I rememba' your mama and daddy, but where in the hell did all this money come from?" he asked again, shoving the cigar between his teeth. Hands moving fast, he opened the top of the sack and looked in, then pulled out several stacks of bills.

I reached and closed the door, suggesting, "Miz Nona, Mister Cal, y'all have a seat, please." I sat at the head of the table with the sack of money in front of me, placing one hand on top of the stacks Mr. Cal had removed from the bundle.

In as few words as possible, I told them how Barbara and I had found the money hidden in our mother's bedroom, but I said nothing about the second chest, still uncounted. Neither Mr. Cal nor Miz Nona spoke. I heard a couple of sighs, and waited, looking at them. Finally, Mr. Cal cut his eyes toward me and said, "Ben, I'm guessin' you wanna pay off what you owe us, and deposit the rest … is that it? That your plan?"

"Well, Mister Cal, I'll certainly pay off my debt; I think I owe you $5,889.32, plus a little interest. Yes, sir, I'm prepared to settle it right away with my farm money." Mr. Cal wiped the corner of his mouth with one finger. "But I've been reading about how the whole country's gonna boom in the next few years," I said, "and I figure I might send what I have here to a couple of investment companies in New York, companies that invest for you in other companies."

"Ah, Ben, Ben, Ben …" Mr. Cal whined, moving his eyes quickly from me to the sack, then back to me. It was then I imagined a little kid whose sucker had been snatched from his lips. Mr. Cal moved his head in circles. "I don't know," he said, still in a whiny voice, "and where you been readin' 'bout that, in some newspaper outta New York?" His thin graying hair was slicked back, looking like it was glued to his scalp. He chuckled and leaned to one side, pulling his crumpled, white handkerchief from his hip pocket. Balled in his hand, he raised the handkerchief and wiped the brown drool from the corners of his mouth. Quickly, he swept the handkerchief across his nose, still chuckling quietly.

"Yes, sir," I said. "In fact, that's exactly where I've read about it. I read it every day."

"Oh," he grunted, looking wide-eyed at me. "Well, Ben, it might be good to send it up to that bunch of hot-shots on Wall Street, but you might be jist as well off leavin' it with us, right here, close by so you can get to it real easy-like." He quickly swiped his handkerchief across his forehead, continuing, "Hell, I can pay you good interest, real good interest. Let's see," and he hesitated before committing himself, quickly turning his big body to glance at Miz Nona, asking sweet-like, "Nona, what're we paying right now on CDs, honey?" He removed the cigar from the grip of his teeth, coughed one little cough, and then cleared his throat. He reached up to his mouth again, placing the soggy end of the cigar back between his parted lips.

Miz Nona pursed her lips, cutting her eyes slightly toward Mr. Cal. "Well, Cal, uh, Mista Evans, sir," she said, "I sold a thousand-dollar CD yesterday and gave them one and an eighth on it. That's about the highest rate anybody'll get today, sir." Miz Nona seemed very nervous as she looked at her boss; it appeared that her eyes sparkled as she spoke, or maybe I was misreading what seemed to me like substantial admiration she held for the rotund little man. She smiled at him, fiddled with a button on her blouse, then looked at me. Finally, she settled her eyes on Mr. Cal. Miz Nona sighed, and when she exhaled, it sounded like a long soft hum coming from deep inside.

"That's about it, Ben," Mr. Cal said, raising his hands from the table as though concluding the matter. I said nothing, just looked at him. "Ah, Ben, maybe an eighth more for this big a deposit, like here in this sack," he said, patting the bundle with his short, fat fingers. "But I don't know what the bank'll do with this big amount of money. Maybe let the farmers buy a few cotton pickers, or finance a few new cars with it." He shook his head, but never took his eyes from the sack on the table.

"I don't know either, Mister Cal, but right now, all I want to do is verify the amount I have here and deposit it in your bank, and I'll work later at moving it to New York, maybe before spring planting." Opening the sack and pouring about half of the money onto the table, I asked, "Can you all count it now, while I wait?"

"Oh, sure," Mr. Cal said, and instructed, "Miz Nona, you write it down on that pad, and me and you'll do the countin'. Ben can watch." He looked at me, grinning, with his cigar sticking straight out from the grasp of his teeth.

The string on each stack of twenty-dollar bills was pulled away, and Mr. Cal and Miz Nona counted fifty bills, then placed a paper strap around them, making a thousand dollars in each strap. Less than five minutes later, Mr. Cal said, "We need to get some help in here." He stood, turned, and stepped toward the door, stopping at my chair. He looked at me sitting at the head of the table, removed his cigar from his lips, and asked sharply, "Ben, how much money you got there? Did you count it?"

"Sure; yes, sir," I said. "I want to see if I counted correctly. I've never seen this much money."

He left the room, and after a couple of minutes, two women came in and introduced themselves as Betty and Marie. I stood and nodded my head while they sat themselves at the table. Quickly, they began counting the twenty-dollar bills.

Only once did I doze during the entire counting. With a deep sigh, one of total relief, like a hum, Miz Nona announced, "That's it." An hour had passed.

"How much, Miz Nona?" I asked, then she slid the pad directly in front of me. I looked closely at the number she had written, and then looked at her, frowned, and exclaimed, "A hundred and fifty thousand dollars? Is that all?" And I let my voice trail up a little, as though questioning her final count.

"Well, that's what we got," Miz Nona hummed, sounding helpless and apologetic.

I slammed my opened hand onto the table top, exclaiming, "That's correct, Miz Nona! Absolutely correct." I grinned and a smile slowly crossed her face. She slumped in the chair as though wilting from exhaustion. "Would you please give me a receipt for this deposit, signed by Mister Cal, and please ask him to come back?" I asked.

Very much a lady, Miz Nona tiptoed from the room while Miz Betty and Miz Marie kept their eyes locked on me. Looking directly at them, and smiling, I said nothing. Miz Marie smiled back, appearing happy and friendly, while Miz Betty's mouth turned down on both ends.

With a signed receipt in my hand, Mr. Cal walked with me to my truck parked at the curb in front of the bank. We shook hands, and I told him I would be in touch in a few weeks. The fat little man in the dark blue suit smiled, with brown drool seeping from his lips. His tongue came out and swished the drool back in.

On the windshield of my truck was a parking ticket, a fine of fifty cents, for having parked beyond the one-hour limit, bought by the lone nickel I had put in the meter when Ava surprised me.

A Full-Grown Man

A hundred and fifty thousand dollars. *A hell of a lot of money*, I thought.

My mind turned to Ava. "Ava Koller," I said out loud. Her name came out smooth and easy as I drove down Main Street.

I turned right on Pershing Highway and passed my old school, going home to Gold Dust.

Thirty-Two

I slowed the truck almost to a stop as I turned into the driveway off the main road coming from the Gold Dust Bridge. After a few feet, I stopped and looked toward my house sitting at the end of the long, straight drive. To the left, about a hundred yards away under several big trees on the bank of Edward's Creek, sat the two houses I built for my workers, Henry Brown and Bo Johnson, and their families. I felt I needed another house, now. Maybe by spring, I thought, with some of the money I had just deposited, I could bring another family to live and work on the farm. I figured that, at the same time, I should build a garage, hire a professional to plan and landscape from the road all the way to the house, and hire another professional to renovate the old house, inside and out.

At the end of the sidewalk, Lucy and Jake were waiting for me. I stepped from the truck, then kneeled to hug my dogs.

"Mista Ben!" I heard someone call my name and I jumped, startled. It was Jessie, Bo's daughter, walking toward me with her arms folded in front of her.

"Oh! Hi, Jessie, you surprised me. What's up?" I asked. I looked at her, waiting for her reply, quickly recognizing that Jessie Johnson was no longer a little girl.

"Mama's not feeling too good," she explained, "so she sent me to do a little cleaning in the house and cook you some dinner. That all right?"

"Sure, Jessie. What's wrong with your mama?" Hattie had taken care of the house and the duties in the kitchen, including keeping up the pantry, since before Mom died, soon after I hired and moved Bo and his family to Bennefield Farm.

"She didn't say, Mista Ben, but she said to tell you I'm gonna help her from now on, if it's okay with you."

"Well, Jessie, you tell your mama whatever she wants to do is good with me. Okay?"

She smiled. "I'm a good cleaner, Mista Ben, and I can cook," she said, pointing her finger at me. "And I'm gonna make you some pancakes for supper. Mama said you like pancakes."

While walking toward the back porch, Jessie followed with Lucy on one side and Jake on the other. I stopped and turned to look at her again. "I love pancakes, Jessie, but you had better check to make sure we have everything you need."

"Yes, sir, I will, but Mama says everything's there."

Never had we locked our door, day or night, and it never occurred to me that anything was unusual about the practice. I told Jessie that she, too, could come anytime she wanted. She looked at me, smiling, and said, "You sure do trust people, Mista Ben, not lockin' your doors." Lucy barked and Jessie patted Lucy's head. Jessie followed me into the kitchen, and I waited at the door going into the hall as she walked toward the sink, gathering dirty dishes from the table. She turned, looked at me, and said, "This is where your Mama killed herself. I sure hate that, Mista Ben."

"Yeah," I said, "it'll be a year in April."

"I remember when she did it. I didn't wanna come in here after that. Do you miss your mama?"

Surprised at her questioning, I hesitated, then answered, "Yeah, I miss her; I miss her."

Jessie brushed away a tear moving slowly down her cheek. "I'd sure miss my mama if she died, and I sure hope she don't kill herself."

"Well, Jessie," I said, "we don't know what goes on inside a person. People do strange things sometimes, even bad things to themselves." I began to fidget, realizing Jessie had stirred images I didn't want to see again, and memories laced with guilt about how my mother died. "It was bad I didn't see what was happening to her. Maybe I could've stopped her, somehow."

"Yes, sir," she said. She brushed another tear from her cheek. "But you did real good, Mista Ben. Everybody says so. Daddy says you're a powerful man, and a good man, too."

"I don't know, Jessie, I don't know," I said, as I left the kitchen for my room upstairs. Standing in front of the closet in only my underwear and socks, I hung my dress trousers on a wire hanger, placed them in the closet, and turned to get a pair of jeans from my bureau drawer. "Oh!" I said, startled to find Jessie standing in the doorway. "Jessie, what are you doing up here?"

"I just wanted to see where you sleep, Mista Ben, that's all. And see if your bed needs changin'," she said, as she moved toward the bed.

"No, no, stop, Jessie, stop!" She turned and looked at me, glancing from my feet to my head. "Jessie," I said, "I'll let you know when my bed needs changing, but you don't come up here except to clean, and that's only when I'm not here." The expression on her pretty face changed quickly. "Do you understand, Jessie?"

"Yes, sir," she mumbled, looking down at the floor. "I understand, Mista Ben. I'm sorry." Abruptly, she turned and ran through the door and down the steps. I sat on the edge of the bed, then fell back completely, covering my face with my hands.

After a few seconds, I heard the indistinct sounds of pots rattling in the kitchen.

Anna is beautiful, and so is Ava. Jessie is beautiful, too, I thought.

Thirty-Three

NEAR TWO O'CLOCK IN the afternoon three days later, the sun was bright and warm, the sky deep blue and cloudless. I grabbed my windbreaker from the hooks at the door on the back porch, to walk the short distance to Gold Dust. Possibly, someone might come to the bridge, someone to talk to.

In the middle of the old bridge, I stopped and looked through the railings down to the level part of the bank where small trees and brush had begun to grow, where Anna and I had spent our evenings. I thought about her and about Benny, trying to imagine their life in New York. *What were they doing at that moment?* I wondered. *What were their plans for New Year's Eve?* The face of the small boy kept popping into my mind, a face peering at me around his mother's legs. I leaned with my arms pressing against the railing, looking to the water below.

"Benny," I said. "My son. *My son.*" There was a ring in the words when I said them out loud, a sound causing emptiness in my stomach and anger at my mother for what she had done. I wished my father was still alive so we could talk about my son, and he could have known his grandson. I wanted him to be happy for me and for Benny. I straightened up and stood tall, looking to the south down Edward's

Creek toward my home and farm. I placed my hands on my waist and spit over the railing as far as I could; a simple little game we had played as boys, but there was no shouting or laughter, no jumping around. *As boys*, I thought, *as boys!* The words rang in my ears. Long ago, I had convinced myself I was much too young to take on this life merely by the fact of being the son of William and Hester Bennefield. Leaning against the railing, again, I spit far out, yelling silently, *Son-of-a-bitch, son-of-a-bitch*, over and over. I spit again.

"Ben! Hey, Ben," I heard, recognizing the voice coming from the direction of the Bartletts' house. James was waving to me. He jumped from the porch and began running toward the bridge.

Thank God, I thought. I needed a friend at that moment, someone to talk to.

"Ben, how are you, boy?" James said, moving closer to me, smiling. He extended his hand and I grabbed it, then we hugged. During the Christmas holidays, we had not made time to visit, for many reasons, most of which were neglect of a friendship. "Hey, man, what's going on around here?" he asked.

"A bunch of nothin'," I answered, "a little winter-time clean up, and getting ready for spring. That's about all." We looked into each other's faces and began to laugh, and then we hugged again. "James, you look great. School's good for you, huh?"

"You bet, Ben. It's been a long haul, but it's been good," he said.

"And the girls, the girls; LSU's loaded with good-looking girls, huh?" I asked.

"Girls? Nah, I don't have time," he said. "And you, you son-of-a-gun, still plenty of girls in your life, I bet."

"Oh, every now and then, but you know what happens here. They leave, or get married and then leave. But I'm still around, hanging in here, and working my butt off."

"Don't lie to me, Benjamin. Dad says everybody for miles around talks about Mister Benjamin Bennefield, the young stud with lots of land, the big cotton farmer from Gold Dust." He hit me on the arm with his fist. "Hell, yes," he said, "everybody knows!"

I flinched at his words, knowing James and I had never lied to one another about anything. We questioned each other, but never lied. And today I felt the guilt of having not held up my end of our bargain, a promise to each other to go off to college, and when Uncle Sam would call, we'd stick together in the army. And maybe one day we'd share in a business of our own. But whatever came about, we knew it would be far away from Gold Dust, from the land, and from cotton. "James, I envy you," I said. "I should've been with you all this time, and we'd graduate one day, together. I'm sorry it didn't work out."

James stopped his raucousness for a second and forced a smile. "Ah, that's crazy, Ben. I've still got a lot ahead of me before I can start living, and sometimes I'm scared, scared as hell."

"Scared? You scared, James? You've never been scared of anything in your life. You ought to be a farmer in Gold Dust. Now *that* would Scare the hell out of you.

"Yeah, I got out of here, and look at me. I haven't got a job; I've got nothing … and, here," he stopped his speech, raising his outstretched arms, "look at what you've done, how far ahead of me you are." He frowned, looking very serious. "And Ben," he said, "I hear you have a kid, a son. What about it?"

Again, I flinched, feeling like I had been hit in the stomach, caught off guard. It was the first time I had had the words spoken to me, plain, simple, and direct: "You have a son!"

"Yeah," I said, hesitatingly, and glanced down at the bridge's floor. "I do, but," my mind was searching for words, "yeah, but he's far away, and I don't know that I'll ever get to know him." My voice became a whisper. "He lives in New York with his mother."

James was standing with his hands shoved in his pockets, looking at me. "Ben, everybody around here knows about him, so you might as well open it up," he said. "Don't shy away from it." He placed his hand on my shoulder.

Again, I looked at the floor of the bridge, then turned my eyes up to face him. "Yeah," I said, "I'll get used to it one day. He's a beautiful boy, James, as beautiful as his mother."

"Anna Mancini," he said. "Sure, I remember her well, our summer 'reward' in Gold Dust. But Ben," James studied my face for a second, "you won her after all those years. Every boy around here had his eyes on Anna, but you were the big winner, boy, of the most beautiful girl we'd ever seen."

"I guess you could look at it that way, but it didn't turn out just right," I said. "I live here and Anna lives in New York." I shook my head. "She married and someday she'll belong to the world, and I'll still be eating dirt right here around this damned old bridge."

"Ah, get off it, boy," James started again. "Get your kid down here every summer when he's old enough. He's yours, too."

"Sure," I said. "I plan to work on that in a couple of years. It'll take a little time."

James's face lit up again. "You've gotta come visit me, Ben, in Baton Rouge. We'll slip over to New Orleans for a day or two."

"Sure," I said, then asked, seriously, "What are you gonna do after graduation next year?"

"Oh, man," he exclaimed, "I've got a debt to Uncle Sam for at least six years, the air force. They paid my way through school, and I'll probably end up in pilot training. Maybe a career in the air force. That's not bad." His words sounded like an apology.

"No, not at all. See the world! What do they say, 'Twenty years the army way, retire young and draw your pay,' or something like that?"

An awkward, uncomfortable silence set in for three or four seconds after the chattering and laughter died. We looked at each other.

James was my friend, a friend since we were old enough to remember, but that day on the Gold Dust Bridge, on New Year's Eve in 1954, both James and I knew I was a much older man, far beyond the years of our youth.

"I have to go, James; a little party up the road a ways." We shook hands, our eyes still holding to each other's face, both of us feeling the estrangement of two old friends. I walked along the bridge's runner, but before I stepped into the gravel at the end of the bridge, I turned back and waved at him. He had not moved. He raised his hand. "James," I called to him, "go with me to the party. It's at Ava Koller's house. She'd like that."

"If you think so, Ben. I'd like to go."

"Sure, I'll pick you up around six."

Thirty-Four

The sky was turning amber and the sun had fallen behind the trees in the west when I pulled the truck to a stop. Several cars were parked on the side of Pershing Highway across from the driveway to the Kollers' house. James commented on the distinguished beauty of the big home, sitting against a backdrop of tall oak trees. Built long before the Civil War, it had been the Big House on the Star Plantation. The house had two fronts: the original faced Edward's Creek and was referred to now as "the terrace"; the second front was built facing Pershing Highway decades later, when the road was cut through the countryside. James thanked me for inviting him to Mr. Koller's annual New Year's Eve *cochon-de-lait*.

"I understand you've been dating Ava for a while, Ben. How's that goin'?" he asked, as we walked along the gravel drive.

"Good. Ava's a nice girl, smart, and I'm sure she's gonna be a good teacher. You know she finished at SLI almost a year ago."

"She's finished ... Yeah, I knew that. What'd she do, take a little time off, or is she gonna stay here and look for a man to marry?" James asked, smiled, and tapped me on the arm.

"Yeah, a little time off, I guess, but she's a teacher, and teaching jobs around here are hard to get; aren't many vacancies coming up, but Ava's determined to teach," I explained.

"Mother says you have to be born into the system, that teaching jobs are handed down from one generation to the next," James said. I figured he would know since Mrs. Bartlett had been a teacher in the elementary school in Bunkie for as long as I could remember.

"So, James, I guess you're gonna come back here and take your mama's place in a few years. That right, big boy?" I hit him on the arm.

James grabbed his arm as though I had really hurt him. "No way, Benjamin, not likely to happen, ever. Not to this fella," he said. "I'm gonna see the world."

Before we could knock, the front door swung open.

"Mister Benjamin Bennefield," Ava announced in grand style, "and his friend Mister James Bartlett, two of the best-looking men in the entire parish." Ava curtsied and smiled, holding a bottle of beer high in one hand. She was striking and beautiful.

James glanced at me, then moved to hug Ava. I followed, kissing her on her lips and putting my arms around her.

"Everyone's on the terrace, Ben; James, I'm delighted Ben brought you. How in the world are you?" she asked, taking my arm on one side and James's on the other. We proceeded slowly toward the end of the long hall to the big doors opening onto the terrace. "How's school, James?" Ava asked.

"Good," James said, "another couple years and I'll be done."

Ava let go of the two of us and delivered us to the terrace, where as many as a hundred people stood around, all with a drink in hand, talking, and laughing. "Ben," she ordered, "show James around. Y'all probably know everyone here." Ava smiled as she patted my cheek. "I have kitchen duties to take care of." She turned and walked toward the kitchen, her perfume lingering around my face. I took a deep breath.

Both James and I watched her move away, and I thought of my sister's words the only time she met Ava: "She's a fine one, Ben," she had said. No doubt, Barbara had judged well.

James and I moved side by side, touching, an old habit developed when we were kids and carried through high school, signifying that, were a fight to erupt in a crowd, and we were caught up in it, we knew we were on each other's side. Every kid around understood, if you had a fight with one of us, he had to fight the other one, too.

I looked to the end of the terrace to my left and saw my new good friend from the bank, Mr. Cal Evans, wearing his dark blue suit with a cigar stuck between his teeth. He was talking fast and motioning at the same time; I figured he was eagerly explaining the workings of simple interest and certificates of deposit. Next to him I recognized his wife, a tall, slender woman standing quietly, and wearing a flowered dress with a lace collar. A cameo graced the middle of the collar at the base of her long neck. A shiny black purse dangled from her folded arm, and in her lily-white hand she held a colorful handkerchief. Had I not seen the two together at other events, I would never have placed them as man and wife. Continuing to scan the party-goers, I saw no one I didn't know by name or at least by sight, all from around the area. And there, at the other end of the terrace, was Miz Nona, another familiar person from the bank. She seemed much prettier than she had been in the bank's dark-paneled room, counting twenty-dollar bills. Standing next to her was a tall man with a two-day beard, wearing a blue and yellow plaid cowboy shirt and blue jeans, with his tummy falling slightly over a big oval belt buckle, shiny like silver. He took a long swig of his beer and looked to the other end of the terrace where Mr. Cal was continuing his long-winded speech. The man leaned toward Miz Nona and said something in her ear. Miz Nona turned slightly and glanced at her boss, frowned, then whispered back in the man's ear. Again, he cut his eyes toward Mr. Cal.

"Well, how're you boys doin'?" A strong, coarse voice pulled my focus from Miz Nona and the man.

"We're doing great, Mister Koller, thanks," I said. "Gonna be a great party, I can tell." James and I reached for the beers held toward us by Mr. Koller. "Thank you, sir," we said in unison. Mr. Koller's eyes quickly scanned both James and me.

"Well, make yourselves at home with all these older folks. The food's comin' out in a few minutes," he said. "Ava's got her job to do, but she'll be finished in a little while." At that very moment, two colored men in long white jackets jockeyed through the crowd with a roasted pig sprawled atop a slab of well-worn cedar. A bright, red apple was in its snout. "Here we go, boys. Dinner's ready. Y'all get yourselves somethin' to eat." Mr. Koller left us and walked into the crowd.

"James, there's a lot of rich folks here, boy. You think we can handle this?" I asked.

"We can handle it, Benjamin, we can handle it." James looked at me, and we smiled a familiar smirk only two longtime friends would understand.

In less than thirty minutes, the roasted pig had vanished, along with several large platters of potato salad and a multitude of foods we ate with our fingers. Ava wandered over to the spot where James and I huddled, nibbling our dinner, and after a few minutes she raised her hand, waving in the direction of the kitchen. Immediately, four young colored girls in long white aprons over black dresses, each wearing a tall chef's hat, walked from the kitchen door. Each held a silver tray heaping with colorful exotic fruits, every bite with a toothpick in it. Behind them came four young colored boys dressed in black shirts and trousers, also wearing long white aprons and tall chef's hats. Each of them carried a silver tray, too, but laden with delicate sweets from the French bakery on Main Street in Bunkie. Smiling as they moved slowly among the guests, they offered their treats.

"Mista Ben?" asked a familiar voice. Turning quickly, I was surprised to find Jessie Johnson standing in front of me with a tray of fruit. She smiled, speaking again, very softly, "Would you care for a bite of my goodies?" Her big, dark eyes slowly rolled up to my face. She smiled, holding my gaze to her eyes.

"Sure, Jessie, thanks," I said. Before I could grasp a toothpick between two fingers, she abruptly turned away, and slowly strutted in the direction of Miz Nona and her cowboy-shirted husband. Jessie glanced back at me, wistfully.

"Hey, boy," James said, poking his elbow in my ribs. Frowning, he cut his eyes at me, asking, "You know her, don't you, big fellow? What's that about?" Subtly he motioned with his thumb toward Jessie.

"Nothing, James," I whispered. "Clean up your mind, boy; her dad works for me. They live in one of my houses."

"Well, okay," he said, "that's good enough for me." Then he added, mockingly, "Mista Ben," with a twist in his voice, and staring at my face. "Ben," he asked, "isn't that Mister Evans, there, from the bank?"

"Yeah, Cal Evans," I said, figuring he would quickly make another comment I had heard many times before.

"Boy," he exclaimed in a low tone, "I hear he's a real scalawag!"

"Maybe so," I said. "I've mostly dealt with Miz Nona when I've needed anything at the bank. Nice lady." At that moment, I saw Miz Nona tugging on the arm of her husband while he pushed his way through the crowd, headed in the direction of Mr. Cal. "Uh, oh," I exclaimed to James. "Something's gonna happen. Get ready!"

Before I could get out another word, Miz Nona's husband slammed his fist into the bull's eye of a big round target: Mr. Cal's face. The big man fell back very hard onto the laps of several ladies sitting in chairs along a knee-high stone wall. The women screamed, falling onto the floor with Mr. Cal.

"He has a gun, he has a gun!" Miz Nona screamed wildly.

A Full-Grown Man

By the time James and I reached the cowboy, he was aiming the pistol straight at Mr. Cal's head. Mr. Cal lay still on the terrace's brick floor, which now was covered with spilled beer, high-balls, tea, and several old ladies. James and I tackled the man at the same time, and the pistol fired. I held him down, straddling him, while James struggled with his arms and pulled the gun from his grasp. Yelling and cursing while fighting to free himself, he threatened to kill both James and me, but stopped when Mr. Koller pointed his shotgun inches from his plaid shirt.

"That son-of-a-bitch," the man yelled, "he's been after Nona long enough, and I'm gonna kill 'im, I'm gonna kill the bastard." He was panting and drooling badly, and I felt as though James and I were struggling with a raging bull, a bull bleeding from wounds inflicted by a callous predator. He was about to lose his life, and he had made up his mind to fight for what was left. Later, we were told the bullet had grazed the stone wall, ricocheted, and shattered the window in Mr. Koller's office.

After a few minutes, the sheriff arrived with two deputies, who nicely escorted Miz Nona's husband to the sheriff's car. Miz Koller and Ava walked among the guests, bidding them goodnight, and the revelers began leaving. Ava came to James and me and, with tears in her eyes, thanked us for having quickly stepped into the fracas, thwarting what would have been a dramatic and deadly ending to a New Year's Eve party. Together, we walked to the kitchen, where several servers were putting away food and drink before they, too, departed Mr. Koller's *cochon-de-lait*.

At the sink in the big kitchen, Jessie leaned on one leg, washing dishes and humming. She turned toward me, smiling, then glanced at Ava and James as we sat in chairs at the kitchen table.

Watching Ava, but hearing little more than indistinct rumblings, I recognized a sparkle in her eyes as she talked with James about what had happened on the terrace.

James was enthralled by the wit and enthusiasm of Ava, a girl we both had known for a very long time. Now, Ava was a beautiful and exciting woman.

The big clock in the main hall began to strike, and I counted, slowly: dong, dong, dong, until the eleventh strike. Before it hit the twelfth, I said, "Happy New Year, Ava. Happy New Year, James." I waited for Ava to stop talking, but she kept on, neither of them hearing the clock nor anything else around them.

I wanted Ava to caress my face with both her hands, hug me, and wrap her arms around me; I wanted to take in her scent; and I wanted her to kiss me when the clock struck twelve, at midnight, the end of another year. But Ava didn't stop talking, and James never stopped listening.

The ride home seemed to take much longer than usual. The first hours of the New Year were very dark for me, and the shine on the suddenly renewed friendship with my buddy had begun to dull. Silence rode with James and me; no words were spoken as I ground my teeth the entire four miles to Gold Dust.

"I hate this damned old bridge," I blurted out when the wooden runners on the Gold Dust Bridge bounced noisily beneath the truck's tires.

"Ben?" James said, in a question.

"What, James?" I said, turning and glaring in his face. "What the hell do you want?" I wanted to hit him.

"Ben," he said, hesitating again for a couple of seconds. "Thanks for taking me, taking me to the Kollers' party. I appreciate it." I said nothing and brought the truck to a stop at the sidewalk in front of the Bartletts' house. James opened the door, stepped out, and stood looking at me through the open door. He raised his hand. "Happy New Year, Ben!"

The wheels spun in the gravel as I pulled away; the door slammed.

"Happy New Year, Benjamin," I said out loud. "It's 1955."

Thirty-Five

"Before the Ides of March," Dad would say every spring. "Get the seed in the ground before the Ides of March," as though we had never heard it before. "That's the time to plant cotton around Gold Dust." Bo, Henry, and I finished the last acres on March fourteenth, around two o'clock, on a windy and cool Monday.

On April Fool's Day, the familiar green lines of tiny plants marked the rows of new cotton, and though exciting to see, they reminded me most of the hard work still ahead of us. Working the fields, with the dust clouds following the tractor and the anxious hope for timely rain, was challenging for any cotton farmer. But the back-breaking job of picking the blossoms at harvest time, arduous to say the least, had become an almost insurmountable task due to the unavailability of laborers in large numbers. The migration of field hands to the cities in the North and to the far West had hurt the area farmers, especially the small farmers with little capital. They had no choice but to borrow money, and make heavy investments in the mechanical cotton picker.

Mr. Charles White was the first of the small farmers to do so, and he rented out his tall red behemoth to roll down the rows of whiteness, growling like an angry dinosaur as it gathered in one day as much cotton as fifty field hands could pick. On winter evenings in the secluded dining rooms around Gold Dust, or around the big iron stove in the depot, we debated whether the mechanical cotton picker eliminated the jobs on the farms and plantations, or whether it was the inevitable result of a desperate need to replace the millions of field hands who fled the South in the thirties and in the years following World War II. After several winters of discussions, most of the cotton farmers began to believe with certainty that the mechanical cotton picker embodied the axiom "necessity is the mother of invention."

For several years, I had hired Charles White to help harvest my cotton. But the time had come, and I ordered my first cotton picker from the implement company in Bunkie. It was the second one around the Gold Dust Bridge. My two men, Bo and Henry, applauded the decision, which diminished their burden of finding laborers for the horrendous bent-over task of picking cotton by hand.

Two days before the July Fourth celebration at the Gold Dust Bridge, the contractor completed the garage at my house and finished the third house on the banks of Edward's Creek. I looked forward to Mr. Ed Moreau moving in with his family, a wife and three teen-age sons, as the manager of what had become known as Bennefield Farm.

"How about right here, Ben?" Ava asked, pointing at two chairs. The Gold Dust Bridge was decked out in red, white, and blue banners across the top, and garlands of red, white, and blue hung from its sides from one end to the other. Two big Stars and Stripes waved beautifully from its peak in the hot summer breeze . The bridge was blocked off on the west end to stop traffic, and on the east end a band of four horn-blowers played what sounded like "Stars and Stripes Forever." Ava opened her umbrella to shade us. "Not many people this year," she said, looking around.

"No," I agreed, "certainly not like during the war, or even a few years back." After a few minutes, I felt a tap on my shoulder and glanced to find Miz Margaret. Behind her, Mr. Frank fidgeted with his trousers, attempting to pull his belt up to fit over his bulging tummy. I stood quickly and offered my chair to Miz Margaret.

"Oh, no, thank you, Ben," she said. "We'll only be here a few minutes. It's too hot in this sun." She smiled. "And this is Ava Koller, isn't it?"

"Yes, yes," I said quickly. "I'm sorry. Certainly you and Ava know each other."

"We do, but I haven't seen Ava for a long time, since she was little girl, I suppose." Miz Margaret smiled and asked politely, "How are your mother and father, Ava? I hope all right."

Ava smiled in the shade of the umbrella. "Yes, ma'am, they're fine. Thank you for asking."

Miz Margaret looked at me. "Ben, I hear you're moving on with your business; you've hired a farm manager and built another house. I know your mother and father would be pleased at the progress you're making."

"Yes, ma'am; we're just working as hard as we can to keep up, but the daily rains aren't helping any," I said, shaking my head.

"I'm so happy for you, Ben." She placed her hand on my arm and asked, "Would you walk with me back to the store, dear? I have something for you."

"Yes, ma'am," I replied, holding my arm for her to take. I looked at Ava and winked. "I'll be right back. Keep the band playing."

Miz Margaret and I walked slowly toward the store, with Mr. Frank behind us, dragging his feet in the sand and gravel, grunting with each step and breathing hard. "Don't go so fast," he ordered. I could hear him gasping for air.

"Ben," she said, "I have a little article for you, sent to me by Aunt Isabella a few days ago. Anna has accepted an invitation to display her work in a private gallery on the *Champs-Elysées* in Paris, two summers from now. Isn't it wonderful?" She looked up at me. "I'm so proud of her." Miz Margaret's face had lit up, talking about Anna.

"So am I, Miz Margaret. I'm proud *for* Anna, very proud," I said. Then, quickly I asked, "What does she say about Benny?"

"Benny is the love of Anna's life, Ben, Anna's letters tell me, and I'm sure he'll be a fine young man very soon." Miz Margaret pressed her hand onto my arm and looked up at me. "He's my grandson, Ben," she said, confirming the unspoken. "You do know that, don't you?"

I'm certain I grimaced, and barely in a whisper, I answered, "Yes, ma'am. I know."

"Ben," Miz Margaret said, looking straight into my eyes, "your son is my grandson, attaching us to each other."

"Yes, ma'am," I said, looking down at the gravel. Our steps were slow and small by then.

"The facts are complicated, Ben, to the people living around Gold Dust," she said, "but I'm satisfied that most are beginning to accept the truth as it is, and people … well, people are a forgiving lot. It just takes a little time." I said nothing, but continued to listen, wondering what else might break out of this conversation, an awkward, and strange conversation, I felt. "Benjamin, from now on let's not run from the facts of our lives," she said. "You and I should talk freely and openly about our link to each other: a beautiful child in New York. I like thinking about him and Anna, and I want to be happy to openly express those feelings." She looked at me. "Don't you think we can do that?"

It appeared to me there was a release of anxiety from Miz Margaret, and I was sure that my friend was giving me the chance to express my own feelings, uneasiness, or fear.

"Without any doubt, Miz Margaret, I'm ready to do that. I want to talk about Benny, to feel free to do it," I said. "I want to be happy about it, all the time, to everyone." We had stopped walking. She stood so close to me, and suddenly I wanted to hug her and thank her. When she smiled, I saw Anna. I knew, too, I could search for a lifetime, but could never find a more wonderful and loving grandmother for my son.

"And Benjamin," she said, asking, "are you and Ava going to marry? That's the word around here." I was stunned by her question, my eyes blinking to clear them.

"Maybe," I mumbled softly. I looked toward the store, away from her face, then back again. "Maybe one day I would marry Ava, but I'm afraid she'll say no, so I've never asked."

"Look at me, Benjamin," she said. "Look at me." She paused while I turned to face her. "You have your entire life waiting to be lived, and it appears you have everything going for you. Don't, Ben, don't misspend it in loneliness, with idle foolishness, waiting away the years hoping for something else to happen. What you do next is what matters. Ben, Ava comes from a good, upstanding family, and I know you like her."

"Yes, ma'am, I know," I said. We resumed our walk.

"Ben, what I said is for your own good, and I have one more thing. I hope you don't mind if I tell you something else I've heard in the store. May I?"

"Oh, sure, Miz Margaret, tell me," and I held my breath, expecting another jolt.

"I've known for many years your mother hid money away, and from what Hester had confided, it was a very large amount," she said. "And I understand from the gossip, you have found the money, and I hope you have." We stopped walking again at the step onto the store's porch. There were no secrets in my life I was sure, not here, not around Gold Dust.

"Yes, ma'am, it's in the bank now. In fact, I've put half in one bank and the rest in the other bank in Bunkie." It felt good to be able to talk about the money to someone.

"That's excellent thinking, Ben, and I want to offer you something, something for you to consider. Okay?"

"Yes, ma'am." Miz Margaret glanced at Mr. Frank, who had finally caught up with us. He hobbled across the porch, opened the screen door, and stepped into the darkness of the unlit store. His pants again were barely hanging on his bottom. He coughed.

Miz Margaret smiled as she glanced at Mr. Frank then turned to me. "My family in Philadelphia is old and very well established," she said, "with a large portfolio of investments. I will gladly put you in touch with people who can invest for you, astute and highly polished professionals who do nothing but take care of money for people from all around the country."

"Yes, ma'am," I said. "I've written to a couple of firms in New York and will make arrangements sometime in a year or so, but right now, I'm leaving it in the banks in Bunkie, until I learn more about investing and my own responsibilities."

"That sounds excellent, Ben; sounds like the beginning of a well-thought-out plan. And if I recall, Hester indicated she had around $300,000, part of which her mother had accumulated."

"Yes, ma'am, that's about right; a lot of money that Barbara and I never knew about, hidden in her bedroom," I said. I waited for her to spill out more information, surprising me, details I thought no one knew.

"Um, that was Hester, all right. Bless her heart. I still miss her," she said. She glanced at my face. "But life goes on, Ben, and that's what I mean about not letting your life be misspent. It can happen to any of us. Believe me, darling, I can speak first hand." Inside the front door, I reached and pulled a string to light a lone bulb hanging from the tall ceiling. We walked to the counter, where Miz Margaret retrieved what she had wanted to give me.

"Thanks, Miz Margaret," I said, as she handed the paper to me. I glanced quickly at the clipping, but I didn't mention I had already seen the article in my paper from New York.

I left Miz Margaret standing behind the counter in her dark store. That July Fourth, she lightened a load I had not realized had burdened me, the weight of having no one to talk to, to hear me, things I had wondered about, and advice and thoughts that might have come from a good father, or possibly, a good mother, had I had them available to me.

When I stepped from the porch onto the gravel, I stopped and looked west toward the Gold Dust Bridge, where the four horn players were blasting out another Sousa march. I stared at the old bridge with all of its banners and streamers waving in the hot summer breeze, and wondered if this might be our last Fourth of July celebration there. I wondered, too, as it appeared, glaring at me, if the Gold Dust Bridge might have a few suggestions for me about my future. Might it give me permission, as did Miz Margaret, to ask Ava to marry me?

Thirty-Six

As I approached the spot where Ava and I had settled, I saw someone sitting in my chair. It was Jessie Johnson, who had walked the short distance, as I had done for all of my life, from Bennefield Farm to the celebration at the Gold Dust Bridge. The breeze had picked up, and dark clouds were rolling in from the west.

Standing to the side of the two of them, I looked at Jessie. Surprised when she saw me, she stood quickly. "Hello, Mista Ben," she said. "You can have your chair back, now." She smiled as she stood.

"Thanks, Jessie." I sat in the chair and looked at Ava. She glanced up at Jessie and then at my face, holding her smile.

"Well, I gotta go now." Jessie raised her hand. "See you later, Miss Ava; bye. Bye, Mista Ben."

"And how was Jessie?" I asked.

"Oh, fine," she said. "Jessie's very good at helping at parties. She's smart, and isn't she beautiful?"

"Yeah, her dad works for me, has for several years. Good family, hard-working people." I took my cap off and ran my fingers through my hair. "It's too damned hot out here," I said, shaking my head slightly, "and look at those clouds."

"Ben, I didn't know Jessie kept house for you, with her mother. And she cooks for you?"

"Yeah, for a long time," I said. I glanced at Ava's face. "What?" I asked. "What did Jessie tell you, Ava? You have to be careful about what she says."

"Oh, she didn't say anything in particular, but she has an awful crush on you, I can tell," she said.

Through the corner of my eye I could see Ava watching my face, waiting for a reaction to her statement.

"A crush on me?" Then I admitted, "Yeah, I can tell, but she's just a kid; and it happens when a flood of hormones drowns your mind when you're growing up." Then face to face, I teased Ava, asking, "Haven't you ever had a crush on someone?"

I touched her cheek with my finger, and again, teasingly, with wanting eyes, I looked into her eyes only inches from mine and moved my tongue across my lips. Her umbrella tilted. Thunder sounded in the distance, rolling thunder.

She pushed away from me. "Stop it, Benjamin, in front of these people!" she said, placing her hand on my thigh. She whispered, "Let me tell you a secret, Ben."

"You have a secret for me?" I whispered back to her, wetting my lips again.

"Yes, Mista Ben, a sweet little secret."

"Great; I love secrets. Whisper it to me, Ava baby." I sat upright in the rickety little chair and held my eyes glued to her pretty face, only inches away, slowly running my tongue across my lips for the third time.

"Jessie's a woman, Ben, a sixteen-year-old, full-grown woman who has a terrific crush on you." Ava laughed quietly and then placed her hand on my cheek, whispering in a mocking and childish tone, "On 'Mista Ben,' sweet 'Mista Ben.'" Her laugh stopped me cold. She parted her lips. "Oh, I'm sorry Ben, I shouldn't make light of it, I'm sorry," she said, "but I hadn't figured you to be so sensitive about a silly teenage crush."

"I'm sorry, too, Ava," I said. I leaned away from her. "I suppose I may be a little sensitive, and it does concern me, very much, because—" I stopped in mid-sentence, wondering if I should confess, my second confession to a strong woman, a woman I cared about very much. "Ava," I said, searching for the right words, "I … I knew a kid a long time ago, a kid who was taken with someone, an older person who didn't quash that teenage crush until much too late, after it had turned into a nearly out-of-control obsession. He caused a lot of problems and a lot of pain for a whole bunch of people, and himself."

"Ben, I'm sorry." Ava's eyes glistened with tears. "I'd heard the story, but I'd forgotten it. And I think I knew the kid." She waited a second then whispered, "I hear he's overcome it now." We looked at each other. "Do you think he has, Ben?"

"Yeah," I said, "maybe he has." I glanced at the sand and gravel in front of us, stood, and reached to help her from the chair. She took my hands, never taking her eyes from mine.

"Most of the time he has, and you need to help him, Ava."

"Let's go home, sweetheart," she said, glancing up to the dark clouds.

Thirty-Seven

WE WORKED OUR WAY past the band and a chorus of teenagers singing "God Bless America," to the west end of the bridge where we had parked Ava's car. Before stepping into the gravel at the end of the bridge's runners, I stopped and turned around to glance again to the south, down Edward's Creek, then to the east bank at the foot of the bridge. Ava was the first girl, other than Anna, with whom I had ever walked the entire span of the Gold Dust Bridge, and I wondered if the old bridge was truly going to make something happen, if it was going to give me a sign of some sort to let me know it, too, approved of Ava Koller becoming my wife.

"What's the matter, Ben?" she asked, waiting a few steps beyond the end of the bridge.

"Oh, nothing," I said. "Thought I heard something, but I guess not." I turned, and hand in hand, we walked to the car. Inside, it was blistering hot, and I had already begun to sweat. I removed my cap, brushed my fingers through my damp hair, and held my eyes set firmly on the Gold Dust Bridge. Still, I waited, expecting the bridge to suddenly burn, or explode, or turn from its rusty red color. Maybe if a flag fell from the top into Edward's Creek; anything, any hint at all. But nothing happened. It gave me no signal, no approval, nothing I could interpret as a sign about asking Ava to marry me.

"We sure don't need any rain," I said, looking at Ava and the gold earrings she wore. I had given them to her last Christmas. *Golden earrings,* maybe they would cast their spell as the beguiling song rang in my mind. I hoped. Just as the car's engine revved, several big drops of rain splattered on the glass. "The cotton's growing too fast," I said out loud, "too much stalk, getting rank." Ava glanced in my direction and kept on driving.

In less than five minutes, in the pouring rain, she stopped the car at the end of the sidewalk going to the back porch. "Pull in the garage and we'll wait out the storm," I said, pointing in front of us.

The thunderstorm with its heavy rain and strong wind had quickly cooled the air, but I worried about how much water the storm would dump onto the cotton fields, already too wet.

As soon as she turned the key to stop the engine, Ava looked at me, smiling, as she slid across the seat toward me. "Mista Ben," she mocked, "let's wait out this little ole storm, honey, in the back seat of this car. You wanna do that, sweetheart?" She took off her shoes and started climbing across the seat to the back. My heart quickened its beat while I kicked off my loafers.

As I followed her over the seat, I could see Lucy and Jake sitting below the open window, their ears laid back, and their tails swinging from one side to the other. Lucy barked. "Hell," I whispered to Ava, "Lucy and Jake are sitting right there at the door."

"Ignore them, Ben," she whispered. "They don't know what's going on, and besides, they certainly can't tell anybody." Ava cupped her hands around my face, kissing my lips before I was completely resolved to the idea that it was all right for my dogs to be so close. "Careful, darlin'," she whispered, "it's tight back here." She wrapped her arms around my neck, and I could feel her breath on my face. "Careful, darlin', slow," she whispered in my ear. "Go really slow, sweetheart."

Lightning flashed and thunder sounded.

"I love you, Ben, I love you," Ava said softly, above the sound of rain pounding the tin roof. Thunder sounded again and again, and lightning flashed.

Sitting up, I pushed open the back door of the car and ordered, "Come on."

In a split second, Ava and I were trampled by Lucy and Jake, barking and trying to lick our faces as they climbed on top of us. We laughed, then Ava screamed while trying to push them away.

"Marry me, Ava," I yelled above the barking, the laughing, and the rain on the tin. "Marry me," I commanded, looking straight into her beautiful face.

Everything stopped, it seemed, all of the sounds, the barking, the rain on the roof, the screams.

"Oh, Ben," her lips were moving but with no sounds I could hear. "No," her lips said as her head moved. She frowned while her eyes blinked rapidly, and then the onslaught of sounds burst out, through my head. "Not now, my darlin'," she screamed, without a trace of a smile. "I can't. And I have something to tell you."

A clap of thunder sounded like a train plowing through the garage, shaking the car. Both dogs jumped through the door and ran into the rain, barking, searching for the noise. I closed the door and sat upright on the seat, looking at the wall in front of the car. All I could hear was hammering on the tin roof, while my mind rambled aimlessly; no thoughts came to a conclusion of any sort, just loose ends flying in different directions.

"It's not the end of the world, Ben," Ava said, straightening her blouse, while I buttoned my jeans. I couldn't look at her. "I'm moving away in August, Ben. I've decided to leave here."

I could think of no words to cry out, neither in anger nor in kindness. There was nothing there.

Only twenty minutes earlier, I recalled, I had given the Gold Dust Bridge two chances to give me a sign about my future with Ava, and it gave me nothing.

We sat in silence on the back seat of the car; I looked through the windshield at a blank wall, a stark, white, blank wall, while Ava watched me.

Maybe silence was the bridge's signal, I thought, *and I should have listened to its silence.*

A strike of lightning brightened the garage for a split second, and another blast of thunder shook the car.

Lucy and Jake began barking again, and again they ran out into the heavy rain.

Go home, Ben, and forget about me. Leave me alone, I remembered a woman saying to me several years earlier. I was a kid, then, seventeen years old. And when *she* went away, she took my heart, and for years I cried.

After Ava said no so quickly and so definitely, I felt a sense of relief, of knowing, but also an awful feeling of rejection. A heavy blanket, it seemed, was smothering me. I glanced at Ava sitting beside me, knowing I cared for her very deeply. I put my arm around her and lightly kissed her lips, then reached to swing open the car's door.

"My fields are flooding right now, and I don't know what's going to happen, Ava. I have to go … I have to go." I stepped from the car and walked barefoot into the storm.

"Ben, Ben, wait," I could hear her calling. Through the deluge of water, under the big trees swaying in the wind, I crossed the yard, then climbed the steps and swung the screen door open. On the porch, I stripped off my soaked jeans, shirt, and my skivvies, and walked into the kitchen, stopping abruptly.

"Pancakes tonight, Mista Ben," Jessie said, smiling, as she looked at me from in front of the stove.

Stunned, like a little boy hurting after a terrible whipping, I ran, naked, up to my room.

Thirty-Eight

ALREADY, THE YEAR 1955 had shaken me badly on the morning of January 1 when James and I left the New Year's party at the Koller home, but mine and Ava's close relationship continued. Months later, I realized I should have adhered to the belief, as my father had done, that the first twelve days of January portend the general weather conditions of the year to come; I would have been far better prepared for the trying events that came. Instead, I proceeded as though farming cotton that year would be little different from the usual exhausting, but most often rewarding, efforts of preceding years.

The rains came early in the growing season and far too frequently for the young cotton. The mechanical cotton picker for which I had eagerly waited came to Bennefield Farm a few days following the July Fourth celebration, and we parked it in the special shed we had built just for it, but the big machine never gathered a row of cotton that year. Until 1955, the worst cotton crops local farmers could recall were in 1949 and 1950, when the stalks grew far above six feet, due to too much rain, dropping its fruit as they grew due also to boll worms and boll weevils. Both pests were uncontrollable again in 1955 because the daily rains washed away the effect of the insecticide we used, Dichloro-Diphenyl-

Trichloroethane. And I was certain the hundreds of small fish frequently washed onto the bank of Edward's Creek were the result of the runoff from the fields, rain water laced heavily with DDT. As was the case, by late August the farmers became resolved to the reality that the loss of that year's crop was inevitable. The fields were soon plowed under.

There were many things I wished could be simply "plowed under," a favorite term in the vocabulary of those who lived the mundane life in the farming communities. It was an expression in exactness when you wanted a bad thing or situation to disappear, to be over with and buried. But it was a saying I didn't particularly like. I was taught early in life by Will Bennefield, my father, that a man must face adversity, under whatever guise it came, adversity created by him or adversity put upon him by others.

On Christmas Day in 1955, I left the church in Bunkie a few minutes past noon to return to Gold Dust. When approaching the Koller home, I recognized Ava's car parked in front and figured she was home for Christmas. She had refused my calls after July Fourth, but I learned from her mother she had indeed moved to Baton Rouge, working in the legislative office of Senator Tom Buckman, in a job for which she had not been trained. The senator and the Koller family had been friends for many years, so I figured the senator was paying for past years' contributions to his campaigns.

When I saw her car, my immediate thought was to stop and see her, though possibly interrupting their dinner. And that was okay, as truly, I wanted to face Ava and I wanted her to face me, with a chance of reconciling a relationship that I had come to relish, and now missed.

I got out of my truck, walked briskly to the front door, and knocked. The second time I knocked, the door swung open. "Hi, Ava," I said, stunned by her beauty that seemed to have bloomed greater and far more profound.

"Ben Bennefield. What a surprise! It's good to see you, darlin'," she said in her usual warm, Southern way. Ava extended her hand to me, and I recognized her glow was that of an expectant mother. Before I could say anything at all, she laughed and brought her hand to her tummy. "Oh, Ben, don't look so surprised, darlin'," she said, as James Bartlett stepped behind her from the dimness of the room.

Stunned to see James suddenly appear, I was unable to speak for a second. He spoke up first. "Ben, it's good to see you. How are you?"

"I'm okay," I said, frowning, and glanced from Ava to James.

He crossed the threshold onto the porch. "I want to talk to Ben. Sweetheart," he said to Ava, as he pulled the door, closing it. "We'll only be a few minutes."

"Bye, Ben; bye, darlin'," she said, raising her hand goodbye.

I felt Ava had dismissed me as she would a child. Her words, I figured, might be the last I would hear from her for a long time, maybe for the rest of my life.

"Ben, let's go to your truck, please," James said, looking squarely into my face, not smiling. "I have a lot to tell you, buddy." There was no need to talk, since it was evident James and Ava had married. We walked down the sidewalk. In the truck, I couldn't take my eyes from his face. I waited, frowning and breathing heavily.

"Ben," he said, his forehead creased, "it looks like a surprise to you that Ava and I are married. I figured you would have heard by now, but I'm glad, because I wanted to tell you in person."

"In person, James, like right this minute."

"The time was never right, Ben, and I'm sorry," he said, somewhat whiney. His voice was shaky.

"What should I have heard by now, James?" I wanted to hear him say directly to my face, in his words, what he had planned to tell me. I gritted my teeth, wanting to hit him in the mouth.

"Well, after Ava arrived in Baton Rouge, Ben, she called me and we got together," he said, moving his eyes beyond my face, looking blankly through the truck's window.

"James," I said, "how much time would it have taken to call me, or write a letter if you didn't want to say it outright?" It was the perfect time, but I stopped, with my fist already pressing into the palm of my other hand. "I should have known something had happened when Ava refused my calls. It doesn't really matter, now, *friend*."

His eyes were glassy, and he was searching for words.

"That's okay, James," I said and shook my head. "Ava didn't want to marry me, and she chose you." I shrugged. "What the hell else you want to say, buddy?" My fist was balled up.

"Nothing," he said, "nothing." His smile was slight, his eyes moist. "We got married in Baton Rouge in September, Ben."

"Congratulations, James. I'm glad for you and glad for Ava. Congratulate her for me."

"Ben," he said. I could tell he was desperately looking for a way to make things right, to say he was sorry, to ask for forgiveness. "I was given a chance, Ben, a chance with Ava, and I took it. And I knew she loved you."

"No, James, you're wrong," I said, sighing quickly. "I asked her to marry me, and without any hesitation at all, she said no. So, I think you're wrong, otherwise we wouldn't be having this conversation right now."

James looked at me, frowning, his eyes wet. "Ben, she had no choice. Don't you know why she didn't marry you?"

"No, I don't. She never said why and right now I'm not sure I want to know. But tell me anyway. Maybe I can fix the problem before somebody else bitches about it."

"Because of your mother, Ben, your mother, what she did." James stopped, his eyes glaring at me.

"What about my mother? What?" I shouted, frowning and beginning to breathe harder. I grasped the steering wheel with both hands, my fingernails biting into my palms. "What about her?"

"I hate to say it, Ben," James said softly, "but suicide is a scary thing for most people. Risky. Ava's family forbade her to even see you, but she did anyway." His mouth was half open, waiting, I suppose, for the impact to clear from my face.

After a long and deep sigh, I looked across the expanse of winter-brown grass to the leafless trees along the side of the long front yard of the Koller mansion. It reminded me of the December morning in the gazebo when I threw the letters away, into Edward's Creek. The trees were leafless then, but I knew spring would come again, a time for a new beginning. But right then, in my truck, and hearing an old friend explain the complex consequences of how my mother's suicide determined mine and Ava's relationship, all I felt was bitter hate.

"I have to go, James," I said quickly. "I have to go."

"Ben, I'm sorry to have been so blunt, but that's the way it is," he said softly.

"Get out of my damn truck, James," I yelled at him. "Get the hell out!" I revved the engine, hoping he would get out fast, before my anger boiled into violence.

James opened the door, stepped out, and closed it. I drove away.

"Son-of-a-bitch," I yelled, gritting my teeth, and slamming the wheel with my hands. "Son-of-a-bitch, son-of-a-bitch." Hester had reached from her grave to remind me again of the power she wielded over the lives of those she controlled, her power over me.

When I reached the house, I drove the truck into the garage and waited in the dimness before walking with Lucy and Jake to the steps at the back porch. In the kitchen, Jessie was preparing dinner.

Once inside, she asked immediately what was wrong with me. I told her about Ava and James marrying. "I knew about it, Mista Ben," she said.

"Why in the hell didn't you tell me, Jessie? That's big news."

"I started to say something, Mista Ben, but I figured it wasn't any of my business," she said, cutting her eyes toward me. "Besides, I thought all along you probably already knew about it. You and Miz Ava were so close; she should've called you, herself. She's the one who should've told you." Jessie rolled her eyes toward me, and before I could say anything, she asked very bluntly, "Did you love Miz Ava, Mista Ben?"

"Sort of," I said, almost whispering, and thinking to myself, *Oh, no, more of Jessie's questions.* But I continued, "Yeah, but it was a different kind of love than just plain ole *love*. You know what I mean, Jessie?"

"Yes, sir, Mista Ben, I think so, but—"

"You ever been in love, Jessie?" I asked quickly, hoping to turn around the conversation.

"Yes, sir," she said, and I could see Jessie squirm, appearing somewhat embarrassed. In the time she and her mother had cooked and taken care of the house, I had never seen her express fear or apprehension. "I think I'm in love right now, but sometimes I wonder why I feel that way, cause nothin' ever happens about it."

"Love takes time, Jessie, and you haven't been living long enough to be in love with anyone, not real love, the kind you would die for." I glanced at her as she moved about swiftly. "They say it happens only once in your life."

"You ever had that *die-for* love, like you said, Mista Ben?" she asked, and suddenly I began to squirm inside.

"Yeah, I did, a long time ago."

I questioned the wisdom of continuing this conversation with Jessie, but it felt good to talk to someone, and Jessie was always a willing talker.

"What ever happened about it? She must've went away and found somebody else? What happened to your *die-for* love, Mista Ben?" Jessie was reaching a point in her questioning when normally I would have ignored the words completely, or left, if necessary.

"Oh, I was really young at the time, and no one around me would accept it." I glanced at the black and white floor, reminding me of my mother.

"Was your heart broken, Mista Ben? Did it hurt?" she asked.

"Yeah, some. Well, a lot, really, but broken pieces eventually heal. Makes us stronger, gives us courage for the next time we have to heal, Jessie. But it makes us scared, too."

It was time to change the subject, I felt, and before she could reply or bluntly ask anything else, I questioned, "How old are you?"

"Sixteen," she said. "I'll be seventeen next June." Smiling, she left the kitchen, carrying my dinner on a silver tray, served on my mother's best china, and I followed. She placed the plate at the head of the dining room table, where two candles had already been lit, with crystal glasses and silver, set perfectly, and a glass of wine. She turned and looked at me. "This is Christmas dinner, Mista Ben," she said. "Merry Christmas." She smiled, and then, with short, fast steps, she headed toward the kitchen.

Standing behind my chair, I could see the streams of heat curling upward from what would have been the best dinner I had had for a long time.

"Sixteen," I mumbled. "Smart, advanced in thought, and exuding confidence; there should be far more for Jessie than cooking my dinner, cleaning my house, and serving at parties for rich white people." She had stirred into my mind, my thoughts, calculatingly and carefully, causing me to think and say things I had never confided to anyone.

While my eyes moved around the long table, where the chairs stood empty, I weighed the silence; there was no chattering, no laughing, and no family gathered at the Christmas table. There was no one with whom I would laugh, to toast with wine, to confide; no one to examine my heart or hear me out. I thought about Ava and James; then I thought about Anna.

I stared at the food on Hester's plate. The kitchen door onto the porch closed with a slam.

I wasn't hungry.

Thirty-Nine

NEAR TEN O'CLOCK ON January 3, 1956, the first day of school after the Christmas holidays, I walked into the lobby of the colored school on the north side of the railroad tracks in Bunkie, just as the bell rang. Immediately, the smell of chalk, pencil lead, and crayons rekindled memories of my childhood. I inhaled a deep breath, held it for a second, and then let it out slowly. Before I could reach the principal's office, a torrent of kids burst from the doors on both sides of the long hall, and I backed against the wall nearest me. Chatter and laughter fought for space in the air; I watched the strong, youthful bodies bump into each other, creating more laughter and excitement. As the students moved through the hall, heads turned my way; it was unusual, surely, for them to see a white man in their school. Equally strange and unfamiliar for me was standing in a school hallway full of faces of varying shades of brown and black, very different from the only school I had known. I was taken aback by the sudden realization that I had never set foot in a colored school, a reality, I knew, of the times into which I had been born.

I eased my way into the front office.

A secretary, looking somewhat surprised to see me, smiled. "May I help you, sir?" she asked, as I scanned the small room.

"Yes, please," I said. "I'd like to see the principal if he's available."

"Yes, sir, hold on." She turned and called toward the open door to her right, "Mista Malone, there's a gentleman here, wants to see you." She watched until a tall man in a brown suit stepped from the door. Mr. Malone had dark skin, and thick black hair, nicely groomed. He sported a clean-shaven face, and a kind and friendly smile.

"Yes, sir," he said, smiling. "May I help you?" His approach was sincere.

"I hope so, Mister Malone," I said, as he gestured toward the door to his office.

"Have a seat, sir. And your name is?" he asked.

"Ben, Mister Malone, Ben Bennefield, and I live down at Gold Dust." I held my cap in my hand while scanning Mr. Malone's educational credentials hanging on the wall behind him. "I have a situation that I'm hoping to solve with your help," I said. He pulled his chair under him and sat down, placing both arms over the edge of his desk.

"Well, Mister ... Ben," he spoke hesitantly, "I'll sure do what I can." Apparently, he hadn't fully gathered the name Bennefield, but he continued. "Tell me what you want me to do, sir." His smile was big, genuine, and welcoming.

"I have a young girl whose family lives on Bennefield Farm," I said. Deliberately, I cleared my throat, repeating, *Bennefield Farm.* "Her dad's worked for me for several years. Jessie Johnson's her name, and I'm pretty sure she quit school after last year."

Immediately, Mr. Malone began nodding and called to his secretary. "Miz Mary, would you bring me Jessie Johnson's records, please?"

Neither of us spoke while we waited, and after a minute Miz Mary handed Mr. Malone a folder, explaining, "Jessie didn't come back in September. I really hated it."

Mr. Malone thumbed through the thin file for a minute. "Jessie was a very good student," he said. "Smart and never a problem in any way. Just don't know why she left us." He shook his head, then looked back at me.

"I suppose the 'why' could be important, but right now, Mister Malone, I want to see if Jessie could start back right away and catch up with her classmates," I said. "Do you think it's possible?"

"It's been done before, Mister Bennefield, and lookin' at this girl's record, well, Jessie finished the eleventh grade last year." He smiled, and said, "She skipped the fifth grade some years back. Smart little thing. She ought to be able to catch up real quick-like, and maybe graduate with her class come May. And we can help her along."

"Excellent, Mister Malone," I said. "Whatever supplies or books she might need, I'll be obliged to pay for them. Would you stand up with me, if need be, to convince Jessie to come back to school?"

"Oh, sure, sure, that's no problem. I'll pass this by the superintendent today; in fact, I'm goin' to a meetin' in Marksville at one o'clock. He'll okay this in a minute."

"Mister Malone," I said, "I appreciate this. Jessie comes from good parents, and I'm guessing she'll be the first one in her family ever to graduate high school, if she agrees to come back."

"Yes, sir, Mister Bennefield," he said. "We need to educate these kids for a new world out there." His smile was broad as he chuckled.

"It's Ben. Call me Ben," I said.

"Oh," he exclaimed softly, still smiling. He shook his head. "No, sir, Mister Bennefield, not now. Time's not right, not here, anyway, sir," he said. "But that's okay, we just wanna get this girl educated as best we can, and I thank you for helpin' to get it done."

I stood then and extended my hand over his desk. Mr. Malone looked at me, somewhat cautiously, but took my hand in his, quickly wrapping his other hand around it. "Thank you, sir, Mister Bennefield."

Around one o'clock that day, my farm manager, Ed Moreau, stood at the bottom of the steps at the back porch. "Come on in, Ed. Bo and Henry will be here in a few minutes," I said. We sat at the kitchen table while Jessie washed the dishes from the noon meal, and I pondered Ed Moreau's value as manager of Bennefield Farm. He was not to blame for the disastrous crop of the past year, but he offered little to prepare us for the coming year and the planting season. I questioned my decision to hire him.

Bo and Henry stepped through the kitchen door. "Have a seat, fellows," I said, motioning to two chairs at the side of the table.

I really didn't know where to start, but I began explaining plans I had weighed for several months, laying them out to these men whose families' livelihood and well-being depended on the continuous success of Bennefield Farm. "We're going to split into three operations this spring and summer." That statement seemed to awaken them from the winter hibernation that had set upon them since October. "I've taken an option on three hundred acres of pasture land on the east side of Gold Dust, Carl McClanahan's cattle farm. It has two large barns, the pasture's in pretty good shape, and there's plenty of water from Edward's Creek. I'm buying Carl's herd, eighty-nine brood cows, and they'll be dropping calves in a couple of weeks. There are eighteen heifers that will stand for the bull in May or June, and two bulls. One of the bulls is pretty well worn-out, and we'll send it to market or butcher it ourselves." While I spoke, Ed never flinched, but both Bo and Henry, I could tell, were beginning to question my wisdom. "The next operation," I said, "will be in soybeans."

Before I could say more, Henry spoke up. "Ben, I sho' don't know nothin' 'bout cattle and soybeans. I never was around 'em." He sighed heavily and shook his head. Henry looked at Bo as if asking for help.

"That's okay, Henry," I said. "We're gonna learn about both, together. It won't be easy, I know, but we can't live with just one crop. We have no choice but to diversify as best we can, and this seems like a good year to start. Cattle farming," I said, shaking my head, "I've studied it for quite a while, and with the growing seasons we have, pasturing two hundred and fifty head of cattle should be easy compared to the dry lands of Texas and Oklahoma. We'll learn how to do it. Working people can afford more meat, and the population's booming. I want to be part of getting meat on their tables, and there's good money in it." I recalled frequent articles in my newspapers, and elaborate layouts of information in ranching magazines, telling of the development of a booming industry. "Some time back," I said, "we had a few cattle on Bennefield Farm, but when my dad died suddenly, Mom sold off the cattle and rowed up the pastures for cotton."

"What about cotton, Ben?" Bo asked.

"We'll have around five hundred acres of cotton that should be at a premium this fall. Cotton farmers all the way from Texas to Georgia and the Carolinas suffered badly this past year. Many have gone out of cotton, going to corn and soybeans." I stopped when Jessie dropped the lid of a pot she was drying. Ed Moreau jumped. When his eyes opened, they lit on my face.

"So," I said, "next Monday we'll take over McClanahan's farm, and see what we're getting into. In the meantime, I'll work on cotton seed and soybeans for spring planting. Won't be long, and we need to get the equipment ready, starting tomorrow morning. Bo, you know what to do there." I stood up. "Bo, I need to talk to you for a minute or two."

Henry and Ed left.

"Jessie, I want to talk to you and your dad for just a minute," I said. "Come sit here at the table." Looking surprised, Jessie moved from in front of the sink and sat next to her father.

"This morning I spoke with Mister Malone at your school in Bunkie, Jessie, and he says they will help you catch up with your classmates if you will go back to school." I had expected a response from either Jessie or her father, but neither said anything. "I would advise you to do it, Jessie. You're young and you're smart, and now's the time to prepare yourself for what's going to happen in our country."

She frowned and turned her head, her eyes squinting. "What?" Jessie asked. "What's gonna happen, Mista Ben? To me!" She looked at her dad, quickly adding, "I'm just a little ole colored girl. You know what that means around here?" A deep-rooted anger, it seemed, began to seep through Jessie; the expression on her face and her tone seemed bitter.

"Hush, Jessie," Bo admonished. "Mista Ben don't wanna hear all your whinin', girl."

"Yes, I do," I said. Jessie moved her hand up to her lips and her eyes began to dampen. "What does it mean around here, Jessie? I don't really know, so you tell me."

She brought her hand down, laying her arm on the table. "Mista Ben, colored girls—" Jessie stopped, then glanced at her father. "Colored girls work in white folks' houses, they raise white folks' kids, and then come home every day to work some more on white folks' land." She wiped a tear from her cheek. "I can do all of that without goin' to school." She looked at her father again, then at me. "If I'm gonna raise kids and work in houses, then I don't need to waste any more time in a classroom." Bo frowned, and shaking his head, he looked back and forth from Jessie to me.

"Jessie, from what I see, everything is changing very fast," I said. "Last year about this time, a woman with an incredible voice sang at the Metropolitan Opera in New York. That was the first time a colored person ever sang there. Everywhere, things are changing, and it can only get better; it has to get better, especially for colored people." Again, tidbits of information I had gleaned from the newspaper and news magazines rushed through my mind. "Tell me some more, Jessie."

She looked at her dad, then at me. Words seemed to form on her lips, but vanish. "I want to write," she said, as she played with her fingers on top of the table. "Mista Ben, I wanna be a writer, write stories. I want to go somewhere, a big city maybe, and be a reporter for one of those television stations in New Orleans, or up in Memphis." Tears slid down her cheeks, but she didn't bother to brush them away. She raised her head, tilted it to one side, looked at me, and asked contemptuously, "Now, Mista Ben, you tell me: Do you think a colored girl from Gold Dust could ever do that, ever?"

"Yes, absolutely, I do," I said, looking at Bo. Tears shone in his eyes as he stared at his daughter. "But Jesse, you have to prepare yourself with education, and learn to be patient. You have to have a lot of patience to wait, a lot of waiting, and hard work." Silence hung over us for several seconds. "I'll tell you what. Both of you hear this," I said. "It's a secret, our secret, and it's a promise, too. Jessie, look at me. Straight in the eye." She raised her eyes to mine. "I promise, if you graduate with your class in May, I will pay your way to college, entirely, including an allowance to live on, for four years, Jessie. That's my promise."

Immediately, Bo began shaking his head. "No, you ain't gonna do that, Mista Ben. Jessie ain't for sale. She's gotta work for what she gits. We need her 'round here, anyway."

"Bo, this is something I *want* to do; I almost have to do it," I said. "Jessie has a seed inside her, which has to grow, or it'll die. She's too smart, and has too much to offer, to let that little seed disappear." Bo's eyes were locked on mine. "It's like cotton, Bo, the same as cotton," I said, "just a little seed, and look what comes out of it, what it does for us, for the whole world, and all Jessie needs is to find her spot. She'll grow like cotton." Tears filled his eyes. "You have to let Jessie go, let her get out of here, out of Gold Dust. She'll have a chance, Bo, and we have to let her take it."

He looked at Jesse, then at me.

Bo stood over his daughter, and after a couple of seconds, he spoke. "Let's go home, Jessie."

No other words were spoken. They left the kitchen. For five minutes, I sat at the table, thinking, wondering if I had meddled too deeply into the lives of my friends.

A few minutes before six the next morning, I was drinking my first cup of coffee and opened the large envelope of documents sent to me by my sister's lawyers in New Orleans: Fisk, Merriman & Musk. I rubbed my finger across the name, embossed in gold on the envelope.

A voice called, "Ben, Mista Ben." I opened the kitchen door and found Bo standing at the bottom of the steps. "Ben, I'm gonna start workin' on the 'quipment down at the tool shed this mornin', me and Henry," he said. "You gonna have to take Jessie to school, and Hattie wants to go with you." He raised his hand as he turned, heading in the direction of the tool shed.

"Fine, Bo, fine," I called to him.

Forty

FISK, MERRIMAN & MUSK
2344 Canal Street
New Orleans, Louisiana

December 30, 1955

Mr. Benjamin Bennefield
Box 12
Gold Dust, La.

Dear Mr. Bennefield:

Enclosed are the necessary documents whereby you are agreeing to grant to your sister, Mrs. Barbara Bennefield Anderson, a ten percent (10%) interest in the land known as Bennefield Farm in Gold Dust, Louisiana. In exchange, Mrs. Barbara Anderson has relinquished any claim to all said properties, including the cash monies that came to you by way of and as a result of the will of Mrs. Hester McGinnis Bennefield, mother to Barbara Bennefield Anderson and Benjamin William Bennefield.

The enclosed documents are in accordance with your request so stated in your letter dated November 30, 1955, to this firm.

Please have your attorney stand as notary to your signature, and return said documents to our office as soon as possible. Upon receipt, we will furnish a copy to Mrs. Barbara Bennefield Anderson, per your previous instructions.

Yours truly,

Adam G. Fisk
Attorney at Law

I placed Mr. Fisk's letter back in the envelope with the documents to be signed, figuring I would get it done after Jessie settled into her school.

The phone rang two short rings, and I wondered who would call so early. Grabbing the handle of the coffee pot, I refilled my cup and walked fast to the hall.

"Hello, this is Ben," I said.

"Ben, how are you so early in the morning?" Barbara asked.

"Barbara," I exclaimed, "I was just looking over the papers Mister Fisk sent a few days ago."

"Oh, Ben, that's very generous of you, but I wanted to tell you again before you send them back, you don't have to do it."

"I've felt terrible about Mom's will, Barbara, and I'm sorry about it, so, no, I want to do this. Besides, you might need it someday. Who knows?"

"Ben, I've said it before and I certainly don't want to sound as though I'm bragging, but we have more than we'll ever need, but I will say this: It's rather nice to know I'll have an attachment to home, and to you. I like the idea, and your generosity is overwhelming."

"I think it's right, so, there we are. Enough said."

"Well," Barbara said, "now that I have a little say-so in your business," I could hear her laugh as she continued, "buy land, Ben. Land, that good, solid stuff no one makes."

"Funny you would say that. I've just taken an option on three hundred acres on the east side of Gold Dust. You know, where we used to ride horses into the woods, past the railroad track."

"Oh, sure, I remember. That's great, Ben, wonderful."

"Cattle," I said. "We're goin' in the cattle business starting Monday morning, bright and early."

"Ben, it sounds like a fantastic venture, from what I read. I'm so proud of you, and for you," Barbara said.

* * * * *

So was I. Proud and excited. The brood cows on the McClanahan Cattle Farm were thin, and some had already dropped calves, which were small-framed and not as heavy as they should have been, due to their mother's poor nourishment through the winter. That Monday morning, I advised Henry we should begin feeding daily with hay supplemented with dairy feed and meal. The hay we had to buy from a farmer near Turkey Creek and have hauled to Bennefield Farm. Unfortunately, many of the new calves didn't survive more than a few days, thus launching our venture into the cattle business on a very disheartening note.

But lessons are sometimes quickly learned, and in the fall of 1956 we sold the entire herd of mixed breeds at the auctions in Opelousas and Alexandria. With the proceeds, I bought thirty registered Black Angus heifers and a young bull from an Aberdeen-Angus rancher in Kansas, sixty miles west of Kansas City, Missouri. On the two-day ride home, we lost one of the heifers, but late each spring, for four subsequent years, we had twelve additional heifers shipped from Kansas. Within that period of time, Bennefield Farm became known as the finest polled Angus farm in the state of Louisiana, and beginning in our fifth year, small ranchers from east Texas to southern Georgia came to buy brood cows to start their own Angus herds. And as early as our third year, Bennefield Farm had won over the processors who supplied the buyers of Angus beef for the finest restaurants from Houston to Atlanta.

* * * * *

When Hurricane Audrey killed nearly four hundred people in the small town of Cameron on the Louisiana coast the following year, Jessie Johnson, my young protégée, as I had come to think of her, was finishing her first year at Southwestern Louisiana Institute, better known as SLI, in Lafayette. I, meanwhile, had already made arrangements to go to Paris for the opening of Anna's show on the *Champs-Elysées* in July.

"Oh, Ben," Miz Margaret happily exclaimed, "I'm so excited you're going, and you'll be with Benny for nearly a week." Miz Margaret bubbled over with excitement, a grandmotherly pleasure I readily recognized. "He's an adorable boy," she said, "and advanced far beyond his years."

Steadying myself on one foot and then the other, I waited anxiously as she jotted down in my charge book a list of the items I'd placed on the counter. "I can remember bein' Benny's age, at least a little," I said, "and it should be fun for both of us." But I wasn't sure. Benny didn't know me, nor did I know him, and I feared too much sudden togetherness might prove difficult for either of us to handle.

"Ben, Anna tells me he wishes to be called by his real name, 'Bennefield' rather than Benny," she warned.

"Oh," I said, barely audible. But I thought immediately, *Bennefield is too long a name for a little fellow. Maybe when he's president of a bank or some big company,* and my mind played with possibilities.

"I love it, Bennefield, the name," she said. "We should so honor his father, don't you think?" Miz Margaret winked at me. *No*, I thought, *no*. I gave no indication of agreeing to call Benny anything but Benny.

"We'll see, Miz Margaret," I said, shifting again to the other foot, thinking and believing there was no need to honor his father. "Well, I'll keep in touch, and if you want to send Benny something, I can take it with me, I'm leaving on July 17." Miz Margaret said nothing as she folded my charge book and placed it in the drawer. "See ya, Miz Margaret." I hustled my two bags of groceries, one under each arm, and left the store for home.

Just as I set the bags on the kitchen table, I was surprised when Jessie suddenly appeared from the dining room, with an apron tied around her. "Jessie!" I exclaimed. "What are you doing here? I thought you were at school."

"Just home for the weekend, Mista Ben, and I thought I'd check to see if anything needs doin' here. You okay?" she asked.

"Oh, sure, I'm fine. Y'all get any bad weather from the hurricane?" I asked while taking the groceries from the bags.

"No, not really, just a little wind and a lot of rain, but no damage." Jessie curled her finger. "Come see, Mista Ben, I want to show you what I've done." She smiled, turned, and walked swiftly through the dining room into the main hall, stopping at the door into my mother's room. She turned the knob, pushing lightly on the door. "I cleaned Miz Hester's room, Mista Ben," she said. "It's spotless, and I'm gonna keep it this way from now on. It's beautiful." Jessie gestured with her hand for me to enter. "Ta-da!" she said.

I stepped through the door, walked slowly to the rug at the foot of the bed, stopped, and looked around the room. Indeed, it was clean and beautiful. Before I said anything, Jessie wrapped her arms around me above my waist, surprising me, and pressed her body against my back.

"Stop, Jessie," I demanded. "What the hell are you doing? Let go."

"No, Ben," she said. "Please hold me, like Ava. Hold me."

"Jessie, stop. Let go of me, please," I said calmly. She wouldn't open her arms. I pulled her hands apart, broke free, and turned, holding her by her shoulders, away from me. "Jessie, this is wrong, all wrong. You know it."

She looked up at me, frowning, and her lips quivered. "No," she said, struggling to break my grasp. "I don't know that it's wrong, and I don't want to know it." She glared at me, asking, "Why can't you hold me like you did Ava and all the other girls you bring out here for me to clean up after?" She began to cry.

"Please leave, Jessie. Get out of here," I said. Releasing my hold on her, I pointed to the door.

She whipped around and ran from the room. My breathing was shallow. I was afraid.

I dropped into one of the big chairs in front of the fireplace. "What the hell's going on?" I asked, then yelled, "Son-of-a-bitch, son-of-a-bitch," while pounding the arm of Hester's damned old chair. I closed my eyes. After a few seconds, I heard a soft whine coming from the front porch. It was Jake, I recognized easily. He was crying.

I glanced around, wondering about the irony of the events that had taken place in this room. My first breath had been taken in the bed right there, and I was nurtured on my mother's breast in the chair where I sat. But before the age of five, I had been forbidden to set foot in this damned place. *You're a full-grown man*, I could hear her say, and the determination in her voice was clear and scornful. *You're a full-grown man*, my mother said on the day we buried my father. *No. I'm a boy*, I had wanted to tell her, *only a boy who needs time, time to grow up, time for his youth, and someone to love him, and someone he loves.* My mother's words seemed a curse on me, haunting me time and again. And the words crashed through my mind again: *You're a full-grown man, Benjamin, Jessie Johnson is only a girl, a young girl.* "No, I'm not, I'm not," I denied, in my head.

"Son-of-a-bitch," I yelled again, jumping up from the chair. I rushed to the front door to see why Jake continued to whine, grating harder on my mind. "What, Jake? Why are you crying, boy?" He lay in front of me then rolled onto his back. Something was wrong, I knew.

I followed my dog to the garage, and the closer we got to their beds, the faster he walked. In the dim light in the back, we found Lucy lying in her bed. While Jake's whimpering became louder, I knelt and rubbed her yellow fur. Jake's crying turned into an unfamiliar howl. Together, we cried.

Before the sun went down, while Jake sat watching, I buried Lucy in a flowerbed beside the gazebo, near the rocks on the bank of Edward's Creek.

For weeks, Jake spent most of his days watching his mother's grave.

* * * * *

Forty-One

When the first rays of the sun shot through the oaks in the front yard, I drove slowly in the new light down the driveway to the main road. Instead of turning toward the highway, I turned to the old bridge. The Gold Dust Bridge seemed steadfast and resolute, and in my mind it stood as *the keeper of memories*. For almost sixty years, it had been the sole owner of *time* in the lives of everyone who lived around it. Secrets, I felt, it favored most.

Stopped in the middle of the span, I stepped from my truck and leaned against the railing to look down to the water, just as the sun began to show through the trees on the east bank. The spot on the old boards where I stood was the place where James Bartlett and I had had our first fight, a blood fight. It was a Saturday morning, I remembered, hot, with damp suffocating air, and already the dust had settled in thin brown lines in the sweaty creases of our necks. James called me a new word we had learned, *bastard*, and I knew whatever a bastard was, it wasn't good. I hit him in the mouth with my fist, and blood shot out of his lip. His eyes opened wide; he was startled by the blow and the bright red blood that dripped onto his naked chest, falling onto his bare feet. He swiped his hand across his face, smearing the blood from ear to ear, and then he began yelling with uncontrollable anger. James picked up a rock and threw it, hitting my forehead, stunning me for a second. When he saw the blood seeping from the cut over my eye, he turned and ran toward his house, leaving his bicycle leaning against the railing. "You're the bastard," I yelled several times, throwing rocks at him, and before I fully thought out the potential repercussions, I picked up his bike and dropped it over the railing into the middle of Edward's Creek. For the entire summer, I peddled while James rode the handlebars on my bike. *And now, thirteen years later*, I thought, *here I am again, standing on that bloody spot, remembering when two good friends had beaten each other up, over the word "bastard."*

I looked down and with the toe of my boot, I made an X in the thick grime on the oak plank, thinking, I know the meaning of that potent and degrading little word. Another hot day, the air heavy with moisture, and I'm leaving my home destined for Paris, France, to meet my kid and be with his mother. Paris, France, a hell of a long way from the "X" I had drawn on the Gold Dust Bridge.

The truck's engine smoothed out and hummed sweetly, while I glanced at the picture Anna sent me for Christmas. "Benny Mancini," I said out loud, thinking again about the bloody fight on the Gold Dust Bridge.

From New Orleans to Atlanta took almost four hours; I changed planes, and from Atlanta we flew to New York, where I had a two-hour layover. I found a bank of public phones and called the number Miz Margaret had given me.

"Hello," a voice said fast and precisely.

"Yes, this is Ben Bennefield," I drawled. "Is this ... this Mister Steinman?"

"Yes it is, Benjamin. Anna left early yesterday for Paris," he said, before I had asked.

"Well," I stammered, "I ... I wanted to check and verify where she and Benny are staying in Paris."

"Oh, sure, I have the information, Benjamin. I'll get it," he answered quickly.

I waited for a second, and he came back. "Benjamin, she's at the Corondulet Hotel, *Rue Lincoln*, right off the *Champs-Elysées*; her number is suite eleven," he said slowly while I wrote the information onto my pad. "The phone number there is 25 62 32 10 83." Very fast, he asked, "Did you get all that?" I had her phone number from Miz Margaret.

"Yes, I did, and I thank you. I hope you're doing well," I said, already feeling a bit of tension coming through the phone.

"Very well, I'm very well, thank you, Benjamin. I hope you have a nice visit in Paris. Good-bye, now," Jacob said, and I heard the click of the phone's receiver. An old image of Mr. Steinman came to my mind, mostly a smile, a broad smile with lots of teeth.

"International flight number thirty-six forty-two, now boarding at gate fifty-seven, concourse D," a female voice said over the intercom, then repeated it again with a smooth, clear, and enticing tone. Listening attentively, I imagined what the woman might look like. Very pretty, I figured, probably with just the right amount of lipstick and coloring, manicured nails, about five feet, six inches tall and dark hair, maybe auburn in color, softly curled. "International flight number thirty-six forty-two from New York to Paris, now boarding at gate fifty-seven, concourse D," the voice said again, further enhancing my image of the lady. I fumbled for my ticket and passport while rushing toward gate fifty-seven. Just when I handed my ticket to the agent, the tantalizing voice began again. "International flight number thirty-six forty-two, now—" and standing beside the ticket agent, I saw a short, stout lady wearing a blue shirt, overstuffed by large, round breasts, and a black skirt whose belt was tucked in, hidden. Her hair was long, brown, and needed washing very badly, while her lips appeared dry and wrinkled under a thin covering of newly applied pink. As she held the microphone with one hand, I examined her short, bulky fingers with torn cuticles and nails that had never seen the color red, "—boarding at gate fifty-seven, concourse D," she ended her announcement. The man handed me my passport and ticket stub.

"Thank you, sir," I said, smiling, and glanced at the lady by his side.

"Enjoy your flight, young man," she said, speaking fast. I nodded.

The smooth hum of the engines seemed comforting, and thirty minutes into the flight sleep crept upon me. I was glad the other two seats in my row were empty. Through the small window on my left, I could see far below, a sprinkling of thin, white clouds. I sighed, recalling a conversation on a cold, winter night in the living room of our home with my dad and mother, an exciting conversation for a young boy who on that very day had seen his first jet airplane, through similar thin, white clouds. It roared very loudly high above, turning in wide banks and circles while James and I watched from the middle of the Gold Dust Bridge.

"Did you see them, Dad?" I had asked excitedly, as the flames in the fireplace burned bright and hot. And I remembered a Christmas tree in the room, lit with a thousand colored lights and hundreds of shiny glass balls.

"Yeah, I saw them, Ben, and heard them. Pretty loud!" my father had said as he thumbed through his newspaper, glancing back and forth at me while we talked.

"I want to fly a jet plane when I grow up, James and I both," I confided in my father.

"Well, you can do it, son. Being a pilot sounds like an interesting and fun job to me," he said.

"Dad, did you know they can go over five hundred miles an hour?" I asked. "And one day they'll go faster than the speed of sound." I waited anxiously for him to offer additional information for me to think about.

"Ben," he said, looking up at me after laying his paper on his lap, "we're gonna have to go to the air base in Alexandria and look around, get a little information from those folks. That would be a good thing to do during the winter."

"Yeah, James can go with us," I said.

My body jerked and my eyes flew open. I sat upright in the seat, glancing around, and realized I wasn't in our living room talking to my father. My heart was beating fast as I turned, looking again through the small window, into the dark.

"Are you okay, sir?" a woman's voice asked, with an accent.

"Yes, yes, ma'am, I'm fine, thanks," I said.

The stewardess reached toward me with a soft drink and a couple of crackers on a folded napkin.

"I hope you're enjoying your flight, Mister Bennefield," she said. "Are you English?" Her eyes were soft, with long black lashes, and sheltered by beautifully sculptured eyebrows.

"Well, no, I'm not; I'm American."

"But your heritage, your name, Bennefield?" she asked, smiling.

"Oh, that. My father's people came from England a long time ago, so I guess I'm English, too," I said, apologetically, having been caught off-guard by her sudden appearance and her questions. "You're Irish, aren't you?" I asked, surprised to see the name—Sarah McGinnis—on the lapel of her jacket.

"Oh, absolutely, Irish all the way, Mister Bennefield," she said, obviously proud, and pleased, it seemed, that I had continued the conversation.

"Well, Sarah McGinnis," I said, looking up at her pretty face, "you might be my cousin, my beautiful cousin."

"Really?" she said, dragging out the word, as she dropped into the seat next to me. "Why do you say that?"

So near to my face, I looked into Sarah McGinnis's blue eyes, very bright and very deep; a beautiful girl, with dark hair, and skin that had seen little time in the sun. Her fingers were long and her nails were painted red; the movement of her hands was gracious and feminine. Her smile was beautiful, and her face was kind. Through the corner of my eye, I saw her cross her legs as she leaned toward me. I leaned toward her.

"Over a hundred years ago," I said, "three brothers left Ireland for the USA, and one of them ended up in a wilderness in Louisiana, where he built a farm. His name was Bardan Desmond McGinnis. He was my great-great-grandfather, around 1845."

"Your mother was a McGinnis?" Sarah asked excitedly, touching her nametag with one finger.

"Yes, a straight line of McGinnises. Tough people from Ireland, but I know very little about any of them." I took a sip of the drink she had brought me, keeping my gaze on her face. "You're beautiful, Sarah, very beautiful," I said softly.

"Well, my husband's family is very old," she said quickly, "from Cork, in County Cork. There's a great number of Desmonds there, but few McGinnis's live there now." Sarah glanced around and stood quickly. "I have to go." She winked at me. "I'll be back. Have a good flight, sir."

I watched as Sarah walked down the long aisle, handing out her goodies to people with heads leaning in different directions, eyes half opened. *Husband*, I thought, glancing through the black window. *Husband. Stewardesses aren't supposed to have husbands. They're supposed to be young and beautiful, friendly, and not married.* One hand held a drink I didn't want, while the other hand held a napkin with something in it, and I needed to pee very badly. I ate the crackers straight from the napkin and drank the cola, then glanced again through the window. There was no land that I could see; no thin, white clouds either. Only blackness, and the roar of engines.

I was sleeping when I felt a hand tapping my shoulder. I opened my eyes to the black window, and a voice said, "Your dinner, sir." A shelf dropped from the seat in front of me, and a stewardess in a long white jacket set dinner in front of me. Sarah McGinnis never came back.

After a smooth landing in Gander, Newfoundland, I fell in and out of sleep for several hours. I sat up straight, regaining my senses as we approached the airport near London.

My flight from London to Paris was quick, and after sleeping in the lounge in the airport in London for a couple of hours, I was excited to arrive in the "City of Lights." I was dirty and wanted a bath.

The cab driver set my bag on the sidewalk in front of the *Hotel de Marquis* on *Rue Marbeuf*, and I tipped him with the smallest bill in my wallet, a five-dollar bill. He removed his black cap and held it toward me as he bowed very slightly. His smile was big and he spoke fast, "*Merci beaucoup, monsieur,*" he said. As he ran around the rear of the cab, his hand raised, and he called out, "*Americain! Americain!*" In a second, the cab sped away. I stood in amazement, wondering if I had given him too much, and figured I should find a bank to exchange dollars into francs. Before I could pick up my suitcase, two young men, pushing and shoving each other, hurried toward me from the front door of the hotel. They struggled playfully to grab the handle of my suitcase, and the smaller one pushed off the larger one. Big boy shot out in rapid fire, "*Salopard! Salopard!*" He raised his fist to the smaller boy.

Long streamers, red, blue, and white, waved from every light post, and banners hanging across *Rue Marbeuf* read "*Jaques Anquetil, Tour de France.*" Jaques Anquetil, I knew, was the Frenchman who had been in the lead of the famous bicycle race, according to the newspaper I had left for Jessie Johnson on my kitchen table in Gold Dust.

In Paris

Forty-Two

THE ROOM WAS SMALL, but nice. A bed covered with a white spread and four pillows stood between two windows on the far wall. There was a small matching chest on the side, with a lamp and a clock sitting on top. To one side of the room was a dresser with a small television, and a mirror hanging crooked on the wall above. A chair and a floor lamp with a crooked shade stood on the other side of the bed, next to the door leading into a bathroom. Tight between the lavatory and the shower stood a toilet made of copper. The shower was shiny white tile and very small. *Perfect for a week in Paris*, I thought, and I smiled, unable to fully comprehend the magic that had taken place between the moment when I stood on the Gold Dust Bridge, and now. I wondered if the old bridge had known I would stare in amazement, nearly halfway around the world, at a strange apparatus made of aging copper, hoping the damned thing worked. Surely the old bridge knew because it, and everyone around it, knew everything about Benjamin Bennefield.

I dialed the number Miz Margaret and Jacob Steinman gave me.

After only one short ring, a small voice said, "Hello?" as clearly and precisely as Jacob Steinman himself.

"Hello," I said. "May I speak to your mother, please?"

"Who is this?" the small voice asked.

"Well," I said, surprised that Benny would answer the phone and immediately ask who I was, "a friend of your mom's."

"Hello," another voice said. "This is Anna Montagne."

"Anna?" was all I said.

"Hi, Ben," she replied happily. "Jacob told me you had called, and I've been expecting to hear from you. How was your flight?"

"Okay." When I heard her voice, my mind left me momentarily, and I was unable to say anything else. After a second or two, I added, "I'm fine; okay; yeah, and … and how are you, Anna?"

"Wonderful, Ben. Everything's going well at the moment. Have you settled in?"

"Yeah, pretty much," I said. "I'm ready to get out and walk, move around. How's your secretary, the one who answers your phone?"

"Benny? Oh, he's great." Then in a whisper, she said, "I told him earlier his dad was coming soon. He's waited by the phone for almost an hour." Then, she said louder, "Benny is great; in fact, he's waiting for someone to come see him. He's looking at me right this second with a smile on his face."

"Thanks, Anna," I said. "How should I do this? It's been a while; you think he'll remember me?" My mind's picture of Anna was clear, but the vision of Benny was clouded and dim.

"Oh, absolutely, Ben. Besides, he has the snapshots you've sent every Christmas. In fact, he brought one with him, a small one in a frame. It's by his bed." She whispered again, "He knows it's you on the phone, Ben." Then, she said, "We're going to a restaurant on the *Champs-Elysées*, about two blocks from here, in the direction of your hotel. Why don't you meet us there in an hour?"

"I think that's great," I said. I had never sent any snapshots to Benny or Anna. *Clever, Miz Margaret, clever*, I thought, *and sent in my name, I'm sure.*

"That will be nice. In an hour. And Ben," she said, hesitating, and then in a whisper said, "I'm hoping during this week you and Benny will become who the two of you really are. It's time, and he wants it and needs it."

With a lump in my throat, I paused, then swallowed.

"Ben? Ben, are you there?"

"I'm here, Anna. What's the name of the restaurant?"

"*Le Restaurant Benoit*," she said.

A few feet inside *Le Restaurant Benoit*, I stood holding a single red rose tied with a yellow ribbon and a box containing a small jet fighter plane made of metal. The maitre d' asked something, but before I could attempt an answer, I saw Anna hurrying toward me with Benny scooting along behind her. She stopped right in front of me, Benny moving to her side. She turned and stood beside me, facing Benny. Glancing back and forth to him and me, she settled her eyes on my face. "Here he is, Benny," she said. I was frozen in time and place.

Benny stood in front of me, his eyes on mine. His brown hair was much longer than mine and streaked with dark; his green eyes were set deep, and they neither blinked nor wavered as they stared at my face. Bennefield Mancini was tomorrow's child, a child I knew, without a doubt, the result of two powerful and commanding blood lines: Irish and Italian. With lips slowly parted, his face haunted me, like looking into a timeless mirror.

"What do I call you, Mister Bennefield?" he asked.

"Call me Ben, if you like."

"Ben? That's okay, but I like 'Dad' better, if you like," the kid replied, mimicking me.

"Dad it is, then," I said, glancing then at Anna, wanting desperately to hug her. She appeared to be exhilarated with this first encounter between me and our son. I extended my hand to Benny. His fingers barely wrapped around my palm, but deliberately, with a firm grip, as he had done at the funeral almost three years earlier; he shook my hand.

I had expected this child to have a handshake suggesting determination and strength well beyond his years. And he did.

"Hi, Ben," Anna said, hugging me. "It's wonderful to see you." I held her close against me until she pushed away. Her hair was no longer blonde, but once again dark auburn. She was trim, svelte, and velvety, and outstandingly beautiful, as I had remembered her always being. "I'm so glad you came." She looked at Benny, who was still standing in front of me, watching my face, and waiting for the next step. "Let's have dinner," she said.

During nearly three hours at *Le Restaurant Benoit*, Anna and I spoke very little to each other. Most of the conversation was directed by Benny, who brought me up to date about New York, the zoo, the park; his likes and dislikes, and a lagniappe of questions about a farm near a village in Louisiana, the name he knew well—Gold Dust. Every now and then, when the conversation seemed to stall, Anna would suggest Benny or I say something specific. I recognized her attempt to have us share information on which a relationship could be founded.

"Two more questions, and that's it," Anna said, pointing to Benny. At every chance, my eyes wandered to Anna, and I had no doubt that neither my mind nor my heart could be trusted.

"Well, Dad," Benny said, surprising me each time "Dad" was spoken, and my mind had to recover its thoughts. "How old were you the first time you left Gold Dust?"

Anna and I recognized immediately his was a trick question, but my answer was easy. "Well, Benny, I never traveled far from home until I was over twenty years old, but that was because I really had no place to go, not far away. Besides, we were country people, stay-at-home kind of people. We had plenty of everyday jobs to keep us busy."

I could feel Anna's eyes staring at me.

"Okay, Benny, last question for tonight," she said, smiling and raising her finger. "Last question."

Benny stood, then moved to stand closer to me, almost in front of me, as he leaned and propped his elbow on the table. "Dad," he said as he lightly placed one finger on his cheek, looking to the floor and then at me, "am I old enough to go to your house and stay awhile?"

"Maybe," I said, and I recognized a frown on Anna's face. "Benny, you might be. We'll talk about it together and decide later. And I have one more question for you." His eyes never left mine. "Can you spend the day with me tomorrow, while your mother's working?"

His smile and his eyes, no doubt, said yes.

Almost three hours into our first visit, and I had been quizzed extensively by a young boy with extraordinary ability to revolve in an adult world, a result I was sure, of his life with two highly intelligent and well-educated people.

As I walked the six or eight blocks from *Le Restaurant Benoit* to the *Hotel de Marquis*, I pondered this new job I had been handed, the job of fatherhood, for which I felt inadequate, but now was eager to dive into. Very much, I wanted to do a perfect job, to do the right thing, first for my son, then for his mother, and finally, for me.

A sweet, light breeze made the bright streamers and banners wave evenly from every light post along the *Champs-Elysées*, while hundreds of people strolled around me with no notice of a man from Gold Dust. *A man*, I thought, and the words, *a full-grown man,* shot through my head with a vision of Hester Bennefield. *Forgiveness*, I thought again, *forgiveness*; and a sudden flash of lightning lit the sky above the *Champs-Elysées*. Maybe this long trip was a journey for forgiveness, like a child would forgive, like Benny had already shown.

Big drops of rain began to fall; another bolt of lightning flashed, then a clap of thunder shook me. I ducked quickly into a walkway laden with flower pots and plants, a walkway about twelve feet long leading toward a door of glass panels.

I leaned with my back against the wall, running my fingers through my damp hair.

This is a wonderful little house, a whisper said in the dark. *It's so charming and quaint.*

Thunder sounded, and lighting brightened the darkness with a flash.

And on a glass pane, I wrote, "Ben loves Anna."

We don't have to do this, Ben, the whisper said.

Covering my face with both hands, I slid to the floor with my back against the wall and sat with my head propped on my knees. I closed my eyes.

And the rain came down.

Forty-Three

After I pushed the doorbell, I waited for only a second or two before the door opened.

"Good morning, Benjamin; your ward is waiting on the balcony," Anna said with a smile, delight showing clearly on her face. She gestured for me to enter her suite. "How about a cup of coffee with hot milk?" she asked.

"No, thanks. We have to get us a good spot before the crowds get too big. *Tour de France* is wheeling in in about thirty minutes," I said, glancing at my watch.

"Oh, that's right! What a treat to be in Paris at this very moment … *Tour de France* and my show. You chose well, Benjamin!" She kissed my cheek, and the perfume she had worn the night before still lingered. "Benny, your dad is here," she called to the open door to the balcony.

That word again; I have to get used to it, I thought to myself. I sighed deeply and shook my head. Anna turned to me, smiling, and in a split second, Benny ran through the door and stopped abruptly in front of me.

"Hello," he said, rather sheepishly.

"Hey, Benny; we've got a lot to do today. Are you ready?" I asked, extending my hand for him to hold.

He held his eyes firmly on my face while reaching slowly for my hand. "Yes," he said, half-heartedly and softly, "I'm … I'm ready." He looked at his mother.

"Bye, Benny; have a nice time." Anna hugged him. Turning to me, she said, "This is all very new, Ben, you'll have to be patient and proceed slowly." She winked. "It won't take long."

"Sure," I said. "I understand." Then to Benny, "Let's go."

He jerked his hand from mine and walked slowly toward the door, not looking back.

Near ten o'clock, and a few blocks up the *Champs-Elysées,* we found a place at the curb where we could wait for the first cyclist to rush toward the finish line. From my pocket, I pulled out the list I had made of the five leading cyclists who were expected to win, and I began to explain the event to Benny. At first he listened, but in short order, without warning, he sat on the curb and looked pensive and guarded. With his fingers, he played with some small pebbles at his feet. Had I done something wrong? I wondered. I sat beside him, very close, crossing my legs, making sure his shoulder touched my arm, and I started again to explain the event while we looked at the list of names. The chatter and laughter around us quieted, and suddenly the crowd began to chant in unison, "*Jaques, Jaques, Jaques,*" waving their banners and flags, some small, some large, but all were blue, white, and red. "Let's stand, Benny," I said when the crowd quieted, and a band nearby began playing the French national anthem. I placed my hand around his shoulders, letting it lay over his chest, and pulled him tight against my thigh as we stood together, listening. He glanced up to my face when the band finished and the crowd burst into cheers.

"That's his name, Benny," I whispered. "*Jaques Anquetil.* He'll be the winner, I'm sure." And I pointed to the name at the top of the list as I held it in front of us.

At that moment, a kid about eight, dressed from head to toe in blue, white, and red handed each of us a small flag and held his fist high, never missing a beat, chanting, "*Jaques, Jaques, Jaques.*" Benny watched closely, as the boy walked on, handing out flags to everyone around him. The crowd became louder, and in less than a minute four cyclists whizzed by within six feet of us. "Wow!" I said, and then I began waving my flag and chanting with the crowd, "*Jaques, Jaques, Jaques.*" Benny's green eyes had brightened, when he looked up at me, facing the sun. "*Jaques, Jaques, Jaques!*" I continued yelling.

"*Jaques, Jaques, Jaques,*" his lips began moving in rhythm with the crowd's chant. Three more cyclists shot by, so close and fast they were merely streaks of colors, and the crowd cheered louder.

"*Jaques, Jaques, Jaques,*" Benny yelled, still looking at me. "*Jaques, Jaques, Jaques,*" he called out loudly and clearly, waving his flag as he chanted, and when we glanced up the *Champs-Elysées*, an onslaught of riders was headed in our direction. His chant became louder, his smile grew bigger, and his flag waved faster.

Jaques Anquetil was the champion of *Tour de France* that day, July 20, 1957, with a time of 135 hours, 44 minutes, and 42 seconds. On the list that I had copied from the newspaper and showed to young Bennefield Mancini, there were no Americans. But though their names never appeared in any story about *Tour de France*, two Americans did win that day; two Americans who had been strangers to each other: one a young boy, and the other a young father. They won big, cheering relentlessly, with an astounding depth of heart, not only for the cyclists of *Tour de France*, but for themselves, in celebration of the end of a long and treacherous ride, their journey in search of each other.

Young Bennefield Mancini looked squarely into my face, smiled, and placed his hand in mine. I held it tight, silently promising to both of us that I would never let go.

The crowd cheered and the band played on.

The sun was still high in the sky when our cab delivered us to the Corondulet Hotel around five that evening.

"Benny, I'll be back around eight to pick you up," I explained. "We'll walk to the gallery. Okay?"

"Dad, why can't you stay with me? I don't want to go to the gallery," he said quickly.

"It'll be nice, Benny, and besides, your mother wants you to be there for the opening of her show," I explained as I pressed the button to the doorbell to Anna's suite.

"No, she doesn't, Dad. Mother said she wanted you to be there when the show opened, not me," he countered.

But when I glared at him, he quickly looked away.

"Good evening, Mister Bennefield, Benny," a pretty young girl in a long black dress said as she stood in the open door. "I'm Teresa Sabatier, Miss Montagne's assistant, and Benny's best babysitter." She reached and tousled Benny's hair. "Come in," she said.

"No, thank you. I have to go. I'm delivering this young man to your care," I said, all the while searching beyond Miss Sabatier for Anna.

"Who is it, Teresa?" Anna's voice came from another room. "Mister Bennefield?"

Before she had completed my name, she rounded the corner and stood in front of us. "Hi, Benny, and Mister Bennefield. How was the day?" she asked, smiling. She hugged Benny. Anna was wrapped in a light blue robe, which I presumed was silk. It was shiny and tight to the skin.

"We had a great time. We saw *Tour de France* and even the Eiffel Tower. How 'bout that Eiffel Tower, Benny?" I winked at Anna, while telling her, "It wasn't our favorite, but we're gonna go there again."

"Wonderful," Anna said. "Tired, I'm sure. Maybe a nap before we go to the gallery. Teresa, would you please?" She pointed to Benny, who held his hand toward Teresa.

"See you later, Benny, in about two hours. Okay?" I called to him then looked at Anna as she stood in front of me.

"Thanks, Ben," Anna said. "You've been a dad all day. How's it going?" she asked.

"He's a fantastic kid, Anna, incredible. You've done a great job." At that moment, I was trying hard to find words that seemed okay to say, knowing I couldn't trust or be guided by the emotions I felt. I merely repeated, "He's a fantastic boy."

"He has all of the personality of young Benjamin Bennefield," Anna said, laughing quietly. "The one I remembered a long time ago, but that kid was a tad bit older." Anna laughed again. "He's a romantic, Ben; he sees and loves everything, and takes it all in, and makes life around him beautiful."

"I see it already," I said, "much like his mother; a good thinker, very rational."

"Oh, but he has a temper he uses wisely," she said, holding up a finger, "and it's controlled very well, thank God. That's fascinating to me, because I've always screamed when things didn't go my way; but anyway, *Dad*," she said teasingly. "I love the word, *Dad*. I never had a dad, you know. I never knew mine." The chit-chat continued, as we stood in the doorway.

I moved my hand toward her cheek.

"Don't, Ben," she said, turning her face away from my touch. "Don't do that." Her lips parted. "I'm sorry, but you shouldn't." She looked at the floor.

"Sorry. I'm sorry I did that, Anna," I said. "Remind Benny I'll pick him up around eight."

I backed out of the door into the hall. The door closed softly.

The walk to my hotel seemed long. It was quiet.

Forty-Four

"What's wrong, Bennefield? Why that terrible frown?" I asked.

"I hate being dressed like this, like a clown," he answered then looked up at me.

"Oh, no, Benny. Look at me, I have a tuxedo on, too. It's appropriate for this occasion. And this is a big show in Paris, France," I said enthusiastically. "Maybe we'll see some real important people, like the president of France, and we have to be properly dressed. Don't you think so?"

"No," he said bluntly, reaching to take my hand as we left suite eleven.

Four blocks from the Corondulet Hotel, we stopped at the broad glass front of the *Amarante de Paris*, and looked in along with several others. Hanging from the ceiling from wires of silver ribbons, were several pieces of Anna's work, spotlights shining on them, and moving very slowly along a track running twenty feet then turning, making the paintings visible in the lobby inside, as well as from the sidewalk where we stood. Benny was impressed, and so was I. "You see, Benny, this is interesting even from out here." He frowned, cutting his eyes up to mine.

Down the long hallway, we could see people standing in twos and fours, talking about particular drawings or a painting. Most women were dressed in long dresses, colorful with small waists and broad skirts. Most wore hats, small ones, but some were larger. Long white gloves were apparently the fashion craze. Men wore black tuxedos.

"Can you understand what they're saying, Benny?" I asked, smiling.

"They're saying how much they hate this place," he grumbled.

The first vacant bench we came to, I sat Benny beside me, taking his hand in mine. "Benny," I whispered, "this show is for someone we love, and we have to be happy to be here, for her. Where's the smile you had all day? Did you lose it at the hotel?"

"No," he said. "I hate this place, and I hate my mother."

"What's wrong, Benny?" I asked, frowning. "You shouldn't say that. What's wrong?"

"Mother's what's wrong. She said I couldn't go to Gold Dust with you. I hate her!" He turned his eyes up to my face, holding his stare.

"To Gold Dust?" I asked, surprised. We had not talked about Gold Dust or my house, all day. "When did she say that?"

"After you left the hotel, I told her I was going to Gold Dust with you."

"Ah, Benny, no, we haven't talked about it," I said. "You shouldn't have told your mother that."

"I'm old enough; I can go. I don't need much care, Dad, and Grandmother's there, too." Big tears started forming in his eyes, sparkling from the spotlights overhead.

"Benny, listen to me," I said. I waited for a second while he wiped his eyes with his fist. "Grown-ups, your mother and I, have to talk about it first, and we have to make the decision, and we haven't had time to discuss it." He sniffed hard, when a drop of water ran from his nose. "Here," I said, "wipe your nose." I handed him my handkerchief.

"Dad, I want to go to Gold Dust with you. Grandmother told me about Gold Dust, every time she came to see us, and I want to go with you." Tears began flooding his eyes.

Maybe I can make a trade-off here, I thought. "Son," I said, and I stopped before I would say another word, realizing what I had called him, like my dad had called me. "Son, if you and I will be happy tonight and enjoy this big event for your mother, I promise I will talk with her tomorrow about you going to Gold Dust with me. Will you take my word for it?"

Benny looked at me, then up and down the hallway, still with big tears on his cheeks, and said nothing. He wiped his face and his nose with my handkerchief. "Here, Dad," he said, standing now in front of me, and handed the handkerchief to me. "I'll take your word for it."

Right at that moment, I knew I had fallen into a trap, for certain, while he stared at my face. When his smile broadened, I saw the door of the trap slam closed.

"Look at this, Benny." I pointed to the four drawings I had seen displayed in the Museum of American Art in New York several years back, except this time they were centered on a wall painted red, twenty feet wide, and now, framed in gold. About twenty people stood in front of the drawings, sipping wine from long-stemmed glasses, and wearing fancy dresses and tuxedos, speaking very fast. I wondered what they thought as they spoke and pointed to the drawings of an old store, a strange little house with a pointed roof, a rail depot with bales of cotton on its platform, and a young boy with a dirty face.

"Who's that boy, Dad?" Benny asked.

"That's me, Benny, when I was about seventeen years old."

"Mother knew you when you were seventeen, Dad?" he asked.

"Yes, she did. That was a long time ago. And that's your grandmother's store in Gold Dust, and that one is the railroad station." I stopped short of saying anything about Doc Foster's garden house.

Benny studied the drawings very closely, placing himself, I figured, on the front porch of his grandmother's store or playing on the bales of cotton on the station platform.

"What's that one, Dad, the little house and the swing?"

"Benny," I stammered, "just a little house, but we need to move on so we can see the entire show and visit with your mother."

"I really like that one, Dad. If I go to Gold Dust, can I ride in the swing?"

"Sure, but I have a swing in my gazebo. We don't have to go there," I said.

"We don't have a swing in our apartment. We have to go to the park to swing."

"Well, that's okay, Benny, not everybody has a swing, so don't feel bad."

"Can I play with Lucy and Jake, Dad?" he asked.

"Lucy and Jake? How do you know about Lucy and Jake, Benny?"

"Grandmother. She knows everything. You sent me a picture of Lucy and Jake. I like dogs, Dad. Do you think Lucy and Jake will like me?"

"Sure, Jake will like you, Benny, but I have to tell you a sad thing." Benny stopped and looked at me. I turned to face him.

"What? What sad thing?" His mouth was half opened.

"Lucy died, Benny, not long ago. I have only Jake now."

"Why did she die? Grandmother said Lucy's Jake's mother."

"Lucy *was* Jake's mother, and she had gotten old, Benny. Lucy had been my dog since I was about ten years old." I was ready to end the question-and-answer session.

"Is my mother going to die? She's old."

"Benny," I said, "first of all, your mother isn't old." I led him to a nearby wall, and then knelt in front of him. "Right now, we have to go through this gallery, so could you please save the questions till later?"

"No," he said, again very emphatically. "If mother dies, can I go live with you in Gold Dust and have a horse?"

"A horse?" I questioned. I sighed. "Benny, what do you know about horses … your grandmother?"

"Yes, she said you have horses and a gun, and you hunt in the forest."

I looked at the boy, figuring Miz Margaret had filled him with notions that I could never imagine. "What else, Benny, what else has your grandmother told you?"

"She said you would let me ride your horse, and you would teach me how to shoot a gun," he said. "Dad, I want a gun, a real one, like yours." I looked at him. "I want to hunt in the forest with you. Are there bears in Gold Dust? Did you ever kill a bear, Dad?" He stared at me, waiting for an answer.

"No, Benny. I've never killed a bear; there are no bears," I said, and he fired another question.

"Do you think Mother will let me go to Gold Dust when you leave, Dad?"

"I don't know, Benny, I don't know," I said impatiently. "In fact, right now, I don't know anything." I stood up, in front of him, frowning and squinting, I asked, "How old are you, boy?" And I knew he was maneuvering the conversation back into another trap in which I would fall.

"I'll be five in February, but you know that, Dad," he said, laughing quietly.

"Yeah, yeah," I said, nodding. "But you sound like a lawyer, Benny, with all those questions, and those answers you already know before you ask the question. I'll bet you're a lawyer."

"No," he said, "but Mother says I ask too many questions. Do you think so?"

"Absolutely, too many questions and at the wrong time. Let's go find your mother."

A Full-Grown Man

We turned a corner and entered the Grande Hall of the *Amarante de Paris*, and I stopped abruptly.

"What's wrong, Dad?" Benny asked. I could feel a burst of excitement inside me, rushing through my entire body, thinning the air I breathed. I inhaled deeply, held it, and let it out slowly.

"Nothing's wrong, Benny, nothing's wrong," I said, speaking slowly while holding his hand, and I looked to the far wall, where Anna stood with twenty or so people gathered around her.

My eyes held to Anna. I couldn't move. She was the woman I once knew, her smile, her movements, her presence. I grasped Benny's hand tighter in mine; my breaths became short, my heart beat faster.

Everything I knew, everything I wanted, I could see in front of me and I was holding in my hand.

Forty-Five

A FEW MINUTES PAST one, I heard the key turn in the lock. Anna walked in barefoot, shoes in one hand and a yellow paper crumpled in the other.

"Oh, Ben, I'm sorry I'm late," she said. "I didn't expect you would wait, and I hadn't expected so many people would stay beyond midnight, but that's the way it is sometimes." She walked to where I stood. "Benny did well, I suppose?"

"Sure, he did great. Teresa put him to bed a couple hours ago." She was reading the wrinkled, yellow paper. "How was the opening?" I asked.

"Fair," she said slowly while still reading, a frown coming on her face. "Something must have happened; Aunt Margaret wants me to call her right away. That's strange."

She handed the telegram to me, and I read the simple message. "Yeah, it sounds urgent. Now would be a good time to call. It's about six-thirty at home."

"Oh, I'm too tired, Ben. Would you place the call?" she asked. "I have to get out of these clothes. Please?"

A Full-Grown Man

I called the desk, telling them what I needed. Finally, a woman who spoke English came on the line. "Yes, Mister Montagne," she said. "I'll call you as soon as we get through to the U.S."

"No, no," I said, "my name is Bennefield. I'm a friend of Miss Montagne."

"Yes," the voice said again. "I'll call you as soon as we get through, sir." She hesitated then said, "Mister Montagne."

"That's fine," I said, giving up on the name. "As quickly as possible, please. Thank you."

Sitting at the desk, tapping my fingers impatiently, I watched the telephone.

After a few minutes, Anna returned to the living room, wearing the same blue robe she had worn the afternoon before. "Are they going to call right away?" she asked, dropping onto the couch, arranging the pillows and herself on one end.

"Yeah, they'll let us know," I said. And quickly I moved from the desk to sit beside her.

She looked at me suspiciously, her eyes wide open. "Benjamin, don't get any ideas," she said. "You're moving awfully fast, but you should be careful."

"I don't want to be careful," I said. "I'm tired of being careful. I just want to be by the most beautiful woman in the world." I leaned against her with our faces inches apart, our eyes looking into each other's. She didn't smile.

She took my hand, held it for a second, and then moved it to her lap. She continued to look squarely into my face, still only inches from hers. "Why did you come to Paris, Ben?" she asked softly, surprising me.

"To get to know our son," I whispered, speaking slowly. "To get to know Benny," I said, as I moved my hand to her cheek.

"Benjamin?" she said. "That may have been part of the reason, but I have a feeling you're not telling the truth. Now, let me ask again, why did you come to Paris, Ben?" She brushed my hand away from her face.

"Anna," I said, while placing one finger over her lips, "I came to be with Benny." I shook my head, slightly smiling. "Anna, you're beautiful, and you make me crazy." I let it out, I said it, then moved to lean harder against her, hoping she would give a hint to kiss her, or let me put my arms around her.

She pushed me away, then stood quickly and faced me. "Forget it, Ben," she said. "I'm not going to fall for, for … your flirting and, and … whatever." She had lost her words, her hands raised awkwardly. "And besides, I'm married, so cut it out, would you, please?"

"Anna," I sighed, dropping my head, shaking it, then looking up at her. "Anna, now you and I both know you have a little piece of paper that says you're married, but that's about all you've got."

"That's none of your damn business, Benjamin," she said, angrily. "And don't bring Jacob into this conversation, it's not fair."

"Why not, Anna? He's part of Benny's life, too, and I just might not like it." There was some truth in my statement, and resentment, I knew. And in the past, if I thought about it, I often became angry, cursing Jacob Steinman and, as I usually did, cursing myself.

"Jacob's a wonderful friend to Benny," she said. As she talked, it became evident the conversation had stirred into old, deep-rooted anger, and it wasn't about Jacob. "Jacob has his life and his friends, and I have mine … you should know that. And—," she stopped and wiped her eyes.

"And what, Anna?"

"Ben," she said, squinting, "what gives you the right to suddenly enter my life merely because it's convenient for you at the moment, and use our son as a stepping stone? It isn't fair to anyone, not even to you." She moved to a chair and sat down, then looked at me with tears in her eyes. I leaned against the arm of the couch, sighed, and closed my eyes for a second. I knew, though it was difficult to admit to myself, Anna was right; but I knew also that now, though unexpectedly and quickly, Benny had become part of my life, and an important piece of what I saw as a new beginning for me.

"Ben," she said, "I have my career and I have Benny, and thank God for both. But I'm tired. I'm dreadfully tired of being on edge, every day, working for the next event, and when it comes, it's just like the one before it." Again, she wiped her eyes with the sleeve of her robe. "Paris … well, this one is identical to the show last spring in Chicago, with a minor exception: the language. But believe me, they say the same things and expect me to say the same words over and over. I'm just tired of this bubble I live in." Anna began to cry softly. "And you're not helping by doing what you're doing right now." The emotion in her voice was raw, but clear. It surprised me when suddenly she returned to the sofa and sat close to me. "Hug me, Ben, just hold me, please," she said, her voice breaking. I wrapped my arms around her and held her. She closed her eyes, and I closed mine. After a couple of minutes, Anna was asleep.

The phone rang. I glanced at my watch. Two o'clock.

"Hello," I said. "This is Ben Bennefield. Hello …"

"Ben, this is Margaret Smitherman, darling; I hope you can hear me."

"I can hear you, Miz Margaret. Is something wrong?" I asked, glancing toward the sofa where Anna was sleeping soundly.

"Oh, honey, Frank died in the clinic in Bunkie late last night. His suffering is over, God rest his soul." The static on the phone became louder.

"I'm sorry, Miz Margaret, and I'm sorry I'm not there to help you. When's the funeral?" I yelled into the phone.

Suddenly the static completely cleared, and Miz Margaret screamed out, "On Friday the twenty-sixth, Ben. Friday the twenty-sixth. His brothers are coming from New Jersey."

"I can hear you now, Miz Margaret."

"Oh, that's better," she said.

"I'll tell Anna in the morning, Miz Margaret. She was played out, and she's sleeping now," I explained.

"Well, what are you doing—?" Her question stopped. Quickly, she said, "Well, kiss our boy for me and say hello."

"I will, and I'm sorry about Mister—" and the phone went dead. "Mister Frank," I said to myself.

I looked at the receiver as though waiting for Miz Margaret's unfinished question to come blaring out. *What are you doing at Anna's hotel this early in the morning?* I shook my head, answering in a whisper, "I don't know, I just don't know, Miz Margaret." Her words from a year ago suddenly ran through my mind: *Don't misspend your life, Ben, waiting for something else to happen. What you do next is what's important.*

I wrote a note for Anna, and left her suite.

As I walked the distance along the *Champs-Elysées* to my hotel, I kept repeating the words, but to the cadence of my steps.

I just don't know, Miz Margaret, I just don't know!
I just don't know, Miz Margaret, I just don't know!

From a block away, I recognized my hotel's small red neon sign on the canopy over the sidewalk and changed the cadence.

I'm gonna find out, Miz Margaret, I'm gonna find out!
I'm gonna find out, Miz Margaret, I'm gonna find out!

Forty-Six

IN A DREAM EARLY the next morning, I was a kid, maybe ten years old, walking along a gravel road and holding hands with Anna. The dew was still heavy on the grass and weeds. My bare feet were hurting from the rocks, making me carefully choose my steps. We stopped to watch several large, black birds, vultures, glide in circles high over a pasture where a hundred black cows were grazing with their newborn calves close by, and I knew they were mine. Suddenly, Anna vanished, and a shadow covered me like a heavy blanket, smothering and hot, and a voice shouted, "She'll never fit into the way we live. You're just like every man I've ever known: foolish, Benjamin, foolish and stubborn, and you're going to pay the price." I was shoved into the wet grass on the side of the road, fell, and rolled down an embankment to the bottom of a rocky ditch. I heard a cry for help.

I opened my eyes. I was lying on the floor, looking at a fine layer of dust inches from my nose, wondering where I was and how I had gotten there. I touched my forehead where it hurt.

A bell rang, rang again, and then again. With light filtering around the edges of the curtains, I finally found the noise. "What?" I yelled into the receiver. "What the hell do you want?"

"Ben?" a voice asked. "Are you okay?" It wasn't my mother's voice.

I said nothing for a second, then answered, "Yes, this damn thing kept ringing and I couldn't find it. I was looking at some dust … no … I … I must have been dreaming." I grimaced when I touched the tender spot above my eye. "I'm fine," I said.

"I found your note, Ben," Anna said, "but I don't know what to do. I can't leave my show, not this early." My mind was flailing as Anna spoke. "Ben, are you there?" she asked.

"Yeah, yeah, Anna, I'm here." I hesitated, then said, "Let's see, you can't go, you say. Well, I'll meet you in an hour in your hotel lobby, and we'll have breakfast. We can talk about it. Is that okay?"

"It would help, Ben. Benny's dressed and waiting for you to come for him. Had you planned to spend the day with him again?"

"Sure. But I need to talk to you without Benny around. At breakfast, if you can get away."

"Okay. I'll see you in an hour. Bye."

Standing beside the bed in the dim light of the room, I looked at only a piece of me in the little mirror hanging crooked over the dresser. "What the hell," I said out loud, seeing the reflection. I looked at the phone in one hand and the receiver in the other. I shook my head, and my eyes rolled back. "What the hell are you doing here, anyway?" I asked.

Walking briskly in the cool morning air, I noticed the traffic on the street was sparse, but hundreds of people hurried along the sidewalks with their luggage and flags. I wanted to say, "Good morning," and ask, "How're you?" as I was used to doing in Gold Dust. I wanted to see a face I recognized, and hear a voice with a Southern drawl, gentle, lazy, and sweet. But no one seemed to see me; no one's eyes caught mine. I felt transparent and wondered why a shadow bothered to walk alongside me. I was lonely and alone, while my mother's scolding kept reverberating in my head.

I smiled, recalling the previous day's events with Benny and the exhilaration late in the evening, of finding Anna, whose presence caused my heart to race. And there I was, on a very beautiful morning on the *Champs-Elysées* in Paris, France, rushing to be with her, and she was waiting *for me*. I quickened my pace, while confessing: I had willingly and gladly surrendered to my old obsession, and now, it was playing without pity with my mind and my heart.

The Corondulet Hotel's lobby was packed with revelers checking out of their rooms, still cheering for their countryman who had won the *Tour de France* only twenty-four hours earlier. Somewhere in the distance, Sunday church bells rang, mixing with the chatter and the cheers. I worked my way through the crowd to cross the lobby and stood at the end of a long line of people waiting to enter the restaurant.

After a short while, I heard my name called and turned to find Anna motioning me from the restaurant's door onto the street. I jockeyed through the crowd and we hugged. "Let's go to the pastry shop down the street," she said, smiling, and I wondered if my feelings were as obvious to Anna as they were to me. The air began to warm while we walked along the *Champs-Elysées*, and quickly we found a vacant table, shaded by a canopy over the sidewalk, at a café nearby.

"There's no way I can go to Frank's funeral. I just can't leave right now," Anna said, somewhat pleadingly. "Aunt Margaret understands, but I hate not to be there for her."

I couldn't help but stare at Anna, and my eyes squinted as I smiled.

"What?" she asked. "Don't start, Benjamin. Why are you looking at me that way?"

"I was just wondering, Anna. Why do you continue to call her 'Aunt'?"

"I don't know, Ben," she said. "I guess because that's what I've always called her. When I was a child, she wasn't my mother, she was my aunt. That's ... that's just the simplicity of it." She looked away as she took a sip from her cup.

"Anna, Miz Margaret is your mother, and she deserves what that word means," I told her. "Call her 'Mother' and see what happens." I moved my hand to touch her fingers. Quickly, she pulled her hand away.

"I'll try, Dr. Bennefield, I'll try," she smiled. "And what do you suggest I do about Frank's funeral? And I'm not going to call him 'Daddy,' so don't even suggest it."

"Why don't we have something with this coffee? I'm hungry," I said. I sat upright, raising my hand to get the attention of the waiter.

"Ben!" she exclaimed, then asked, "What is that terrible place above your eye? What happened?" She reached to touch the spot.

"Nothing," I said, leaning away from her finger. "Hester clobbered me last night. She's getting violent."

"Hester? Hester, your mother?" she asked, reaching again to touch the spot as if it would magically stop the hurt.

"Don't touch," I said. "It's sore, and yes, Hester Bennefield, my mother; she did it."

"Oh, Ben, sweet Ben," Anna said teasingly, leaning back in her chair, folding her hands together in front of her and laughing. "That was your dream this morning right before I called, wasn't it?"

"Yeah, Hester pushed me out of bed, headfirst onto the floor." I took a bite from the croissant the waiter had set in front of me.

Anna laughed again and shook her head. "Wow, I wish someone would dream so intently about me."

"There's someone who does," I answered quickly, "or he used to; not quite so violent, but no less physical." I looked her straight in the eyes. She shook her head and her lips parted, then closed. Her eyes rolled back.

She reached and took a flower from the vase in the middle of the table, holding the tip of the stem between two fingers. Anna leaned forward, touching the flower to the spot above my eye, and asked softly, "Does he ever dream that way, anymore?"

"He hasn't for a while, but he's sure the dreams will be coming back real soon, the way things are going at the moment."

"I wonder," she said, then lowered her face, "if he would like to dream again?"

"No, not dreams. He'd rather have a chance at the real thing," I said.

I took another bite, locking my eyes on her face.

"A chance?" she asked, her voice wavering. She frowned, squinted, and dropped the flower onto her plate. "He had a chance and walked away from it," she said, a snappy comeback that I had not expected. "He gave up before he even started." Sudden anger showed, with pain and torment in her words and tone. She held her stare on my face.

"He was just a boy, Anna, just a kid who knew very little about anything; he didn't even know himself, or what he was doing." She continued to stare at me. "And worse than that, he didn't know the rules." I leaned back in my chair. "And there were a lot of pressures on him, some mean and dark, and he was locked in the dark."

"I don't know about all of that," she said, "but I hope to God he's learned something by giving up on the chance he had." She sighed, and before I could say anything, she continued, "Benjamin, I'm scared to death right this minute, looking at you." She pointed her finger toward me. "Because you frighten me; it's like finding a part of my past that was misplaced, and it scares me to suddenly find it sitting across the table from me."

"With your determination, Anna, and the power you have over people, I scare you? You must be kidding!" I couldn't help my words; they came out louder. I pointed my finger at her. "And by the way, it wasn't a 'chance' I was given, Anna, so don't say that. It was a chance that was *taken away*, and everything I wanted went with it. My life changed, too, and my whole future just disappeared, vanished before

I knew what was happening." She looked puzzled all of a sudden, questioning what she was hearing. "And scared? I was scared as hell then, and I'm scared as hell now." I hadn't realized I had stood, looking down at her.

"No, Ben, stop," she said as her eyes began to tear, looking up at me. "I'm sorry." She grabbed my hand and pulled on it. "Sit down, Ben, please," she whispered. I sat down and waited as she nervously fumbled with a button on her blouse. She glanced around, then looked at me, saying softly, "It appears to me we've both misplaced our past, Ben, and neglected it as though it was never there. And Ben, there's something dark and mysterious hidden in it somewhere, almost sinister, and until we discover what it is and lay it out in front of us, we're going to stay scared, maybe forever."

Anna was right, and I said so to myself, but I didn't want to admit to anyone, including myself, that I didn't understand *why* my life had been taken over, ruled by other people for so long, and now, those thoughts kept me angry, making me eager to fight back. But I knew that one day, in the midst of merely living from one day to the next, somehow, I had to get Hester Bennefield off my back, and bring her to trial.

"I'm sorry, too, Anna," I apologized, realizing she, too, had been hurting for as long as I had. I placed both hands over my face. "I need to get out of here, go home. All of this," and I thrust my hands high and spread them wide apart, "is too far away. It's too far away from the way I live. A little bit is a whole lot for me, and this is just too much." She said nothing as she wiped her cheeks, looking at me. "I'm sorry," I said, "but I need to get back to my spot, my place, where I belong."

"To your spot, your safe place, Ben?" Her smile was slight as she continued to speak softly. "Where you feel good, secure, Mister Bennefield?" she said sarcastically.

"Yeah, I suppose you're right, Anna, a safe place, where—"

"You're still a boy, Benjamin, still a kid," she interrupted. "You look like a man, but you're still the kid you were the last summer I spent in Gold Dust." She frowned and shook her head. "You're going to have to settle a lot of things about what happened between us, and in your life, I'm guessing, before you're really a man; believe me, you're the only one who can do it."

I leaned back in my chair and looked at beautiful Anna, then closed my eyes for a second. I knew that suddenly, I was forced to look at myself on the slippery edge of a rocky and dangerous cliff, glaring into a precipice that I had feared and shunned, and knowing that one day I must cross it. I looked at Anna but did not see her. Her words pressed on my thoughts, confirming what I knew. I had to rid the deepest corners of my mind of all the remnants of my mother, about how my father died, what Mother had done to my sister, and how she had manipulated and controlled *my* life. Until I was able to get beyond Hester Bennefield, forgive her and get over her, I'd remain within her reach, making me guilty for my summer with Anna, and guilty for not stopping her from killing herself. Until then, I would never forgive myself. I would never be a full-grown man.

I looked around at the people under the dark green canopy, feeling as though every eye was on me. "I have a lot to do, Anna," I said, leaning closer to her, "and I thank you for this."

I reached to touch her cheek, but again, she moved away.

"Thank me?" she questioned. "Ben—"

"No, I thank you. Let's leave it there, thank you," I said. "And I want to remember this moment, these words, when you come to Gold Dust."

"I'm not going to Gold Dust," she replied. "You can stand in for me with Aunt Margaret, with Mother, at Frank's funeral."

"Come to Gold Dust and get Benny," I said. "I'm taking him with me."

"You're taking Benny with you?" She frowned, her eyes got dark. "Did I hear correctly?"

"Yes."

"Until I return to New York?"

"Yes."

"Only," she emphasized, "until I return to New York, Benjamin?"

"Yes," I said.

She waited a second, nodding, and said, "I'll go to Gold Dust."

Forty-Seven

I watched Benny for indications he would change his mind about leaving his mother in Paris for a period of time that, to a young boy, might have seemed long, but there was no indication, nothing at all. The three of us stood looking through an expanse of glass at the tremendous size of the plane waiting about fifty yards away. Benny wouldn't let go of my hand.

"How much longer, Dad?" he asked, for the fourth time.

I glanced at my watch. "Oh, in about six more minutes. I'll bet the pretty lady there will be telling us real soon to get ready," I said, discreetly pointing toward a black-haired young woman talking to the man who would take our tickets. "Hold on to your ticket and passport, Benny."

"Benny," Anna said, "maybe you should let your dad hold those for you."

"He can handle it, Anna. Don't worry," I said, almost in a whisper. "He wants to do it. He'll do fine."

Anna looked away, and I figured she could very possibly change *her* mind about allowing Benny to go with me. She turned toward me, smiling, then lightly kissed my cheek. "Thank you, Ben," she said. "I really wish I were going." I didn't say it, but I really wished she was going, too.

The young lady with the black hair finally spoke, calling the passengers to flight seven thirty-two at gate twenty-four. Benny jerked my hand, "Let's go; it's ours, Dad," he ordered.

Anna hugged him, then straightened his collar and hugged him again. "Have a good flight, you two," she said, stepping back a little. Benny and I headed toward the counter where a short line had formed. Glancing back, her eyes had filled with tears.

Twenty-two hours later, I placed our bags in the back of my truck in the parking lot at Moisant International Airport, fifteen miles west of New Orleans. "Well, Benny, we made it. Back to hot Louisiana." The air was heavy.

"Dad," he said, frowning. "Are we going to ride in this old truck?" he asked. "Where's the car?"

"No car, Benny; all I have is a pick-up truck. You'll like it," I said, waiting for another question.

"Do your pigs ride in here, Dad?" he asked, while climbing up to the seat.

"No, Benny, I don't have any pigs, but Lucy and Jake used to ride in here. Just Jake, now," I said. "But he prefers to ride in the back."

"I like it, Dad," Benny said, while rubbing the dust and grim on the dashboard. "Can I ride in the back with Jake?" he asked.

"Yeah, on the farm. You can ride in the back," I said. "Benny, we're gonna take a little detour this evening and surprise your aunt."

"I have an *ant*, Dad? What kind of ant?"

"You have an 'Aunty,' Benny … my sister. She's your aunt, your 'Aunty.'" I could plainly see the confusion on his face. "Never mind, Benny, I'll show you in a little while."

Long before we reached Audubon Park in New Orleans, Benny had fallen asleep with his head on my lap. Several turns and I found Newcomb Boulevard. Only once, almost ten years earlier, I visited at my sister's house, but I felt sure I would readily recognize the old mansion that had been their home since Barbara married Dr. John Anderson. "Wake up, Benny. I think we're here."

He roused and sat upright, then looked through the window. "This is pretty, Dad," he mumbled, yawned, and then asked, "Does my aunt live here?"

"Yeah, I'm pretty sure she does," I said. "And Benny, you can call her Aunt Barbara. Okay?"

With Benny standing beside me, I rang the doorbell and watched through the door's beveled glass until a person dressed in white came to open it. A light-skinned lady in a maid's dress asked nicely, "Yes, sir, may I help you?"

"Yes, is this where the John Andersons live?" I asked.

"Yes, sir, it is. May I tell Mrs. Anderson whose calling?"

"Please tell her Ben Bennefield is calling," I said, smiling.

Immediately, the lady's face lit up, "Oh, Mister Bennefield, you're Mrs. Anderson's brotha', who sends us the steaks from Bennefield Farm." She smiled and chuckled.

"Yes, I am."

"Come in, come in, Mister Bennefield, y'all come in. I'll go get Mrs. Anderson," she said. "She's not gonna believe me when I tell her." The lady walked briskly to the far end of the long hall and turned right. I heard mumbling, and then Barbara came out into the hallway with a book in one hand and stopped; she looked at me and glanced at Benny, then again at me.

"I can't believe it, I just cannot believe what I'm seeing," she said as she hurried toward us with a big smile. "Oh, Ben, what a delightful surprise! What in the world has brought you to the city?" She hugged me, and after a second or two she let go, stepping back, with her eyes set on Benny. "Benjamin, who … who might this young man be?" Tears had already gathered in her eyes.

"This is Bennefield Mancini, Barbara. This is my son."

She set her book on the table beside us and bent to hug Benny. He pulled toward me, looking cautiously at Barbara. "This is the aunt I told you about Benny. Give her a big hug." Slowly, he moved to let Barbara hug him, but never offered to hug her back.

"Bennefield Mancini. What a beautiful name, and they call you Benny, don't they?" Barbara said as she hugged him again and then kissed him on his cheek. Quickly, he wiped the place she had kissed, then looked up at me, frowning.

"Let's go to the den," she said. "We can see Mary Ann and her friends in the swimming pool." Barbara led the way to the far end of the hall and into the family room. Through the back windows was a clear view of the entire garden that stretched far beyond the pool. "Benny," she said, "I bet I can find a nice swim suit for you if you want to go swimming." She looked at Benny and asked, "Would you like that?"

"No, we have to drive to Gold Dust in a little while," I said. "We'll save that adventure for later." I sat beside him on the sofa.

While we talked about the flight and the drive into New Orleans, Benny's eyes closed, and I laid his head on my lap.

"Tell me about it, Ben," Barbara spoke softly. "At Miz Montagne's funeral, the last time I was in Gold Dust, I suspected a relationship with this little fellow, but you were upset and angry, so I dared not ask."

"Yeah, you suspected correctly," I said.

"Why didn't you tell me, Ben?" she asked, then motioned to Benny. "How old is he, six, seven?"

"He'll be five in February. He's a big boy; very advanced … has a super mom."

"Anna Mancini. I recall the name, now," she said. "Am I the last to know, Ben?"

"I suppose so," I said. "I didn't mean for it to be that way."

After an hour with my sister, spilling out, for the first time ever, the events of five years earlier, I felt a weight was lifted from me. Of the people I cared about, Barbara was the last to learn about my son, and now, everything was on the table. I could breathe easier and see clearer.

"Well, Ben," she said, "I would think you've crossed another threshold in your life. Now, you can talk openly and happily about your son and about his mother." She laughed and jokingly said, "There're fewer ghosts in your mind … a good feeling, isn't it?" She laughed. "It took a long time, but I got rid of mine. There were several, you know."

A glass of tea and a hug from Mary Ann proved excellent for me; however, Benny had been handed far too much. He slept with his head on my lap as the truck's engine hummed, and the tires clapped every twenty feet against the joints across the concrete highway. *Another threshold*, Barbara had said. *Fewer ghosts in your mind.* And I remembered Anna's words only a day earlier: *You're going to have to settle a lot of things, and you're the only one who can do it.* In the darkness, I looked back and forth from the highway to the face of my son, and smiled as I listened to the constant applause of the highway home. Clap, clap, clap.

* * * * *

After Frank Smitherman's funeral on Friday, we returned to Miz Margaret's house for lunch, along with a few close friends.

"Well, Benny," Miz Margaret said as she poured him a glass of water, "after three days in Gold Dust you're already looking like a real little country boy. I like that."

Benny sat next to me, and Mr. and Miz Bartlett sat on the other side of the table. Benny said nothing.

"His summer's just starting, and we have to get him some short britches and T-shirts tomorrow," I said. "And we're gonna go to the bridge tomorrow evening and look around while the sun sets. Then, he'll really look like a Gold Dust boy. Right, Benny?" Then he smiled.

"Ben, darling," Miz Bartlett said, "you should see my Catherine, so beautiful. She's just like her daddy, and nothing like Ava."

"She's how old, over a year now?" I asked.

"Fifteen months, now, and a gorgeous little girl. Her coloring and hair reminds me of Benny … makes me lonesome to see her." Miz Bartlett smiled and continued to stare at Benny.

"When you write them again, say hello for me. How does James like the air force and California?" I asked.

"Loves all of it … a born pilot, loves to fly, and pretty sure they'll make a career of the military. He always wanted to see the world." She took a sip of tea then said, "Well, Margaret, we have to go, dear. Again, I'm very sorry about Frank, God rest his soul." *God rest his soul,* my mind said, *God rest his soul?* Frank Smitherman has a soul?

"Thank you, Helen," Miz Margaret said. "I'm so glad you all are here, close by. Your friendship means everything to me … over thirty years. And I appreciate you so very much." Mr. and Miz Bartlett hugged Miz Margaret and left.

"Who are those old people, Grandmother?" Benny asked.

"Two very good, old friends, Benny. I love them dearly. Don't they seem nice?" she asked.

"Yeah, they're okay," Benny said and looked at me. I shrugged, raising my hands.

"Ben, don't you think Benny should say 'Yes, ma'am' and 'Yes, sir' to older people, to show respect? That would be nice, don't you think so?" Miz Margaret looked at me. "Benjamin," she said, knocking her knuckles on the table, "don't you think so?"

"We'll try, I suppose, but it'll take a while," I said. I turned to Benny and said, "And we don't have a long time this summer, but we can start, can't we, Benny?"

"Yes, sir, I think so," he said.

Miz Margaret smiled, winked at me, and turned up her chin.

"Thank you, Benny," she said.

"Yes, ma'am. You're welcome, Grandmother," Benny said, smiling.

"See," I said, "you just have to work at it. Sometimes it goes fast and sometimes not."

* * * * *

The summer of 1957 would forever be heralded as the summer of new beginnings. Miz Margaret began her life completely alone in this little town far away from her few remaining family members in Philadelphia; but as she saw it, Gold Dust was her home, and she, too, would one day be buried next to her mother and her husband in White's Cemetery. My life, meanwhile, took on new meanings, a purpose other than farming, other than cotton and cattle, other than the demands of the legacy thrown over me. That summer I became a real father, a dad, with, no doubt, a lot to learn, and my son quickly became the most important person in my life.

And Benny. He took his first swim in a creek with flowing water; took his first horseback ride; and woke for the first time with brown rings of dust in the creases of his neck. By the first week of August, his entire body had begun to brown in the hot Louisiana sun, and streaks of blond appeared in his light brown hair. He showed delight when he drank a tall glass of milk with a peanut butter and jelly sandwich for supper, and after playing till the sun went down with kids whose skin was far darker than his—Henry Brown's little girl, Karen, and her big brother, Junior—Benny would sleep next to me as soundly as a puppy. Often he ran races with Jake, never winning, but always earning a cut or a bruise from running with bare feet. Along with "ma'am" and "sir," he learned to say "y'all" as easily as a kid who had been born and reared in the southland. Bennefield Mancini, it seemed, by the end of one grand summer, had quickly found his place in Gold Dust.

"Dad?" his voice wavered, tipping upward. I knew what the question was going to be.

"No, Benny. You have to go with your mother. Next summer, I'll come to New York to get you."

"Yes, sir," he said.

I watched as Anna turned the car onto the main road, heading for the airport in New Orleans.

It was the end of another summer, and like other summers before, Anna slipped away, once again taking my heart, and this time our son, too.

Forty-Eight

I LOOKED AT THE paper then laid it on the table, face down. *This damn war*, I thought. Twice in the middle of the night I had awakened. I would think about James, about what had happened, imagining terrible things. I remembered when we were kids, how he would reach and shake me to tell me about a bad dream he had just had. I wished this was a dream, too; that he would shake me and we could talk about it. But the headline in the newspaper hammered the truth into my mind. I waited for a few seconds, then picked the paper up again, hoping somehow the headline had changed. But it hadn't.

THE
PARISH COURIER

DECEMBER 16, 1966 Vol. 0002321083

LOCAL MAN KILLED IN NAM

Major James K. Bartlett, USAF, died when his plane was shot down in the jungles in the East Asian war zone of Vietnam.

Major Bartlett was born and reared in Gold Dust, Louisiana, and graduated from Bunkie High School and Louisiana State University in Baton Rouge. Major Bartlett leaves a wife and a ten-year-old daughter ...

How could this happen, I wondered, *and why ... why? He was my friend, all our lives, and we weren't supposed to die, not now. We're too young to die.*

The phone rang twice. I crumpled the entire paper into a ball and shot it toward the trash can in the corner of the kitchen, then hurried to the main hall.

"Hello, this is Ben Bennefield," I said.

"Hi, Dad, what's going on?" Benny asked, excited, in a loud voice.

"Hello, Benny," I said, taking a deep breath. "Not much, son, other than some terrible news from Vietnam."

"Yeah, it's going to get worse, according to the *Times*," Benny said.

"Well, this bad news hit home, Benny. An old friend was killed in Vietnam almost two weeks ago. His parents were notified last Tuesday." My voice had trailed off to a whisper. "We grew up together, my best friend."

"I'm sure sorry, Dad," he said. "But I wanted to wish you a happy birthday; Mother says happy birthday, too."

"Thanks, Benny, but right now I feel a hell of lot older than thirty-two," I grumbled.

"Thirty-two, yeah ... you and I are getting closer to the same age every year, Dad. I'll be almost half your age in February." Benny laughed quietly and asked, "How would you like to have a little company for Christmas? You think you can handle that?"

"Absolutely, I can handle it. Get your mother to come with you," I suggested, hoping.

"No, she has a show opening in Williamsburg in a few days, on the twenty-first, in fact, so she'll be in Virginia for most of the holidays, and I'm out of school until January ninth."

"Sure. You come on. Let me know when to meet you in New Orleans," I told him.

Around three on Sunday afternoon, we arrived in Gold Dust from the airport in New Orleans. I turned the car into the driveway from the main road and stopped. "Look around you, Benny," I said. We looked south, scanning toward the west, across the wide flat fields, brown and dreary from wetness and winter.

"When I was your age," I said, "my friend James Bartlett and I stood right back there on the bridge and made a promise we'd stick together, through high school, college, and our time with Uncle Sam ... whatever that might be."

"But it didn't work out that way, did it?" Benny said. "I guess you can say you were the lucky one."

"Lucky, or whatever you want to call it," I said, "but I don't feel lucky right now. I neglected my friend, Benny, just pushed him aside, deliberately, and mean like, and now I'll never be able to tell him I forgive him." I grimaced. "He'll never see these fields turn green in the spring and white in the summer."

"I'm sorry, Dad," Benny said.

* * * * *

With Miz Margaret beside me and Benny on the back seat, I pulled the car near the entrance to White's Cemetery and turned off the engine. Several mourners had already gathered under the green tent sheltering the grave where James would be buried. I guessed nearly a hundred friends and family members were awaiting the arrival of the personnel from the air base in Alexandria.

"Here they come now," Benny exclaimed, pointing across hundreds of headstones toward Pershing Highway. A long line of cars with lights shining through the cold, misty rain followed a black hearse led by two military cars the color of the dirt in the fields. Hurriedly, I stepped from the car and opened my umbrella to shelter us as we walked to the tent.

The casket was carried from the hearse to the grave by six gentlemen in black suits, and followed by four airmen in dress uniforms. In his upright hands before him, the leading airman carried a folded flag. Under the tent, they draped the flag over James's casket, covering all four sides.

Ava Koller Bartlett and her daughter, Catherine, holding her mother's arm, were the first of the family members following the casket, to step under the tent, moving to the chairs beside the casket. Next were James's parents. While everyone stood, an air force chaplain stood at the podium, speaking for two or three minutes, then the minister from the White's Chapel Church took the chaplain's place.

Tall, and dressed in a black robe, he glanced across the crowd, holding his Bible opened in one hand. He spoke with clarity, in a Southern accent. "Please be seated, ladies and gentlemen," he said. His demeanor, stature, and tone of voice commanded attention and concentration. He glanced across the mourners, bowed his head a little, and began:

"From the beginning of time, men have differed on many thoughts ... thoughts about life, about their neighbors, about country, about the world, and about Jesus Christ. All men agree that no man's fame can ever reach the pinnacle where Christ stands in our world, where his grip on the human heart has no equal, where his word is as powerful and as mighty as the greatest armies ever known to man. To those who follow him, Christ is the way, the truth, and the light. He's the light on the hill, a star shining brightly on a dark night. He beckons to all mankind to come, come to the goodness, and come to the redeeming love of our God."

Opening my eyes into thin slits, I looked toward Ava, who was holding Catherine close, with an arm around her shoulder. Catherine was a beautiful child, a compliment to Ava and James.

The minister continued, "Forgiveness is not about forgetting. Forgiveness is for the forgiver, for the one whose life cannot move forward, whose life will remain still, silent, and cold until the heart speaks loudly and clearly, and says, I forgive. Until then, joy is lost, and love is locked out."

James, I thought, *wasn't a mean or bad person*, and I figured there wasn't much for anyone at his funeral to forgive him for. Again, I looked at Ava and Catherine, thinking, *Ava wouldn't have married me anyway, according to James, because of my mother. And long ago I forgave James and Ava for having married when I had wanted Ava to marry me.* I closed my eyes completely, wondering why the preacher had chosen words about forgiveness and redemption at my friend's funeral. James was a good man, I knew.

The minister continued speaking while my mind wandered, and suddenly I recognized he had come to the closing: "… who taught us to pray," he said. Then the entire group began in unison, "Our father, who art in heaven, hallowed be thy name, thy kingdom come, thy will be done on Earth as it is heaven. Give us this day our daily bread, and forgive us our sins, as we forgive those who have sinned against us …"

My mother's name shot through my mind, and the words I had just spoken pierced my heart: "as we forgive those who have sinned against us …" *Hester McGinnis Bennefield*, I thought, almost saying her name out loud, and I asked myself if I really meant the words I had just said, or were they merely words rushing through the shallows of my mind, only words from a beautiful and commanding prayer?

"Amen," the minister said. Quiet fell, except for the soft patter of raindrops on the tent; then a trumpeter in a blue uniform played

"Taps." Silence followed, and then chatter, hugs, hellos, and good-byes, all at once, over and over, drowning out the patter of the raindrops.

"Hello, Ava," I said as I approached her. She hugged me, attempting to smile. Her eyes were teary and red.

"Ben, how are you?" she asked, speaking softly.

"I'm fine, just sorry … so sorry about James," I said.

Before I could add to my condolences, a voice very close to my ear interrupted. "Hi, Mrs. Bartlett, I'm Bennefield Mancini, this man's son." Benny motioned to me with his thumb, smiling.

"Oh, yes," Ava said quickly; her smile was big and genuine. "You're Benny." She hugged him and backed a step away, exclaiming, "And boy, do you ever look like your father!" Suddenly, Ava changed … her demeanor, her smile, and the pain on her face had vanished. She stood taller, it seemed, and her movements became deliberate. She turned to Catherine, by her side, and said, "Ben and Benny, this is Catherine, my daughter." Ava glanced at me and then to Catherine. She smiled.

Catherine smiled. "Hello," she said timidly.

"Benny," I suggested, "take this beautiful girl and introduce her to your grandmother. She's been talking about Catherine." The two began walking toward Miz Margaret, who was embracing James's mother, Miz Helen.

I looked at Ava, who was smiling as she watched her daughter and my son move slowly through the crowd under the tent.

"Well, Ava," I said, "your daughter is beautiful, like her mother, and I hope all is going to be okay for both of you."

"At the moment it isn't, Ben, but I know time takes care of a lot of ills, and we'll move on."

"Ava, I'm sorry. He was my friend and I loved him. I'm so, so sorry, and I feel like I need to do something; I want to do something."

Her lips quivered. "Thanks, Ben. James provided well for us, and we're going to be okay. The changes will be difficult, the decisions that must be made so quickly, and without James to help me."

"Are you going to remain in California?" I asked.

"No, that decision was already made when James left for Vietnam. Catherine and I will be coming home in a few weeks," she said.

"To Baton Rouge or to here?" I asked pointedly.

"Here, Ben, to my family, until I can find a teaching job, hopefully in the area." Ava glanced toward James's mother and Miz Margaret, who were talking a blue streak to their grandchildren. "And what about you, Ben?" she asked.

"Farming, cotton, and cattle, right there at the Gold Dust Bridge. We're moving right along." I looked at Ava and smiled. "I've had Benny every summer for several years, now, and he's turning into a country boy. He likes the farm."

"He's certainly a handsome kid. What about his mother?" Ava asked.

"Anna's still in New York, and travels," I said, "peddling her art around the world." I didn't want to talk about Anna.

Ava placed her hand on my arm, and asked, "Isn't she married to an art dealer?"

"She was, but they're divorced, for several years now. Jacob Steinman is his name, and he moved to a gallery in San Francisco some years back." *Enough!* I thought, and about that time, Miz Margaret and Miz Helen approached us with Benny and Catherine behind them.

"Ben," Miz Helen said, "we have to go, darling, and Margaret will ride with us to help me. Several people are coming by the house. We'll see y'all there." Ava said good-bye, then she and Catherine followed Miz Bartlett to their cars.

The tent had emptied quickly, except for Benny and me. I sat in a chair facing James's casket, with Benny sitting beside me.

He nudged my arm with his elbow. "Hey, Dad," he asked, "what did you mean by wanting to forgive your friend?"

With all my heart, I wanted to tell him why I had needed to forgive James. My eyes held to James's casket: I felt winded and made no attempt to answer his question.

"What did he do for you to be angry with him?" Benny asked. After a second, he said, "Do you not want to talk about it?"

"Yes, I *do* want to talk about it," I admitted before thinking, still staring at James's casket. "I just don't know how, I guess."

"Say it in plain words, Dad, just plain words. That's all."

"But it isn't plain, and it isn't simple, Benny, it's complicated," I said, shaking my head.

"Try me, Dad, try me. I'm a good listener."

The misty rain turned to drops, sounding on the tent like a thousand tiny drums being tapped, far away, over a hill maybe, down the road someplace. My head was pulsating with every beat, every raindrop.

"Go ahead, Dad, it's just me, and I'm on your side, regardless."

"Well, a long time ago, I wanted to marry Ava Koller, and without knowing why or even when, my good friend James married her, took her away from me," I said, still holding my eyes on the casket. "My life had already been torn apart by things I had done and many things another person had done, hurting a lot of people, including me." I turned, looking in Benny's face.

He didn't move for a second, then pulled up the collar on his coat and squinted, looking at me. "Dad," he asked, his forehead creased, "why didn't you marry my mother, a long time ago? She loves you, you know … instead of asking Ava?"

I sighed deeply, looking squarely into his face. "Your mother was already married when I asked Ava, and there were other reasons; complex and far-reaching events had taken place, and sadly, neither your mother nor I knew most of the events had even happened."

"Was I one of those events? You didn't know about me, when I happened?"

"No, I didn't," I said, locking my eyes on his. "Truthfully, I didn't know about you until you were nearly three years old."

"Why not? Why didn't you know about me?" His voice raised in volume. "Mother said she told you."

"That, Benny," I said, "is another complicated matter, a series of things your mother never knew about, involving other people. But yes, she did tell me, she wrote letters to me."

Benny frowned, his lips forming words that didn't come out. Finally, he asked, "Why don't you marry Mother now, Dad?" His face was troubled. "You know about me now, and you know what I am, don't you?" He stared at me, appearing annoyed, with deep grooves across his brow.

"I don't want to hear that, Benny, please. It tears my heart out and it's too late. You're my son; our names are different, but the blood inside is the same, and nothing can change it."

"Hello, sir?" A loud voice behind us startled me.

"Yes!" I said, standing quickly and turning around.

"We're waitin' to close up this grave, Mista Bennefield. Y'all 'bout ready to go?" the groundskeeper asked.

"Yeah, we're leaving right now." I opened the umbrella. We ran to the car.

On the drive home, Benny sat pensively looking through the side window, biting on a fingernail, concentrating, I was sure, on the conversation we had just had. He was brooding.

"I'm sorry, Benny." I looked at my son: tall, strong in body and in mind, and I thought about myself, when only a few years older ... the summer with his mother, remembering *I was a kid, young and innocent, and ignorant, and hammered by a selfish and conniving mother.*

"Forgiving is for the forgiver," the minister had said about an hour earlier. *Maybe so*, I thought.

"Dad," Benny said, looking at me. "You know something?" He moved his hand quickly with a finger pointing in no particular direction. "The older I get, the more I see there are people I might need to forgive some day."

"Yeah," I said, glancing at him and back at the road. "I think you're right, son," I said, my voice fading. "I think you're right."

The windshield wipers bounced noisily, squeaking across the misty windshield.

* * * * *

Forty-Nine

"Hello, this is Ben Bennefield," I said.

"Ben, he's on his way to Gold Dust, and he's very angry with me," Anna said, almost in panic. Her words were flying faster than I was able to comprehend.

"Wait, wait, Anna, go slow, sweetheart; take your time."

"He left, Ben. He left school and said he was going to live with you."

"What happened, Anna? Did he say why, anything at all?"

"Only that he's tired of the winters in Maine, and he wants to go to LSU. That's all he said, and I can't understand it," she said. "He's very angry." I could tell she had begun to cry.

"Well, maybe he's tired of the winters in Maine and wants to go to LSU," I said, thinking possibly a little light-heartedness might ease an obviously strained situation.

"Benjamin, now is not the time for an asinine comment. I have too much going on, damn it," she said, barely catching her breath. "You turn him around at New Orleans and send him back to New York."

"Wait, Anna, let's talk about this for a minute. I'm sorry to make light of the predicament, but Benny's an adult." I could hear her breathing. "He's capable and old enough to make his own decisions … we can't order him around like he's still a child."

"Well, you handle him any way you choose, but I need a little peace and quiet in my life," she shot back. "Handling Isabella's will and this Mancini estate are driving me crazy," she said, "and my friend Andy is sending the art world in New York into a new stratum. I'm sick of all of it, and tired." She cried, sobbing.

"I know you are, Anna, and I'll do whatever I can. Do you want me to come to New York?"

"No, Ben … no!" She seemed to have calmed a little, but was still crying. "No," she said, again, and I waited for her to let loose with something else.

"What, Anna? What's troubling you?"

"Ben, Jacob has died in San Francisco," she said softly, "and I was listed somewhere in his information as the responsible party. Ben, I just can't handle everything, not with Benny having left college, running off." Her crying became distinct, less distant.

"What happened to Jacob?" I asked.

"They don't know," she said. "They've categorized it as pneumonia, some kind of virus, but it's not important at the moment. He was only fifty-six." Anna sniffed, then continued, "His death and my not wanting to go to California was what really caused Benny to explode. But Jacob was a good friend, and he loved both of us when we both needed loving very badly."

Her comment, even after twenty years, struck at my heart hard and heavy, but I quickly imagined a woman I cared for, the mother of my son, in distress. I said nothing for a few seconds.

"Ben?" she asked.

"Yeah, yeah," I said. "You need help, Anna. Tell me what to do."

"Oh, Ben, I know you never cared for Jacob, but if you can lay everything aside, it will solve a lot of problems for me if you would go to San Francisco and finalize the details with the people there,"

A Full-Grown Man

she said. "He's to be interred in Connecticut, where he's from, and I'll handle that part."

"Sure, Anna, anything for you. Call me back with information. Benny can go with me," I said, hoping she would agree.

"Ben, no. Send him home, please," she pleaded.

"Leave him alone, Anna. Spring semester is nearly over; maybe he needs a long break. Come to Gold Dust in August, and he'll go back with you."

"The two of you are just alike, do you know that?" she said softly. "I feel as though I'm pulled and torn continually, twisted and thrown about every time I'm around either one of you. And the two of you together, then I have no chance at all."

"It's because we both love you, Anna. With everything we've got, we love you, and always will." It seemed easier to say those words when I said "we," but I meant what I said.

"Stop it, Benjamin!" she screamed.

The phone went dead. But before I could leave the front hall, it rang two consecutive rings.

"Son-of-a-bitch," I complained, but quickly answered, "Hello, this is Ben Bennefield."

"Dad!" Benny's voice was loud and excited. "I'm in Atlanta and will arrive in New Orleans in about three hours. Can you pick me up?"

"Oh, Benny," I dragged out his name then said, "I don't know about that."

"What do you mean, Dad? What's wrong?"

"Benny, you're a runaway now, and you have people looking everywhere for you. I think the police in Maine have a bulletin out on you."

"Come on, Dad. Mother called you, didn't she? I'm not going back right now."

"You're not? Are you sure, Benny?"

"Yes, sir, I'm sure, so come pick me up. Would you, please?"

"No, I won't, but I'll tell you what," I said. "When you get to New Orleans, take a cab to the Paillasse Hotel in the French Quarter, and I'll meet you there tomorrow for lunch. We're gonna go to San Francisco."

There was a pause. "That'll be good, Dad," he said softly. "It's nice of you to do that, and I'll be proud to go with you."

Fifty

Being a little late, I walked briskly from a parking space on Bourbon Street to the Paillasse Hotel. I stepped through the door into a bustling lobby, stopped, and looked around. In the far back, I recognized Benny standing in front of a tall red chair, motioning with his hands while talking to a woman standing in front of him. Moving toward him, I could see his jeans were held up by suspenders over a white dress shirt, and as I drew nearer, I saw that he wore black loafers with no socks. *It has to be a college fad*, I thought. When he saw me coming toward him, Benny pointed to me, smiling as he spoke to the woman. She turned quickly, flung open her arms, and began to laugh.

"Mista Ben!" she exclaimed as she wrapped her arms completely around me, rapidly moving her hands up and down my back. "Oh, how wonderful to see you," she said loudly in my ear, then pressed against me a second time. Finally letting go, she stepped back. Tall and beautiful in a red suit and red high-heeled shoes, Jessie Johnson was stunning.

"Jessie, Jessie, Jessie," I repeated while shaking my head. "How in the world are you?"

"Couldn't be better, Mista Ben, and this is the biggest treat I've had in a long time, to find you and Benny here in New Orleans. I love it," she said loudly. "I almost died when Benny tapped me on my shoulder."

"You recognized him, Jessie?" I asked.

"Oh, sure, it's only been a little while, but look at him. He's the spittin' image of his daddy. Just look at that boy." Jessie quickly put her arms around Benny's neck and pulled him to her, kissed his cheek, and said, "I fed this little ole boy every summer and saw him growing up, and now," she shook her head as she scanned Benny completely, "he's a full-grown man." Benny said nothing, smiling from ear to ear while his face reddened. "And you, Mista Ben, you're still the same. Wow!" Her smile vanished and then came back. "How are my mama and daddy doing?"

"They're doing fine, Jessie, but you need to come see them," I said. "We see you on television but you need to come hug them and kiss them."

"Time is short, Mista Ben, but I'm going to Gold Dust as soon as I can." Jessie became very serious, looked at my face, and then spoke to Benny. "Benny, boy, you don't know how important your daddy is to me. Maybe I should tell you." She smiled, looking at me. I shook my head slightly, hoping Jessie would recognize a "No, don't go there" signal. She caught it, then without missing a beat, she laughed, "Benny, I've seen your Daddy naked two times, butt naked, and I bet he hates to hear me say that to you." She laughed while Benny's eyes floated to mine with a questioning look. Again, I shook my head, rolling back my eyes in disbelief. Benny smiled and punched me on the arm. I smiled back, but said nothing in defense.

"I needed some good stuff, Jessie," Benny said, smiling. "In fact, it will help me today when I make excuses for coming to Louisiana. Thanks!" He reached to hug Jessie.

"Well, Mista Ben, I'm sure you're thinking, enough foolishness," Jessie said. "But I do have some good news, and that's why I'm on cloud nine, besides the fact of seeing y'all here."

"Tell us, Jessie," I said, as we sat down in the two red velvet chairs. Face to face, Jessie Johnson and I were at the same level; the distance between us when she considered herself a mere "colored girl" and I was a young cotton farmer was no longer there. We were two friends with the commonality of a place and time unique to us, a place called Gold Dust, and while I slowly moved my hand back and forth along the soft, smooth velvet, I knew I had well judged an angry little girl whose spirit had been suppressed and hidden deep inside her. Without a doubt in my mind, I knew that what I was going to hear from this young woman was the announcement of another big step in her life. And I was sure that, some day, greatness would come to Jessie Johnson.

"Minutes before Benny found me," Jessie said, as her lips began to quiver with emotion, "I signed a contract with the biggest television station in Atlanta to host their new morning talk show. They wanted a new face, Mista Ben, to 'plow new ground,' as my daddy would say, and I'm gonna be that new face." She hesitated, and I could see the tears gathering in her eyes. "A long time ago, you told me the world's changing, and I took your word. Now, I'm getting started in the new world." She smiled, took my hand, and glanced up to Benny standing beside me, then back to me. "Thank you," she whispered and blotted her eyes with her finger.

That day, I said hello to the woman Jessie Johnson had become.

* * * * *

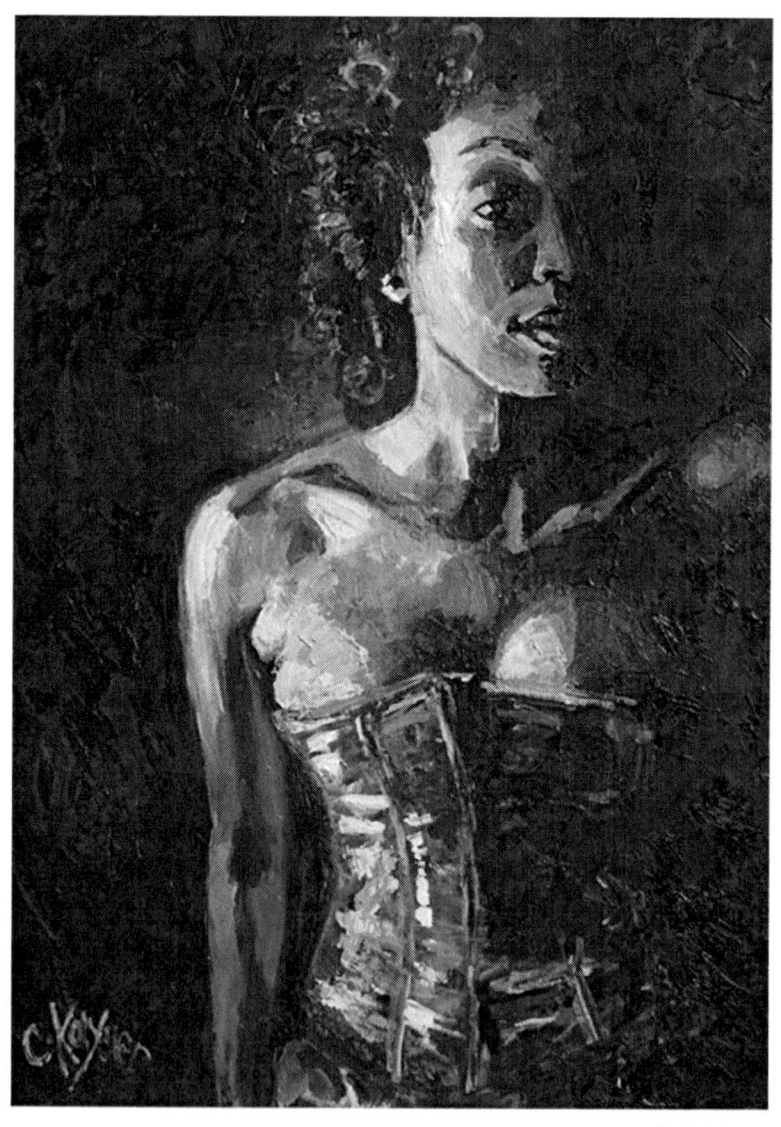

Jessie Johnson

Fifty-One

"Anna?" I said when I heard no one on the other end.

"Yes, Ben," she answered. "I dropped the receiver. I've been waiting for your call. Did everything go all right?"

"Yes. Benny and I will fly out of San Francisco on Friday morning, but in the meantime we're gonna look around the Bay area, and maybe drive to Big Sur for a day or two."

"Benny's okay, I'm sure; what about Jacob, Ben?" her voice faded.

"The body should arrive there tonight." There was a quiet pause, and then I continued, "The Health Department has given the funeral home permission to release the body, and the funeral home in Connecticut will handle the details on that end. You'll be contacted in the morning to make arrangements for burial." And again, another pause.

"What's wrong, Anna?" I asked.

I could hear her breathing. And then she said, "I don't know, Ben. It's as though I've just arrived, exhausted, after a dreadfully long and tiring trip, and suddenly home seems soothing and wonderful, and I don't feel guilty about it."

"Just take it, sweetheart. Plow under the past and go with the feeling," I advised. The moment I said those words, I knew I should write them on paper and carry them in my pocket, referring to them often, for my own sake.

* * * * *

Near sunset on Friday evening, Benny slowly turned the car into the driveway, bringing to a close a gesture of benevolence toward a man I never knew, a job I had done for a woman I loved, and for our son.

"Stop, Benny, stop here," I said.

I felt an urgency to be set free, to be let go, to breathe deeply. I was home. I stepped from the car; the tires squealed on the asphalt as it pulled away. Stretching while I stood, I looked to the west across the big field of dark green, the long rows of cotton about twelve inches high with leaves tilted toward the setting sun.

The April sky was darkening, and far away in the east, clouds were tall and still, looking like mountains in the distance, glowing pink and yellow up high, lit by the sun, and amber and gray where they touched the trees on the far horizon. Slowly, I walked to the old bridge and waited until a car completed its crossing, leaving Gold Dust. Stepping along the wooden runners, I reached the middle of the span and looked around. Once clean and emerald, the banks along Edward's Creek now were overgrown with brush and saplings whose branches draped over the rocky shallows. In the darkness of the trees shading it, the water appeared black and foreboding, having lost its blue-green color.

I looked up along the road; Miz Margaret's store was now the last of the small businesses that had thrived in our town; the post office had closed many years earlier, and past Miz Margaret's, the once fine railroad depot was now mostly hidden by volunteer trees growing against its walls, having waited for years for the wrecking crew to take it down. But the Gold Dust Bridge was still there, tall, erect, and far rustier. Its peak still caught the sun when it was low in the sky. I glanced up into the bridge's massive iron, studying it for the thousandth time, then to its east end and to its west end, and wondered about time, the years, and about the thousands of people who had crossed it from one side of Edward's Creek to the other, going somewhere, their passage granted by the old bridge. Sadly, most of the people never came back. And all around the Gold Dust Bridge, from tree line to tree line in three directions, Bennefield Farm now stretched over three thousand acres. *What for*, I thought, *and why?* "Why?" I yelled as loudly as I could, and a soft muted sound echoed back to me from the trees and the water in Edward's Creek: *Why, why, why, why,* and died away. Leaning against the bridge's railing, I spit as far as I could and watched as the whiteness hit the dark water and disappeared. Quickly, I walked from the spot where I had stood and heard the echoes again, very softly: *why, why, why.* I ran, stopping at the mailbox at the driveway going into Bennefield Farm.

I thumbed through several pieces of mail, then pulled out an item whose return address spelled out "Catherine K. Bartlett." With my thumb, I opened the flap and removed the note, reading it as I walked toward the house.

YOU'RE INVITED
**Please come celebrate
my sixteenth birthday
with family and friends.
STAR PLANTATION
6 o'clock in the evening
April 7, 1972
CATHERINE BARTLETT**

With the invitation was a handwritten note.

Ben,

I tried to call you but there was no answer.

Hope you can come to Catherine's big sixteenth.
Call me sometime.

Love, Ava

Love, Ava. The words bounced around in my head, and I wondered why I had not been able to talk but randomly to Ava during the five or so years since her return to Bunkie. "Love, Ava," I whispered, smiling as I placed the note back in the envelope. Suddenly, the sounds of feet pounding the asphalt in front of me made me stop and look up as Benny and his two dogs ran toward me.

"Where've you been, Dad?" he huffed, leaning forward with his hands on his knees and breathing hard. Sadie and Kaiser began barking and jumping around their master, wanting to run some more. Benny knelt and hugged both dogs. They licked his face.

"To that damned old bridge," I said, laughing quietly.

"Look around you, King Ben," Benny said, spreading his arms wide. "You should be proud, Dad, you're the king of an empire. There's nothing from Long Island to Boston that compares with what you're looking at right this minute. A three-thousand-acre empire," he laughed. Then he quickly added, "I'm coming here to live. Bennefield Farm is where I want to live for all of my life. Look at that sky!" he yelled. "This is freedom, Dad; this is the purity of life, what every man searches for." I had never heard anyone say these things, nor had I looked at Bennefield Farm as anything more than a means to a living for myself and those who worked for me. "Look at this place." Benny drew in a deep breath, rolled his eyes, and yelled, "You can smell it, it's fresh, it's clean, and it's home!" He closed his eyes and in a second they opened, staring at me. His smile was big.

"Well," I said, "that's good to know, Benny. You've made a lot of decisions in just a few seconds. Very decisive. That's a good trait. In the meantime, there's school to throw in there someplace."

"I'll go to LSU, Dad, starting in September," he said. "I've already been in touch with them; in fact, they'll have my records by next week."

"What're you saying, Benny? You've planned this for some time, right?" I asked, as we walked.

"Yes, sir ... no, yeah, I have," he said, "but Mother doesn't know I've been planning it."

"When are you gonna tell her?

"I plan to write a long letter, outlining my ideas and plans. Once she knows what the facts are, Mother will accept it. She's inflexible at times, but her reasoning power is great," Benny explained.

That fact is good to know, I thought. "It seems like a fair enough plan, but I would suggest, before you finalize anything with LSU, that you have your mother's blessing, entirely, in person, and not through letters and telephone calls."

Approaching the sidewalk to the back porch, Benny said, "I need a job, Dad. All summer."

"We have jobs, son, plenty of them. Run over to Bo's and tell him you want a job. He'll give you one in less than a minute."

I smiled, knowing full well Bo wouldn't relish training a college kid from New York on how to work cattle or plow the fields. But I knew Benny would have the best teacher in the state of Louisiana.

Benny eventually agreed to go with me to Catherine's birthday party, and I assured him that once there, he would have a good time and would meet some of the finest, from Bunkie down to Gold Dust and Whiteville.

"But how do you explain me, Dad?" Benny asked, in the car. "My first name is your last name, and my last name is Italian; how do you explain it?" There was annoyance and some deep-seated anxiety in his question.

"I don't explain it, Benny," I said. "Most people won't ask or say anything, so don't worry. Neither of us owes an explanation to anyone."

"Wow," he exclaimed as he brought the car to a halt, parking on Pershing Highway. "Some party; I bet there's a hundred cars here." We walked the long driveway to the old mansion, the Koller home. I remembered a similar walk many years before, with my friend James Bartlett, on New Year's Eve, the night he stole Ava from me. The thought still made my heart sink. I closed my eyes, and then opened them to glance at Benny, remembering it was also the day when James told me to be happy about my son, to love him, to go get him in New York, he was mine, too. Without a doubt, my friend James had given me good advice.

The front door opened after the first knock. I had expected Ava to be there and hug Benny and me, but Mr. B. F. Koller swung the door open wide. "Come in, come in, Ben." He scanned Benny quickly, from head to toe, and asked, "This your boy, Ben? From New York?"

"Yes, sir, this is Benny Mancini; Benny, this is Catherine's grandfather, Mister Koller," I said.

"Good Lord, Ben, I could've picked him out anywhere," Mr. Koller said. "Y'all follow me. The old ones and the young ones aren't mixing, but they're all out on the terrace." He stopped halfway down the hall, turned toward us, and raised his finger to Benny. "I know you're older, young fellow, but anybody under sixteen don't get anything but cola or orange soda." He held his finger toward Benny with a frown on his face, then he smiled, turned quickly, and began walking again, mumbling, "But I figure what the bartender don't know is his fault."

Benny looked at me, smiled, then put his hand on the side of his mouth, whispering, "I like this fellow, Dad."

The north end of Mr. Koller's terrace was decorated with bright banners spelling Catherine's name and announcing the occasion. A hundred colorful balloons were tethered at the center of the large table holding the food and goodies, including an ice sculpture of a young girl holding her skirt out with both hands. A band with an overzealous drummer blasted the stillness. Strings of colored lights crossed the entire terrace from north to south, and at the south end, dressed in suits, jackets, and dresses from stores in New Orleans, Dallas, and Atlanta, stood 90 percent of the wealth of an area ten miles around the Gold Dust Bridge. In the middle, and surrounded by several ladies, was a very familiar figure: my longtime friend Mr. Cal Evans and his lovely new wife, Miz Nona.

I stopped and stared directly at Mr. Cal in his brown and beige plaid polyester suit: He chewed on his cigar, gesturing, and I figured he would never forget the New Year's party years ago when Miz Nona's ex-husband tried to kill him. I was glad and happy for Mr. Cal and Miz Nona. They were survivors, having lived through divorces and the gossipy little town's chatter that hung over them for years. Both had retired from the bank, and according to the continuing chatter, they lived happily in their retirement.

"Ben Bennefield," Mr. Cal yelled, and all eyes turned to us as we stood on the steps going down to the terrace. As he approached, his smile grew bigger; he grabbed his cigar from between his teeth and pitched it over the heads of thirty people, into the yard beyond the knee-high wall at the edge of the patio.

"Huh," I warned, looking at Benny. "Be careful, Benny, this guy's tricky." I smiled at Mr. Cal, extending my hand.

"Well, well, well, Benjamin Bennefield, Mister American farmer himself. How in the hell are you, boy?" While he shook my hand, he continued with his fast-paced words. "A world traveler—" He stopped, glared at Benny standing beside me, and asked, "Hell's fire, who's this you got here, Ben? Damn, you been duplicated, boy."

"Mister Cal, this is my son, Bennefield Mancini, and Benny, this is Mister Cal Evans."

"Good God a'mighty, young man, where'd you git a name like that? You from where? 'Cross the ocean?" Mr. Cal asked, laughing very loud.

"From New York, sir, and I'm named after my grandfather," Benny lied. "He was a great, world-renowned artist from Italy." I watched the scene with amusement.

"Oh," Mr. Cal grunted; his smile diminished. "Well, it's a pretty name anyway. What'd you say it was … Man … Man … what?" He squinted at Benny.

"Mancini," Benny said. "M-A-N-C-I-N-I."

Mr. Cal wasn't fazed by Benny's sarcasm, as he fumbled through his jacket pockets and pulled out a cigar, which at first glance appeared to have had one end already chewed on. He glanced at the used cigar for a second, blew on the chewed end, then stuck it between his teeth. "Your daddy," he said, with the cigar poking straight out of this mouth, "has a hell of a lot of money, young man, and don't you let him tell you otherwise."

I rolled my eyes back, shaking my head.

"Yes, sir," Benny said, and quickly, he leaned toward the short little man, brought his hand to one side of his mouth, and whispered loudly enough for me to hear, "and my mama's got a hell of lot more money than my daddy." Benny smiled and glanced at me, nodding.

We waited for Mr. Cal's next move.

The next move didn't come quick enough, as Ava stepped beside me and placed her arm around my waist. I placed my arm over her shoulders. It seemed familiar.

"Hi, Ben," she said. "I'm delighted you came." She leaned to look at Benny on the other side of me. "Benny, I'm glad you came, too. You want me to take you over to the young side of this terrace?"

"No, ma'am, I see Catherine. Thanks anyway," Benny said, and before he could move, Mr. Cal grabbed his arm.

"Come on, boy," Mr. Cal ordered. "I'm gonna take you over there. You need to git to know some of these little Southern fillies. Besides, I wanna dance some." Mr. Cal, short and stubby and laughing heartily, directed Benny to the north end of Mr. Koller's terrace. Ava and I heard his voice high above the drum beat as he introduced Benny. "All right girls, here's that Bennefield boy y'all been squealin' 'bout."

Ava tucked her arm through mine, laughed, and said mockingly, "Come on, boy, you need to get to know this old Southern mare." Ava led me to two chairs. After a few seconds, she said, with a half-hearted smile, "I need a friend, Ben. A close friend like I used to have." Through the corner of my eye, I watched her. "Can you ever forgive me for what James and I did a long time ago, and be my friend?"

"I've forgiven you, Ava," I said, not looking at her.

"But I've been home a long time Ben, and our paths have crossed many times in this little town," she said. "Maybe you *haven't* forgiven me."

"You ran away from me because of my mother, Ava." I looked straight into her face.

"I'm sorry James told you. He shouldn't have," she said.

"I wish he hadn't, but he did. And there's no way for me to defend my mother or change what happened."

"Well, I've changed, Ben," she said.

"I think I can see that, but—"

"You haven't, Ben," she interrupted. "You've changed very little, if any at all."

I looked across the crowd quickly, then back to her. "What do you mean, Ava? Time changes everything, and I think I've changed a great deal." I sat up straight in my chair, crossing my arms over my chest.

"Benjamin," she said, "you're still twenty years old, and obsessed today like a kid, about your first love, that boy's mother."

I followed her eyes as she looked at the two young people standing separate from the crowd on the north end of the terrace, talking …

obviously enthralled with each other. I gasped for air, as I watched them. I closed my eyes for a second, opened them, and then lowered my head.

"Do you think—" she said, then stopped. My breathing became shallow as I stared again at Catherine and Benny, waiting for Ava to speak. "—I could help you get over that old fixation you have, and we might pick up the pieces, Ben?" She smiled. "I would really like that."

"If you think we could, Ava. If you think so," I said softly.

She moved her hand to touch mine. And I looked quickly again at Catherine and Benny, at the body language of a young man thrusting his charms upon a young birthday celebrant enamored with him. The lights strung across Mr. Koller's terrace flashed colorful streaks, like a hail of stars falling through the blackness of a midnight sky, and my heart beat faster. Anxiety inside me ran rampant.

My eyes held to my son and Ava's daughter. "Yeah," I said. "I … I would like that, too. I sure would."

* * * * *

Fifty-Two

Weeks after Catherine's party, late in the evening, I walked out onto the front porch, letting the screen door slam behind me, and sat in the first chair I came to. Hearing the noise, both Kaiser and Sadie came charging to the porch, stopping in front of me, sitting at attention, and waiting for a command or a handout. I leaned forward and wrapped my arms around the two boxers, both trying to lick my cheeks. Water dripped from them.

"They're good dogs, Dad," Benny said as he stepped onto the porch in his swimsuit. Wet and breathing heavily, he dropped into the chair next to me. Through the summer, his hair had become mostly blonde, bleached by the hot Louisiana sun that grew our cotton and the abundance of grass that fed our cattle. His skin had browned, and his green eyes were bright, set deep ... he was a man, no doubt; certainly not a kid who needed protecting. "The water's cold, but great," he said, and I remembered having spoken similar words after swimming with my dogs in Edward's Creek. *Water is always cold on a hot day*, I thought.

Darkness crept around us, and the constant hum of the cicadas in the big trees lulled us into a daze even as we talked. "Benny, it seems like yesterday when I'd walk with my dad to the gazebo late in the evening. He'd hold my hand while we dangled our feet in the water, which was always cold for a little while, but he held my hand, and I felt safe. It was a good feeling, and I loved being with him. After we got used to the cold water, he'd bring out the soap and towel and we'd bathe in Edward's Creek." Benny looked at me and shifted his bare body in the chair, then ran his fingers quickly through his damp hair. "I wish you could have known your grandfather, Benny," I said.

"What's on your mind, Dad?" he asked teasingly, cutting his bright eyes toward me. "There's something you have to say, right?" He smiled and shifted again in the chair, sitting upright, watching me.

"Well, Benny, this has been the best summer I've had in a long time, and I thank you for spending it with me," I said.

"And?" Benny held up both hands, smiling. "And?"

"During the past couple of months, Ava has returned to my life, and I'm very glad," I said, waiting, feeling sure Benny would have something to say.

"And?" he asked again, pausing for a second. "Dad, I've been here every day. I can see what's been going on. I've just waited, figuring you'd say something when the time was right."

At that moment, I felt like a child again, dangling my legs from the gazebo while the water and the cold crept higher. "Benny, I'm going to ask Ava to marry me," I said, watching his face. The light was dim.

He fell back in the chair. I could see only the white of his eyes glaring at me. Suddenly, the warmth of my dad's hand holding mine was gone.

Neither of us spoke.

"Why?" he asked, breaking the silence. "Just shack up with her; you don't have to get married."

"That doesn't work, Benny, not for what I'm looking for, and not for Ava," I said. "And not around here. Besides, Ava has a daughter, you know."

"Yeah, I know, Dad, I know," he said, moving his hands in circles. "You want to marry the mother, but you forbid me to date the daughter. What kind of deal is that?" Benny's voice became stronger, and his words were rushed.

"There's no '*deal*,' Benny. Ava and I had a love for each other a long time ago, and it didn't work out then, but we're older now, and—"

"And what, Dad?" he broke in. He stood up, directly in front of me. "My mother loves you. Why don't you ask her to marry you?"

"God, this is complicated," I shook my head and sighed.

"It's damn simple to me," he said, his voice getting louder. "We'd be a family, a real family, my mother, my father, and me … and I wouldn't be a 'bastard,' Dad, a bastard. You know how hard it is to be a bastard?" He wiped his mouth. "You and Mother," he said, "two selfish people who think of no one but themselves and what they want." He took a deep breath.

I looked away from him, through the dim light filtering through the trees. The August air was hot and stifling, sweet with the aroma of honeysuckle. I hated what he said. His words hovered over me like the hot air, smothering me, and boiled inside my head.

"Sit down, Benny, and calm down." Again, he slumped into the chair next to me, breathing hard, and angry.

The sound of the cicadas had turned into a piercing scream, when suddenly, Sadie and Kaiser jumped to their feet, barking. Barely visible in the darkness under the trees, Bo was walking toward us. He called out, "Ben, it's jist me." Hearing a familiar voice, Sadie and Kaiser ran to meet him. After a few seconds, Bo stepped onto the porch. "Ben, I sho' hope I ain't interruptin' here," he said, "but I need to talk you. Won't take long."

"Sure, Bo, what's on your mind?" I asked. My voice was unsure. My hands were shaking.

"Ben, I'm glad Benny's here 'cause it's 'bout him, and I want 'im to hear what I gotta say," Bo spoke clearly.

"Sure," I said.

Benny sat up in the chair, watching Bo.

Bo took his cap off and rubbed his head with one hand. "I sho' hates to say this, but I gotta stop it befo' it's too late," he said, speaking softly. "Ben, Henry says Benny's been playin' 'round with Karen for three or four weeks now, and he's gonna hav'ta move off if somethin' happens." Benny flopped back into the chair, looking away from Bo. "It ain't like Henry to bring up these things … he didn't wanna say nothin'." He went on, "But I figure Benny oughtta stop what he doin' before he ruins that girl, and we lose a good man and his family."

"What's going on Benny? What're you doing?" I asked, frowning and looking at Benny.

Benny closed his eyes, shaking his head. He wouldn't look at me; his eyes turned up, showing only white, glaring at Bo.

Silently, I pleaded, please God, let the answer be no. "Is Karen pregnant, Bo?"

"No, sir," Bo answered. "Essie say she ain't, not now. They's scared Karen's believin' stuff that ain't neva' gonna happen. This ain't the big city, Ben. Lord, she ain't even seventeen. Ain't even finished high school," he said. "If it ain't stopped, they'll jist take their family someplace else. And this is they's home."

"Benny'll take care of it in the morning, Bo; I'm sorry this has happened," I apologized. My head was pounding. "Tell Henry and Essie I'll talk to them tomorrow. Tell them it'll stop. Please tell them." I sighed very deeply, then looked past the man into the dark.

Bo turned and started toward the steps. He turned again and walked back to the chair where Benny sat. "Benny, you a fine young man," he said, "but you older than what yo' daddy was when me and Henry moved our families here." Bo stopped and put his cap on, fixing it properly as though preparing for his final statement. "And Benny, I can't say I's sorry I told yo' daddy, cause all of us here watched yo' daddy pay a big price for the things he did before we come here." My head pounded harder, and my eyes began to water. This man, a bystander whom I had never considered to have been aware of the events of my youth, was opening a door that I had never allowed to be looked through, a door I forbade even myself to open.

"Ev'ybody," Bo continued, "owns some love somewhere, the good love, that 'die-for' love, and till they find it, they stay locked in a box that's jist full of air. But, Benny, a man jist can't pick it up and put it down when he wants to, 'cause somebody's gonna git hurt like that. What you playing with here can't ever be that love like ev'y man on this Earth wants, the kind of love that makes you happy all day long." Bo hesitated. "Happy, Benny," he shook his head, "happy ain't happy 'less you got somebody to share happy with."

Bo's words pierced my brain like an ice pick jabbed through my skull.

He continued, "You needs to talk to yo' daddy 'bout what you doin'." I sighed deeply, closing my eyes. "I gotta go see Henry and Essie right now, and I'll tell 'em what you said, Ben." He turned again toward the darkness in front of us. "You fellas have a good night," he said.

Both Sadie and Kaiser jumped up and stood at the top step, watching as Bo walked into the darkness under the trees and disappeared.

I stood from my chair, only a few feet from where Benny sat, looked down at him, and asked, "What in the hell have you been doing, you sneaky little bastard?" Just as my voice exploded with the word *bastard*, I knew in the anger and anguish of the moment, I had badly misspoken. My breath left me.

Benny jumped up, moving into my face, and yelled, "Yeah, I'm your bastard son; just look at what you did a long time ago, and—"

On impulse, I swung, hitting him squarely in the mouth, causing blood to fly in all directions. The blow sent him backward off the porch, into the bushes several feet below. I stood, glaring down at him, and watched him struggle to get up from the bushes. He stood, looked at me while holding his hand to his mouth, and then turned and ran toward the gazebo. Sadie and Kaiser chased after him, barking wildly. Quickly, I ran down the steps and rushed in the direction they had taken. The sound of a splash into Edward's Creek echoed in the darkness, and then two more; the barking stopped. By the time I reached the gazebo, only two heads were bobbing on the water; Sadie and Kaiser were swimming in circles, whining, searching. *What have I done? What the hell have I done?* I stripped off my shirt and jeans and was ready to dive into Edward's Creek when I heard the rustling of water about thirty feet into mid-stream.

"You're a liar, Mister Bennefield." I could hear Benny's gasps. "You lie all the time, to yourself, Mister Bennefield. You're not a man ... you weren't man enough to take care of what you did ... not nearly man enough to marry my mother. You didn't even try, you never tried." His head disappeared below the ripples.

I dove into the creek and found him, hoping with all I had inside me that he was holding his breath. I grabbed him, then encircled my arms around him, and we both gasped as our heads shot into the air.

"Stop it, Benny, stop it!" I yelled. He coughed a couple of times, spitting water from his mouth, then swirled his head, slinging the water from his hair. "You're right," I said quickly, "you're right." We treaded water, clinging to each other. "I've lied, you're right." Calming a little, his body relaxed while I held him. "Let's get out of here," I pleaded. Slowly we made it to the edge, then pulled ourselves onto the floor of the gazebo, where Sadie and Kaiser stood waiting.

We stood motionless and silent for several seconds, while the constant hum of the cicadas cut through the stillness and quiet, and looked at each other. Wet and trembling from anxiety and fear, two men, a father and son, mirror images in ways evident and unseen, had unexpectedly opened old and bleeding wounds. We sat in the chairs.

"Benny," I said, "until you know, I suppose, neither your mind nor your heart will ever be still. And believe me, it tears me up when I tell you." I waited, still breathing hard, and glanced at his face, which glared angrily back at me. "I'll tell you, all of it."

"Then tell me, I'm waiting. But I have to have the truth. Tell me the truth." He touched his lip with his finger. His eyes searched my face suspiciously.

Slowly, my breath came back.

He leaned forward in his chair, holding his eyes on mine. I told him about my dad, about whom I had spoken very little, and purposefully so.

After a few minutes, Benny asked, "He died of a heart attack, is that right?"

"That's on his death certificate, but Benny, I'm going to tell you something that no one knows except me, not even my sister." I wondered if I should go so deeply into this history, which I now looked back on as terror, bordering into insanity, knowing the blood inside *him* was that of Hester McGinnis, his grandmother. I hesitated and took a deep breath. "The truth," he had said a few minutes earlier.

Benny shuffled in his chair, then leaned closer to me. "What?" he asked.

"When my father died, Mother didn't ask for an autopsy. From all indications, he died of a massive coronary, which I believed also, at the time it happened. Two years later, when mother shot herself, Bo and Henry cleaned the kitchen and found a half-empty container of rat poison—arsenic—hidden on top of the cabinet. Thinking back, for several weeks before he died, even months, Dad had complained of problems I recognized later as symptoms of arsenic poisoning."

"Are you saying you think Grandmother *killed* him?" Benny asked in disbelief.

"There's little doubt in my mind she killed him. That fact has often tortured me, making me hate my mother. And Benny," I said, "it's the first time I have ever said those words. And I'm sorry that I have to share them with you." My hands were shaking.

He said nothing. In the moonlight, I could see him taking in the information. "I wanted the truth," he said, barely getting the words out before his voice dropped off.

I told him about Anna's letters hidden from me for years; how I had found them in my mother's room. I told him about the heartache and the disappointments; giving up my senior year of high school and relinquishing my plans for college, a future away from Gold Dust.

Two hours later into the evening, he asked, "But why didn't you run away, get away from Gold Dust? Go to New York, and marry my mother?"

"I was a kid, Benny, less than eighteen, and I knew nothing about any place but where I lived, right here in Gold Dust, nothing about life and what to expect in the outside world. And I had nothing. After Dad died, I felt like my choices and my chances went with him, and my mother made sure of it. Hester knew it. She knew how to deal with an ignorant kid she wanted to lock up and punish for being who he was," I said. "And Benny, by the time I found out about you, your mother had married and moved on with her life; her career had bloomed beautifully, and you and Jacob were part of her picture, and I wasn't. All of that was the result of my mother's plans, the result of her selfishness and the hate she carried around with her."

Benny looked brooding, and again touched his lip with his fingertip. "Until you came to Paris, Dad—" and I sighed deeply, hearing *Dad* for the first time since the beginning of the encounter on the porch, "—I didn't know anything about having a father. Jacob was a friend, just a friend who took me walking or to the park. And I've wondered, why did you come to Paris?" he asked.

"Well, to be perfectly honest ... I went in pursuit of a woman, your mother. She was all I could think of for years. Every day, I spent my life in a dream about loving someone. I went to Paris to find Anna Mancini, the Anna who had made up that old dream, years before. But you were there, and after a day or so, I realized I had suddenly found part of me that had been missing." I smiled, but Benny held fast. "I found part of myself in that kid, in you. And you know something? What I saw was better than anything I figured I could ever do again." I looked at Benny's face; a question was forming on his lips.

"Dad, how did you *ever* persuade Mother to let me come to Gold Dust with you?" He shook his head. "Looking back," he said, "that was strange for her to agree to." He laughed quietly. "She always seemed angry about you."

"I felt a particular need after I found you. All of sudden, I wanted you to know there was another world out there, apart from the way you lived in New York, and part of you had come out of that other world. I was proud of it, Benny, and I wanted you to know about my life and where I came from. And I wanted you to be part of it with me." Before Benny could ask another question, I added quickly, "And in Paris, I resolved in my mind that your mother was never going to be part of my life." I shook my head. "She'd always be the mother of my child, that's all, and I accepted that for the first time after all the years of wishing. And I knew I had to stop waiting for something to happen."

"So," he said, "you're going to move on, aren't you? Asking Mrs. Bartlett to marry you?" His voice held sarcasm, which I figured would remain in his psyche forever.

"Yes," I said. "I'm going to do it."

He reached to pet Kaiser's head, and promptly Sadie moved between Benny and Kaiser, whining. Benny looked at me and smiled. "I guess you just can't make everybody happy, huh, Dad?"

"Early tomorrow morning, son, you owe Henry, Essie, and Karen an apology."

"I know, Dad, I know, and I'm very sorry for what I've done," he whispered.

We sat in silence in the darkness of a night with a moon as big as any I had ever seen. It started as a harvest moon, big and yellow, rising through the trees over the far bank of Edward's Creek. *A little early this year*, I thought, but the cotton was ready. I leaned my head against the back of the chair and stared into the sky. It was the kind of moon about which songs are written. The kind that makes you believe you're not alone in this big world, yet the kind that silently lets a man know he is less than a second in the scheme of time.

Moonlight filtered through the trees. Plainly, tears glistened in Benny's eyes, and I watched as they ran down his cheeks. I reached and placed my hand over his. His hand was warm, and mine, too.

"After the dew dries tomorrow," I told him, "we'll start picking on high ground."

Ava Koller Bartlett Bennefield

Fifty-Three

THE NEXT MORNING, SATURDAY, August 19, 1972, at 8:55 in the morning, in a booth with red plastic seats in a cafe in Bunkie, Ava and I sat looking at each other, waiting for the waitress to bring fried eggs, ham, and biscuits. She appeared surprised when I said, "Marry me." After the words came out, and knowing it was the second time I had made such a demand of Ava, I waited with my lips half opened, and waited, and waited. I closed my eyes, covering my ears with both hands. I opened my eyes, and then asked tenderly, "Will you marry me, Ava?"

"Yes," she mouthed, smiling. I brought her hand to my lips and kissed it.

A week later, having survived the summer with a few scars, Benny left to begin his junior year at Louisiana State University in Baton Rouge. He didn't have to say anything, but it was obvious he still harbored anger deep inside. Since the night of the encounter on the front porch, Benny had become quiet, spending long days, late into night, on the cotton picker Bo had assigned to him. The long hours, sometimes sixteen at a stretch, were self-punishment, I figured, and a plea for forgiveness for his indiscretions with Karen Brown. By the end of the first week of picking, with three mechanical pickers running through the white fields, we had sent over three hundred bales of cotton to the gins around Gold Dust.

After Benny left, I took his place on picker number two, in our rush to harvest a crop that would prove to be the biggest ever on the nearly two thousand acres of cotton on Bennefield Farm. "White gold," Bo and Henry rejoiced. But the price of cotton on the gin platforms suddenly dropped to only two thirds of its usual and expected price.

"Ben," Bo said in his attempt to console me, "look around us. Right here 'round the Gold Dust Bridge, thirty years ago, there wuz forty farmers on little old fifty-, hunderd-, and two-hunderd-acre places. And today, big farmers done eat 'em all up, not jist here, but all over. Now," he bragged as Henry smiled, "we gittin' two bales to the acre, not like it used to be when you wuz lucky to git just one if you could git it out the fields befo' the rain set in."

I knew Bo was right, but I decided to try something different, something unheard of in the world of cotton farming around Gold Dust: to warehouse the bales in the cotton markets of Memphis and Dallas, and wait till spring to put it on the markets, selling it directly to the mills. It was a gamble, but we had the money to wait till the price went up.

*****

Fifty-Four

It was the end of the second week in December when we returned to Gold Dust. I turned the car into the driveway, tired and ready to be home at Bennefield Farm. After nearly three weeks in Rome, Paris, and London, the old house looked inviting and welcoming. "Home," I said, "we're home, Ava."

She roused from sleep, opened her eyes, and looked straight through the windshield at the big white house, which stood tall and quiet, behind the oak trees. The lights in the two front rooms were on and beckoned a warm and exciting welcome. I stopped the car at the steps, opening the door. Immediately Hattie came through the front door onto the porch, her hands clasped together at her waist. "Welcome home, Ben, Miz Ava. We been waitin'," she called out as she walked to the car. She was smiling.

"I'm gonna get her some white uniforms," Ava said under her breath, then pushed open the car's door. In a second, Bo came down the steps, walking to the rear of the car to get our luggage. I shook his hand and hugged Hattie. "Good evening, Bo, Hattie," Ava said.

Bo tipped his head to Ava, nodded, and smiled, then he and I gathered the suitcases and took them to the main hall and set them at the bottom of the stairs. "I got it all ready, Ben, and it's beautiful, jist like always," Hattie said, smiling proudly.

"What, Hattie?" Ava asked quickly. "What's all ready?"

"Y'all's room, Miz Ava." Hattie opened the door going into my mother's bedroom. Red flames danced in the fireplace, and the crystals on the chandelier sparkled, casting sharp spots of colors in a thousand directions across the walls and ceiling.

Ava walked into the room, then to the foot of the bed, still holding her purse as she turned. "This is unbelievable, Ben," she exclaimed. "When did you do this?" she asked as she stepped closer to the blazing fire.

"This was Hester's room, sweetheart," I sighed. "It's been like this for sixty years, maybe longer."

"I had never seen this room, darlin'. It's wonderful."

"Neither had anyone else, but it's gonna be our room now. It's time for Hester to give it up," I said. About that time, Bo began turning down the bed, arranging the covers and pillows. Ava watched him. "This is great, Hattie, Bo, and we appreciate it," I told them.

"Y'all welcome, Ben, and we sure glad y'all had a good honeymoon. I can tell," Hattie said, smiling, her eyes shining. She and Bo left the room, closing the door behind them.

"No uniforms, sweetheart," I whispered to Ava. "These are my friends who've taken care of me for over twenty years. Uniforms will insult them, will separate us."

"We'll see, darlin'," she said, with a frown, "but are we supposed to stay in here, or what?" She looked at me. "I'm dead tired, but I need to walk around, and I'm hungry, besides," she whined.

I grabbed her and kissed her, holding her close to me as we stood in front of the fireplace. Ava wrapped her arms around my neck. "They'll call us in a little while, sweetheart," I said. I picked her up in my arms and brought her to my mother's bed, laying her very gently on the turned-down covers. "Welcome home, Ava." Then quickly, I lay beside her, wrapping my arms around her completely, and closed my eyes. Sleep came quickly, but in less than a minute, my entire body jerked, jarring me, with eyes wide open. I glanced across Ava's shoulder, but Hester's face had vanished. I hugged Ava tighter, flexing and holding my body against hers.

"In a couple of weeks," Ava whispered, "I'm gonna hire an architect and fix up this old house."

"You are?" I asked. "That's good," and I hugged her tighter, flexing my body again.

"Stop it, Benjamin," she whispered, "you horny rascal."

"Y'all come eat supper, Ben," Hattie's voice came from the other side of the door, but I didn't want to move.

* * * * *

By the time Ava and her architect had completed the overhaul of the old house and the three houses facing Edward's Creek, over $80,000 had been spent; Benny graduated from LSU that spring, his first step toward becoming a veterinarian, and with three friends, he departed in early June for three months hitchhiking across Europe. Catherine was graduating from a private school for girls in Missouri. Like her mother, she would be a teacher, and if she chose to return to the area, Ava would relinquish to Catherine the fifth grade she herself had inherited from Miz Helen Bartlett, James's mother, eight years before.

* * * * *

By 1975, it became clear that the ideas and events of the 1960s had moved on. Our trust of government was fading badly, making us leery of anyone sitting in power in the state houses and our nation's capital. We realigned our values, and advanced civil rights throughout the country, thus changing the old social and economic orders by which our lives had been lived for generations. Even Gold Dust, where I lived all of my life, was changing faster than many of my neighbors and friends cared for. But the sweeping ideas of the sixties gained acceptance, and what we read, the music we listened to, and the movies we watched reflected the changing times. Television's broadcasts of events around the world, meanwhile, gave us almost instant anxiety and fears, which heretofore had never been a part of our daily lives.

The vast changes were evident for miles around the Gold Dust Bridge: the absence of the rural family, farm hands, and tenant farmers, as well as small land owners; their flight to the cities of the North and the far West in search of a better life. Once-great homes, the plantation Big Houses, the shacks in old plantation quarters, and homes up and down Edward's Creek had long ago begun disappearing from the landscape, rotting away in the wet winters and hot summers in the semi-tropics of southern Louisiana. And in Gold Dust, the thriving village of my childhood, the last small store, Miz Margaret's, had burned down. With Miz Margaret's small house, only four or five others remained, and they were lived in by those few who, for reasons of their own, had chosen to live out their years in quiet solitude. Hundreds of people born and reared in the area had made their final passage across the Gold Dust Bridge. Never, I figured, would they return.

Very early on a morning in late July, the light of the sun glowed orange and pink through the trees on the far bank from the gazebo where often, in the cool morning quiet, my day began with a cup of coffee. That morning was different, however. There were no birds, no little animals scurrying about: absolute silence, except for the occasional sound of the ripple of water. "Hey!" I yelled, and after a few seconds a soft echo returned: *Hey, hey, hey,* from atop the blue-green water. Kaiser and Sadie sat upright and looked back and forth from me to the water downstream, then lay back down at my feet. After a few seconds, the sun rose, a tremendous red ball, its light glowing softly. Dust in the air, high in the atmosphere, I decided. As the big red ball became more visible, both dogs barked a couple of times. They looked at me, barked again, and then headed toward the garage to hide in their beds.

"Ben," Ava called from the porch. "More coffee?"

"Yes, please, another cup."

"What a strange sunrise," she said a few minutes later, as she crossed the gazebo to sit in the chair beside me.

"Yeah, an omen of some sort, I guess."

"I doubt it, Ben, it's just unusual, and beautiful," she laughed and took a sip from her cup.

"Why are you up so early, Ava?" I asked.

"Oh, nothing really, but I do have a request, darlin', before your day gets set in stone." She glanced again at the red sun. "It is beautiful … makes me feel funny." Her body shook for a second.

"You name it, sweetheart. I can do anything you want," I bragged.

"Drive me to Alexandria. Dr. McMinn suggested I see an oncologist there. His office set up the appointment yesterday."

"An oncologist?" I asked. "Why, sweetheart?"

"Run some test, do a little probing, I guess," she said, shrugging. "I'm just tired much of the time, and my periods are heavy, really difficult."

"Why haven't you told me, Ava?"

"I didn't want any interruptions, Ben, just ignored it, looked the other way."

"And how long has this been going on?"

"A while, but it's become much worse." Ava took another sip from her cup then looked at me. My eyes had not left her face. "Oh, don't worry, Ben," she said. "It's just a routine thing." She laughed quietly.

"But you're worried, I can tell."

"Well, a little," she said. "Really, a lot, I guess you'd say." She sighed, then looked away from me, toward the tall birch trees on the far bank, and the red sun.

The drive home from Alexandria seemed like a thousand miles. Few words were spoken, but there was a constant flow of tears while Ava sat close to me, resting her head on my shoulder. Outside of Bunkie, and going south on Pershing Highway, streaks of red, orange, and pink clouds crossed the horizon in the west, while an incredible red sun began its slow fall behind the trees. "Turn in here, Ben," she said suddenly. The tires squealed on the pavement as I braked quickly, turning into the long driveway of the old mansion on the Star Plantation. "What in the world's gonna happen with this place?" she asked, quickly adding, "I want to go inside, Ben."

Since her mother's death and, soon after, Mr. Koller's, the mansion, and its furnishings had remained as they had always been. "Are you sure you want to do this, Ava?" I asked as we crossed the porch. She said nothing; I unlocked the door. Slowly, it opened.

Feeling the pain of heartache, and in an attempt to ease it, I quickly moved to the inside. I turned to face Ava, announcing, "Mister Benjamin Bennefield, and his friend Mister James Bartlett, two of the best-looking and most desirable young men in the entire parish." And as Ava had done on a New Year's Eve night many years before, I curtsied, smiling.

Her lips parted, quivering. She began to cry. I realized I should not have mocked an incident whose consequences were still vivid in her mind and in her life. I grabbed her quickly. "I'm sorry, sweetheart. I'm sorry." I held my arms around her for several seconds before moving into the hall, closing the door behind us. "I didn't mean to upset you, Ava. I'm sorry," I said. The old house was musty.

She wiped her eyes. "I'm sorry, too, Ben. Memories at this moment are difficult to handle." She glanced down the hall to the doors onto the terrace, then moved to touch a gilded mirror near the door into the living room. "Thirty minutes before guests began arriving for that party on New Year's Eve, I stood in front of this mirror while my parents forbade me ever to marry you, Ben, and I knew I loved you," she said, wiping tears from her eyes. "An hour later, you showed up with James." She shook her head slightly, closed her eyes, and then opened them, looking to the far end of the hall. "Right after the shooting on the terrace that night, Dad told me, 'That other boy's a fine young man; go get him.'" She stopped and looked directly at my face, holding her eyes on mine. "'Go get him,' Dad told me, Ben, like I should just throw you away and carry off the man who looked better to him." She shook her head again. "For a long time afterward, I disliked my father, and only after James was killed, did I finally forgive him."

"And Catherine?" I asked quickly.

At first glance, I thought she would ignore my question or evade it, but after a few seconds, she smiled slightly and looked at my face; holding her eyes to mine, she said, "Beautiful Catherine." She began to cry again. I wrapped one arm around her shoulders, and together we moved into the dark living room. Ava turned on a lamp then pointed to the couch. After a few seconds, she looked at me, blotted her eyes again, and smiled slightly. "Catherine Bartlett, beautiful Catherine," she repeated. "You're asking about Catherine? Well, my darlin', you already know … Catherine's your daughter, Ben," she whispered. "I'm pretty sure you figured that out a long time ago." I sighed and moved closer to wrap my arms around her as she cried. "I was never able to talk about it because of the guilt I felt for having trapped James into marrying me," she said. "Bless his heart. What a good person he was, and a good dad." She smiled and said, "I never told him, Ben, but he knew I was pregnant when we married. All those years and I never told him. He died not knowing for sure whose child she was, his or yours." Ava's crying turned into sobs, broken-hearted convulsions, and I kissed her cheeks. She calmed a bit and said, "And the guilt of having taken your child away from you, Ben; all of this just comes out at a time like this." She smiled slightly. "I guess the best I see right now is that you and Catherine have each other, and she has a brother, too. That fact excited me the first time I met Benny, at James's funeral." She wiped her eyes with her finger. "And you and Catherine finally have each other." She looked at me. "That's good, isn't it, Ben?"

"That's good, Ava. Yes, that's good," I said, then asked, "Does Catherine know?"

"I've never told her in so many words, but she suspects something, I'm sure." Ava continued to cry, while I held her. "Since she's known Benny, and since you and I married, she's bound to have recognized the similarities, there's so many."

"She needs to know the truth, Ava."

"I wish I could tell her, Ben." Her crying had subsided. "I just don't know how, and there'll be a lot of blame I don't want to have to deal with. That's been the problem all along." Ava began to relax, laying her head on my chest. "Catherine can be difficult," she whispered.

The room was stuffy and hot. The red sunlight that had filtered through the curtains was gone. Darkness had set in.

"Let's go home, sweetheart," I said.

* * * *

Fifty-Five

"April showers bring May flowers," I had heard since childhood, and the rhyme ran haplessly through my mind. The last five days of April had brought far more than showers: a deluge of rain that ran Edward's Creek to overflowing in the low areas. Many places along the narrow roads following the creek's banks from Bunkie to far below Gold Dust and Whiteville were badly damaged or washed out completely, impassable. Broad fields of young cotton stood in still water six inches deep, while our cattle had to be herded onto higher ground in the flooded pastures. But May 1, 1976, bright and sunny, with a blue sky washed clean of clouds, was the day we buried Ava Koller Bartlett Bennefield.

With Benny on my left side and Catherine on my right, at home, we greeted friends from Bunkie and surrounding towns and people with whom I had done business from Houston to Atlanta. Two couples had come from California, friends of Ava and James's. When I glanced to the far end of the main hall, Miz Margaret stood tall and elegantly, with several people around her, very beautiful in a black dress; her hair was curled as she had always worn it, but now as white as snow. She wore the pearls and diamonds she had received after Isabella Mancini died. Bo and Hattie scurried in and out through the hall door to the dining room and living room, directing the caterers from Alexandria, obviously proud to have in their midst, working alongside them, their nearly famous daughter Jessie from Atlanta. My sister, Barbara, stood in the living room, smiling and talking to people she pretended to remember, and when she turned my way, our eyes locked. She shook her head in astonishment, while she mouthed, "I can't believe this." But I could, because Ava had left her mark in the hearts and minds of hundreds of kids and their families, both as a teacher and a friend.

When I looked away from Barbara, I heard "Hello, Ben," and my breath left me. It was a voice I had not expected to hear, but one I knew well. Locking my arms around her, I closed my eyes and held her close to me, and I couldn't help that my throat ached. My body trembled; I took a deep breath. I didn't want to open my eyes or let her go. "Anna," I said. "Anna."

Around four o'clock, Hattie and Bo said good-bye to Jessie and to the caterers. Benny had gone with his mother to Miz Margaret's. Hattie brought coffee to Catherine and me in the living room, and after a few minutes, I heard the door from the kitchen close.

I felt it was a perfect opportunity to cross a bridge that needed to be crossed quickly, now that the link between Catherine and me had been broken by Ava's death, and I didn't want to lose Catherine again.

"Catherine, there's something I'd like to talk to you about," I said, a bit anxious. Catherine lowered her head and smiled a little, but said nothing. "I apologize for being so forward, Catherine, but I'm desperate we don't lose each other in everything that's happened."

"For a long time, Ben, I've suspected you're my father," she said. "That's the urgent subject at the moment, isn't it?" She looked squarely at me. "Ben," she said, "I've had no reasons to be happy about it, or sad, for that matter ... It was never discussed, as you know. But I want to be forward, too. Let me ask you this: Do you know who I am, Ben?"

"Barely," I said. "I barely know you, but I do know you're my daughter."

"Well, I'm glad to hear those words, but they've come to me quite late," she said. "It appears I'm probably one of the last to have confirmation of who I really am."

"You have my blood, Catherine, Koller and Bennefield blood."

"That's nice, Ben," she said as she smiled. "It's very touching to suddenly have verification of my ancestry."

"I'm sorry your mother and I never told you, but too many things have come about so quickly," I said. "I need to tell Benny, too."

"Oh, Ben, obviously he knows. I fell in love with him when I was sixteen, and he evaded me all of a sudden." She smiled.

"I had forbidden him to date you, Catherine, a long time ago."

"So, Mister Bennefield, you knew a long time ago, and of course, mother knew at the onset." She shook her head, smiled, and said, "My poor dad, so innocent … my real dad, Major Bartlett." Our eyes met. "You know, Ben, I can't believe the web everyone lives in around here. They attempt to hide in their webs, moving their secrets from one little strand to another, as though no one can see them." As she spoke, she wove an imaginary web with her fingers. "And the entire web, and the secrets they hide and run from, are of their own making."

"Yeah, I realize that. Sometimes the truth is hard to face, Catherine," I said, "and that's why I wanted this conversation with you as soon as we could have it."

"It's done," she said, slightly raising her arms in the air, then leaned toward me. "Ben," she said, "this will scare the hell out of you, I'm sure, but I'm planning to burn the Big House on the Star Plantation, just as it sits, everything in it, and sell the acreage."

"Burn it, real fire, burn it down?" I asked, incredulously. "Just sell it, Catherine, if you don't want it. But it's part of your heritage. You're the fourth generation there."

A Full-Grown Man

"I want nothing to do with it, Ben, that's why I want to burn that damned old house and get rid of the land. I want to *see* it burn, and I hope the wind's blowing hard, so there's no doubt in anybody's mind that that side of my life is gone." She stood, glaring straight down at my face. "I'm starting a new generation, a new life, away from the Kollers, the Bennefields, away from everybody and everything around here." Her hands were balled into fists, she was burning inside, and I was struck by the meanness of her words. "None of you are my family. I have no family." She took a breath, then pointed her finger at me. "Everyone who loved me, or whom I chose to love, left me. My dad was killed halfway around the world, and we buried my mother after a horrible death. And when Benny's mother showed up, I knew truly, without a doubt, I would forever be the bastard at the family reunion."

I cringed, closed my eyes, then opened them, and looked into the beautiful face of a person I didn't know at all. My stomach churned; I felt hot and sweaty, and I wanted to vomit. I closed my eyes again, feeling beaten and helpless. I heard her steps as she left the room. In Catherine's gestures, in her movements, and in the meanness of her words, all I could see hovering over me was Hester Bennefield; she was young, she was angry about what life had handed her, and she wore a dark green dress.

When the front door slammed, the crystals on the big chandelier in Hester's bedroom sang for several seconds.

Most of the night, I lay awake, watching the darkness in the room and listening to the yelping of a dog, far off. Early, I had decided to return to my upstairs bedroom and let Hester have her bedroom back, keeping the door locked. Later in the night, I changed my mind. It had been Ava's room and mine for over three years, and I wasn't going to give it back. When the glimmer of the sun shot through the trees, I was drinking my third cup of coffee in the gazebo, after dragging all of Hester's furniture from the bedroom onto the front porch. And when Bo came, he held the ladder while I pulled that damn chandelier from the ceiling.

"But Ben," Bo said, "you can't burn all yo' mama's stuff. Put it in Benny's house, there, or we can store it in one of the barns."

"It's gotta go. I don't want it anywhere around, Bo, nowhere on this farm."

"Sell it, Ben. Those antique people'll buy it up in two minutes," he argued as we stood on the front steps, looking across the porch laden with furniture. The gold on the green chest gleamed in the bright sun. "Git something for it, Ben."

"I can't sell it, Bo. That'll just complicate things for me." I knew if I made a dollar on her stuff and put it in my pocket, Hester would tear my pants off. "Burn it, Bo. That's the only thing we can do." My eyes caught the sparkle of the prisms as the chandelier lay awkwardly on the floor at the top of the porch steps. It was then I remembered Jesse saying a long time ago, *I cleaned Miz Hester's room, Mista Ben. It's really beautiful.*

"Bo, go call Jessie. If she wants it, load it up and you and Hattie take it to Atlanta. Jessie will like it," I said.

"Lawd have mercy, Ben, I ain't wantin' to drive to Atlanta, but I sho' don't wanna burn Miz Hester's stuff." He shook his head and started walking up the driveway. His steps were short, almost shuffling, and as he walked away from me, I realized my friend Bo Johnson was no longer the powerful young man I had relied on during every phase of my life, the good ones and bad ones. He knew it all, and he had taken care of everything that mattered since I was eighteen years old. I glanced at the furniture on the porch, then quickly looked back at Bo just as he turned and called out, "Ben, I got somethin' to say." He came back to where I waited. "Ben, I'm really glad you gittin' rid of Miz Hester's stuff, here. Maybe you can git some peace, and Ben, Miz Ava was a good woman, we all knows it," he said. "But Ben, you needs to git that otha' woman back in yo' life."

"What, Bo, what are you talking about?" I knew what he was going to say.

"Miz Anna, Ben. You go git her. You done spent most of yo' life waitin' fer her. You got the chance now, and you gotta do it, else you ain't neva' gonna be no full-grown man."

I looked at my friend, figuring he was right. "Yeah," I said, "I'm gonna do that, Bo," nodding in agreement. "I'm ... I'm gonna do that."

Bo looked straight into my watery eyes, but said nothing else. He left.

Ascending the steps, I glanced at the furniture, stepped through the front door, and went into the bedroom. Four walls, naked windows, a bare floor, and a ceiling where two wires dangled from the center; "Yes," I said out loud, then yelled "Yes!" my voice echoed in the openness. "And it'll stay this way till she marries me," I yelled again.

Skipping several treads with each step, I rushed upstairs to my old bedroom.

By the time I had awakened enough to realize the ringing in my ear was the phone, it stopped. I looked around the room, trying to figure out where I was. The clock by the bed said ten o'clock. I wiped the drool from around my mouth, realizing I had slept cross ways on the bed, in my blue jeans and T-shirt with my boots on. The last time this had happened was on a summer morning in New Orleans on a trip with James to the wilds of the Crescent City. "What the hell?" the thought hit me, "I have to check on Ava," and I jumped to my feet. "Ava? God, no, no, no ... Ava is dead. Ava is *dead?*" With both hands over my face, I sat down on the bed, my elbows on my knees. The realization of having buried my wife only the day before hit me; it had been a violent roller coaster for nearly a year, and I never got off. Time and things were blurred by the speed and the ups and downs. As my insides churned, I knew the end was somewhere in front me, but all I could feel was the helplessness of a free fall into a big black hole. I hit bottom. Ava was gone, and I cried.

Fifty-Six

SADIE AND KAISER BARKED. I moved to the window and pulled the curtain back. Bo and Hattie were standing on the sidewalk leading from the back porch, talking and motioning, but their words were indistinct. I rushed down the stairs, quickly through the kitchen to the outside.

"What's wrong, Bo?" I asked, glancing in all direction. "What the hells going on?" I yelled, excitedly.

"I talked to Jesse, Ben, and she wants everything your mama had. Me and Bo just tryin' to figure out when to go," Hattie explained. "That's a lot of fine stuff there, Ben. You sure you wanna git rid of it?"

"Yeah, I want it away from here, Hattie. Everything," I said, "the sooner, the better." When I remembered moving the furniture onto the porch, it was like a dream in which I was a spectator. "Y'all work it out." I left them to go inside. When I opened the kitchen door, I looked around then walked to the stove. I touched the salt and pepper shakers, which always sat on the cabinet near the range top, picked one up, and looked closely at the sticky finger prints. They were Ava's, I was sure. Then I moved to the large iron A hanging next to the door going into the butler's pantry. I touched it, too, remembering I had given it to her when she had finished the kitchen. In the dining room was an arrangement of dried flowers from last fall's garden, sitting beautifully and perfectly in the center of the table, right where Ava had placed it, and along the top of the server were four fresh plants sent as remembrances from friends. Quickly, I gathered them in my arms, rushed them to the front porch, passed the furniture, and emptied my arms making a pile at the bottom of the steps. I returned to the living room, picked up four or five more plants, and rushed them, too, to the pile out front. Back in the living room, I arranged the pillows on the couch, the red one on the end and the blue one in the chair near the window. After completing my tasks, I stood at the bottom of the front porch steps, looking over a heap of jars, flowers, plants, and over two hundred get-well cards scattered across the top. I walked up the steps, opened the door, and crossed the threshold. I took a deep breath. I held it for a second then let it out. "Now," I mumbled. "That's a little better." Slowly, I climbed the stairs, and by the time I reached the middle of my room, I had stripped to my underwear. The clock said eleven-fifty, near noon on Monday. I fell into bed and slept till the sun lit the room the next morning.

It was a new day.

After the third ring, Miz Margaret answered her phone. "Hello," she said, dragging the "o" into a short verse of song.

"Good morning, Miz Margaret, how are you?" I asked politely.

"Oh, very well, Mister Bennefield, and how are you?" she answered, still in singsong.

"It's amazing what eighteen hours of sleep will do for a person," I said. "I'm fine."

"Well, Benjamin, I'm going to let you talk to Anna while I refill our cups. She's right here." And there was little doubt in my mind that, as always, my friend Miz Margaret was truly on my side. Waiting for Anna to come on, I smiled.

"Hi, Ben," she said. "I hope you're rested and feeling well."

"Yeah, but I have a problem and need a little help, Anna. Will you be available in about an hour?" I asked, with a note of pleading I knew was in my voice.

"Oh, sure, Ben, I'll do what I can. I hope nothing's wrong," she said.

"No, nothing's wrong," I said. "Meet me at the bridge in an hour. Okay?"

"Yes, I'll do that, Ben."

"Wear slacks, Anna."

"Sure," she said.

I held the receiver to my ear until the dial tone sounded.

Near ten that morning, I stood in the middle of the Gold Dust Bridge, holding the reins from the bridles of my two favorite riding horses. I looked to the north side of the old bridge, where the trees and overgrowth along the bank of Edward's Creek had been cleared down to the dirt, and to the pilings standing ready for the floor of the new bridge. The deluge of the last days in April was still evident in the depth of the creek and in the brownish color of the usually blue-green water. It was time I assessed the havoc the rains had wrought on my cotton and the thousand acres of pasture along the woods in the east. And horseback was the only way it could be done. At this point, and regardless of the prevailing customs for grieving widowers, unabashedly I admitted there was no one who could help me more than Anna Mancini. Excited and anxious, I waited in the middle of the Gold Dust Bridge.

I watched her walk toward me from Miz Margaret's front door all the way to the end of the old bridge. Tall and trim, and with a cap over her auburn air, I could see her smile as she shook her head. "No, Ben," she called out from where she had stopped, looking at the horses. "It's been too long."

"It's like swimming, Anna, you don't forget," I called back to her, while she walked toward me. After a few seconds, standing only inches from me, she stood on her tiptoes and lightly kissed my cheek. "Thanks for coming," I said, smiling.

"Where are we going, Ben?"

"Well, I figured I needed to look around the farm, and a few words of expert advice would help me a great deal." Before I finished speaking, Anna had stepped to the railing, and leaned against it. She looked at the concrete pilings standing tall in the brown dirt along the bank.

"Oh, Ben," she exclaimed, "they're going to take down the old bridge; it won't be long." She turned and faced me, appearing as though she might break down and cry at any second.

"In a couple of months. The dedication for the new bridge is on the Fourth of July," I said.

"Oh, Ben, that's awful." Anna glanced around, shaking her head. "Why?" she asked. "We don't need a new bridge, especially a big concrete slab. Everyone's gone anyway."

"Not everyone, Anna. I'm here, and your mother, and when Benny finishes vet school, he'll live here, too," I said, adding quickly, "so not everyone's gone."

As if she were praying, she placed the tips of the fingers of both hands to her lips, and again, her eyes scanned the area as she crossed the bridge to the other railing. "Bennefield Farm comes right up to there, doesn't it, Ben?" she asked, while pointing to the trees on the west bank. "It touches this old bridge, doesn't it?"

"Yeah," I said. "Always has. Let's go, the horses are ready." And so was I.

For over an hour, we rode slowly along the muddy turn-rows through the fields. As near as I could figure, we had lost more than three hundred acres of young cotton, scalded by the hot sun and lingering water. What I felt when I realized the havoc the rains had wrought upon Bennefield Farm apparently showed on my face. "What are you going to do, Ben?" Anna asked.

"Plow it under," I said. "That's all we can do, plow it under. Put it behind me, out of sight, and start over."

Knowing their way through the labyrinth of dirt roads and cotton rows, the horses needed little guidance from their riders. They turned and walked slowly up the driveway toward the house. "What a gorgeous setting, Ben. This is beautiful," Anna said.

"Thanks. Ava gets the credit. She cleaned up the yards and did the gardens. They were her love," I said.

The sounds of the horses' hooves on the asphalt brought Sadie and Kaiser running toward us, barking. I called to them, and they stopped at the front porch, waiting for our arrival.

"What in heaven's name are you doing, Ben?" Anna asked while motioning to the furniture strewn out on the porch.

"I've kicked Hester out of the house completely, Anna," I said, smiling. "And you know something? I feel a hell of a lot better already."

The horses held their slow pace straight to the stables a hundred yards behind the house. I removed their saddles, curried them, then let them into the pasture. Anna and I walked slowly to the house and into the kitchen, where, in a few minutes, I had prepared two sandwiches. "Pour the milk, Anna, would you please?" I said, handing her two glasses, then pointing to the refrigerator. "Let's have a picnic in the gazebo."

"No wonder Benny intends to set up his practice here and live here. Look at this setting," Anna said, as she stood awestruck in the middle of the gazebo. Turning slowly, she looked in all directions, my eyes following hers.

Shadows danced across the expanse of green under the spreading arms of the great oaks in the front yard. And Ava's flowers in the garden, from the gazebo past the driveway to the back porch, suddenly awakened me with the brilliance of color; the soft breeze moved the pale green leaves of the river birch on the far bank, all, it seemed, in beautiful harmony with the sounds of the water rippling down Edward's Creek. I sat in one of the chairs at the table, realizing that the beauty that Anna was seeing for the first time had been mine for all of my life, and Ava had made it better. Lazily, Kaiser and Sadie dozed at the edge of the gazebo floor.

"This, Ben, is what stories are written about," she said, sitting across from me. "It's what my friends are always wishing and searching for." She smiled and took the first bite of a peanut butter and jelly sandwich on fresh white bread. "Oh, this is wonderful," she said with her mouth full. "I love it."

"Yeah," I said, smiling, "it's a love potion I've made for years." I watched her face closely for a reaction. She pretended not to hear. I continued to smile, chewing hard.

Anna set her napkin beside her plate and took a sip of milk. She leaned back and almost said something, but didn't. She looked at me, placing her hand over her mouth. "What, Anna?" I asked.

"Oh, nothing, Ben," she said.

"Yes, there is. You seem nervous all of a sudden. What is it?" I asked again.

She glanced across the creek, sat upright in the chair, then placed both elbows on the table with her hands clasped together. "My trip to Gold Dust began as a mission, Ben, something I felt compelled to do." She lowered her hands then brushed one across her brow. "And all of sudden, it's turned into considerably more, and I don't really know what it means."

"What was the mission, Anna?" I asked.

She leaned to one side, reaching into her hip pocket, and brought out an envelope folded in half.

"This," she said. "It's mine, and yours also, Ben. My mission was to bring it to you, to make sure you received it, but I hesitated to give it to you, until you called this morning." She blinked a couple of times, "Only then did I feel you should have it, too." I reached, but she made no effort to place the envelope in my hand. She held it firmly between two fingers. "Ben, I received this several weeks ago, and I've read it many times. I know it almost by heart. It's a message between two women." I frowned, my mouth half open. "You can have it," she said, "but first, I want a promise from you. You have to promise me something."

"Sure," I said. "I promise, Anna," and I quickly held up my hand, in an oath. I didn't like promises, I knew, but with Anna I would promise anything.

"I'm going to set it on this plate and walk away. And when I turn at the end of the drive and you can no longer see me, take it. But you must promise you'll not read it until I'm out of sight. Do you promise?" she asked.

"Why wait till you're gone, out of sight?" I stammered.

"I don't want you to be influenced by your so-called 'love potion,' with my sitting in front of you. That's why, Benjamin," she said, smiling. "You must promise, Ben." She held her eyes straight on mine.

Seeing the tears and the quiver of her lips, I realized that for Anna this was far more than a casual meeting of two friends, as it was for me, also. I hesitated, but then I sat upright in the chair, raising my hand again. "I promise," I said, "no peeking till you're out of sight."

I looked toward the trees on the far side of Edward's Creek. Kaiser and Sadie raised their heads from the floor only long enough to see Anna walk away, then lay back down. I closed my eyes and lowered my head, praying to God, without words. After sitting still with my eyes closed for what seemed like an hour, I reached for the envelope. I recognized Ava's handwriting. I hesitated before taking the letter out.

A Full-Grown Man

March 15, 1976

Dear Anna and Ben,

You are my best and dearest friends. One of you I've loved for a long, long time. The other—you, Anna—I've never heard your voice nor have I seen your face, and you don't know me. But Ben has loved the two of us for much of his life. Good friends always have things that bind them; we have something, too; we have each other, and the love we've shared.

Ben had a secret, a burdensome secret, and only when he held my hand while sitting beside my bed did he let his secret go. And I've decided now, to tell my other friend, Anna.

Twenty-five years ago, Anna, when you needed him more than anyone else in the world, you wrote him letters. Those letters were hidden from him for a long time, causing him to believe, with a broken heart, you never wanted him again. When the letters finally reached him, your life with his child, and his life without the two of you, had been set, each on its own course, carefully charted, and well designed.

In a way few men could have ever done, Ben, in your own very special way, you have loved two women. And when the first was maliciously denied you, you hid the pieces of a broken heart deep inside. I know the pieces were there, Ben, and you shared them in a special love for me when I needed you more than you could ever have imagined, and I'm grateful.

This letter, sent with all of my love and good wishes, is an invitation for you, Ben and Anna, to come together at Bennefield Farm when we celebrate my life. The date is forthcoming.

Ava

Leaning back in the chair, holding in one hand the letter Ava had written only weeks before she died, I was overwhelmed with sadness. I looked to the far bank where the trees rustled in the breeze, then glanced at the letter again, realizing the depth of heart it took for Ava to write in the waning days of her life. Through the tears, I read it again. *To come together at Bennefield Farm*, she had written. But Anna had mysteriously left. I glanced to the end of the driveway. Quickly, I folded the letter and put it in my shirt pocket.

Fifty-Seven

When I stopped the car in front of Miz Margaret's house, she was already walking toward the steps from the swing at the far end of the porch, waving something in her hand. "Ben, thank God you came," she said, holding an envelope toward me, meeting me at the steps. "Anna gave me this letter, Benjamin, and I'm supposed to mail it to *her* in tomorrow's mail if you didn't come get it right away," she spoke fast. "I was about ready to take it to your house myself, to make sure you got it today, Ben," she said, sighing. "Something's going on with her. Anna was like a schoolgirl getting ready for her first date when she drove away."

"She's gone?" I asked, looking around for her car.

"Oh, she was packed and ready when you called this morning. Then she became excited about meeting you at the bridge," she exclaimed. "What's happening, Ben?" she asked, nervously wringing her hands.

"I don't know, Miz Margaret," I said, looking at the envelope, and hesitating. On the front was my name.

"Well, open the damn thing and read it, Benjamin," she ordered. "I've become a nervous wreck waiting for you. You should have been here twenty minutes ago." Obviously, Miz Margaret's patience had thinned to a point I had never seen. Quickly, I tore open the envelope.

May 3, 1976

Dear Ben:

Meet me at noon on Thursday, June 24, in the Tower Room at the Museum of American Art in New York.

Love, Anna

"What is it, Benjamin?" Miz Margaret asked, impatiently. "What's wrong? What did she say?"

Shaking my head, I looked at her, frowning. "I don't know, Miz Margaret. Anna didn't say what's wrong." I turned and walked the few steps to my car, got in, and sat behind the wheel, reading the note again.

"You're not going to tell me anything, Benjamin?" she called to me. I looked through the open window.

"No, ma'am," I said. "Not till I know something real." I raised my hand good-bye and started the engine.

* * * * *

Fifty-Eight

SIX WEEKS LATER, AROUND ten on a Wednesday morning and with a suitcase in hand, I hurried from the back porch to the garage. After a couple of minutes, I turned the car toward Gold Dust, stopping in the middle of the old bridge. I stepped from the car, slammed the door, and moved through the mist, to stand with my arms over the railing.

Only a few workers remained, putting the final touches on the wide, concrete slab crossing Edward's Creek. The new bridge was spotlessly clean, with fresh blacktop joining the old road to each end of the new bridge. Within a minute I had completed my study of its boring simplicity, its hardness in dull gray concrete.

For months, the noise and the movement of the big equipment only fifty feet away had shaken the old bridge, vibrating its iron and its wood. The floor lay speckled with flakes of paint that had fallen from the beams above. Some were blue, others were gray and crimson. For my entire life, the bridge had been only one color: a deep, dark red. But somewhere there had to be souls who remembered it as blue or gray, and all of them, I figured, would forever remember the unique hospitality of the Gold Dust Bridge. I took Anna's note from my pocket, opened it, and then looked up through the iron beams into a sky that was gray and wet. Out loud, I read her message so the old bridge would know. It had to know what was happening in our lives; it had to feel what I was feeling; and it must hope, too, for what I was hoping. And more than anything else, I wanted its blessing for my trip to New York.

"You betta' tell that old thing good-bye, mista," a raspy voice said. I found him; a kid about twenty, shirtless, and browned by the sun. His hair was long and tied in a ponytail. He wore cut-off jeans and high-top boots. The kid stood atop the concrete guard rail on the new bridge, with a brush in one hand. "You betta' cross it fer the last time today, cause it's gonna blow at eleven in the mornin'," he said. "You comin' to watch?"

I didn't want to comment, but I raised my hand, waving a salute, and softly, the old bridge moaned. I smiled when I heard it, a wonderful cry I had heard a thousand times. Looking up through its iron frame, I felt the mist on my face. I opened the car door and sat with both hands gripping the steering wheel, looking through the windshield down the wide, dark ribbon of asphalt leading to nowhere now, but which once led into a vibrant little village. For the thousands of travelers who came and went, the old bridge had been merely a means to cross the creek. But to the people who grew up under the shadows of its framework, it was the ruler of our history, a monument to time and to lives, and it had granted passage to hundreds in their search for a place in the outside world.

After sitting silently for several minutes, I shifted into reverse and backed the car into the direction from which I had come. "Never," I spoke out loud, "am I consciously and intentionally going to make a final passage across the Gold Dust Bridge." I shouted to the kid with the ponytail, "Never!"

Fifty-Nine

ANXIOUSLY, I RUSHED UP the steps of the Museum of American Art and pulled on the glass door. Inside, I glanced around while removing my raincoat and folding my umbrella. A dozen or so people wandered about. Across the lobby, I paid the attendant and picked up a brochure at the marble counter. Being a few minutes early, I walked slowly, glancing at the current rave in the New York art world displayed along the walls in Carrigan Hall, and moved steadily into Weston Hall. After twenty-two years, little had changed other than the paintings and drawings themselves, a very different style of art from what Anna had displayed there in 1954.

When I turned the corner at the end of Weston Hall, both wide doors into the Tower Room were open, and I could see several people standing near the railing in front of a big painting lit brightly on the far back wall. On the bench facing the painting was her silhouette. I quickened my pace, and only a few steps from her, I said, "Hello."

Quickly, she stood, turning to face me. "I'm sorry," I said. "I thought you were someone else, someone I knew."

The young woman wiped her cheek with her finger. "You're not from New York, are you?" She looked at me while draping her raincoat over her arms.

"No, ma'am, I'm not."

She smiled again. "Then you don't know, do you? And you've come from far away to see *The Gold Dust Bridge.*" She motioned toward the painting with her thumb.

"Know what? Has something happened?"

"Yes," she said, "and I'm upset about it. The story was in the paper this morning; the museum's sold *The Gold Dust Bridge.*"

"I'm surprised they'd do that, but it's been here for a long time," I said. "In fact, over twenty years; I was here on opening night."

"So was I. I was ten years old."

"Well, that *is* a coincidence," I replied. "I bet they paid a hefty price for it. Did they say how much?" I was glad to see her smiling.

But tears came quickly to her eyes again, and I reached toward her with my folded handkerchief. "Thank you," she said. "No, no price, but it did say it was the artist who bought it." She sat down on the bench, and I sat beside her as she adjusted her coat and purse on her lap. *The artist bought it*, I said to myself. I looked at the big painting, thinking, smiling, *Anna bought it.*

"I'm an artist, a struggling artist," the woman said. She, too, looked at the painting, motioning toward it with her finger, never raising her hand from her lap. "I'm an artist *because* of this painting." She stopped talking and wiped her eyes again with my handkerchief. "I'm sorry," she said, "just a little emotional, but *The Gold Dust Bridge* has been an inspiration to me for a long time, and I hate that it's leaving us. This is probably the last time I'll see it." She sighed, smiled, and stood up. I stood up, too, facing her. "Your handkerchief, thank you," she said, and handed the handkerchief to me. "It was nice to be able to tell someone how I feel, and to have them take the time to listen. You were kind, and I thank you very much." She began walking to the door going to

Weston Hall, stopped, and turned toward me. "Enjoy New York," her voice echoed in the emptiness of the big room. I watched until she reached the corner.

I was alone in the Tower Room, in the quiet. The shadows with the stillness seemed to make the silence weigh on my mind while I waited for Anna. Spotlights illuminated *The Gold Dust Bridge*, its every bright color and brush stroke. *And Anna had bought it.* The thought made me smile. Moving slowly toward the painting, I jumped when the clock in back of me sounded the first chime, and I turned, facing it. *Twelve o'clock; it's twelve o'clock in New York*, and I remembered what the kid with the ponytail had said. My breathing stopped. I closed my eyes and covered my ears with my hands. I heard the explosion blowing up the old bridge and watched it tumble into Edward's Creek. The water ran red.

I gasped for air and opened my eyes.

"Ben, are you okay?"

"The ... the bridge. It's gone, Anna." I wrapped my arms around her.

"I know, Ben."

"I'm never gonna let go of you, Anna. Never."

"Is that a promise, Ben?" she asked.

The clock struck twelve.

THE END

Printed in the United States
151592LV00002B/2/P